Never Have I Ever

Never Have I Ever

L.V. Hay

HODDER

First published in Great Britain in 2019 by Hodder & Stoughton
An Hachette UK company

3

A CIP catalogue record for this title is
available from the British Library

Paperback ISBN 9781529337723
eBook ISBN 9781529337730

Typeset in Plantin Light by Palimpsest Book Production Limited,
Falkirk, Stirlingshire

Printed and bound in Great Britain by Clays Ltd, Elcograf S.p.A.

Hodder & Stoughton policy is to use papers that are
natural, renewable and recyclable products and made from
wood grown in sustainable forests. The logging and manufacturing
processes are expected to conform to the environmental
regulations of the country of origin.

Hodder & Stoughton Ltd
Carmelite House
50 Victoria Embankment
London EC4Y 0DZ

www.hodder.co.uk

For all my teenage friends in 90s Devon. It might be the land of fields and cream teas, but we were ALL bad girls (and boys)!

But also, for Alfie, who owes his literal life to such blatant shenanigans. I'm glad you're not as bad as us, son (or if you are, that I know nothing about it).

One

In my dreams, I always hear crying.

I awake with a start. Primed and ready for Caleb's wails, I rush through to his bedroom. The cold flutter of anxiety in my chest forces my feet into action. In the few seconds it takes me to cross the landing, my brain jumps forward, ahead of my body. In my mind's eye I see an empty cot, an open window, a fluttering curtain in the breeze.

No, there he is: my precious boy, asleep, arms raised over his head. My heart melts at the sight of him; his angelic blond curls, his rosebud lips. He's just thirteen months, but I can't imagine life without him: it's unthinkable. He could be a cartoon baby, he is that perfect. All mothers say that, but in Caleb's case it's one hundred per cent true. Even strangers stop me in the street to tell me how gorgeous he is.

I know it's all accidental; I couldn't possibly have controlled the genes and cells that make up my only child. I didn't have much to give him by way of good looks, anyway. My dark hair is greying; my face is too angular, my nose more of a beak. I am tall for a woman and have nice wide shoulders, but also an ample bum that's far too big. Hopefully Caleb will take more after his dad. Though he is also a little thicker round the waist than when we met, Mo still has a pleasing look of a blond surfer about him.

Not that he's ever ridden a wave in his life. He's not the outdoors type, but a house mouse.

Even so, strangers telling me how lovely my baby is still makes me puff up my chest with pride every single time. It makes all the sacrifices worth it, not to mention the sizeable dent in our bank balance. Mo is joking when he calls him the 'million-pound baby', but in real terms Caleb might as well be. We'd near bankrupted ourselves to get him. I don't care. I would do it all again.

With a groan, I realise I'm totally awake, all hopes of a lie-in forgotten. I pad over to the bedroom window and peek through the curtains at the early morning sun. We'd chosen this house because of its high position: I could see right across the valley, down across the town towards the pier. The arriving boats with their midnight catches look like toys. I sigh at the beauty, my breath frosting the window pane. I'd missed this, the whole time I was in London. That sense of peace that only watching the sea, undulating back and forth with the moon, can provide. Lakes and rivers might be beautiful too, but for me they are not the same.

I wander out to the landing. Discarded socks, pants and wet towels mark where Mo had already been. Downstairs, there will be a dish half-full of cereal left on the counter; a barely drunk coffee next to it. Mo's entire life is summed up by a detritus of crap he leaves behind him; mine by picking up after him. He'd got up at four to make it to Bristol airport for six. His flight wasn't until eight, but Mo has always been punctual to the point of ridiculousness. He's flying out . . . where? I can't remember. It will be marked on the calendar.

I trudge downstairs, to the open-plan living room and kitchen, avoiding the boxes on the landing. The carpet

2

beneath my feet is grubby with age; there's nineties lime-green décor throughout that stretches all the way down into the living room below. It's why we'd got the house at a knockdown price. We'd had to consolidate and go bargain hunting. As well as five years of IVF, a combination of university loans and Mo's failed first two businesses had left our finances in the crapper. For all of Mo's fevered procla-mations of needing to 'take massive action to get massive results', we'd simply ended up with massive debt. Don't get me wrong, my husband has many admirable qualities and works hard at his consultancy business, but for all his 'blue sky thinking blah blah blah', Mark Zuckerberg he ain't.

Sure enough, I find Mo's leftovers on the side in the kitchen. I pick them up to rinse them out, flicking the radio on by the sink as I do so. The rhythmic, all-encompassing guitar sound of a Foo Fighters song springs into life. Panic bursts through me as my brain makes the connection, recognising the song. I wrench the radio plug from the wall, silencing Dave Grohl's dulcet tones forever.

The kitchen returns to silence. Shallow breaths catch in my throat; I laugh at my over-the-top reaction. When I was a teenager, Foo Fighters were my favourite band. But I can't listen to them these days, too many memories. But I'm overreacting, probably because I'm back in Ilfracombe. Either that, or I'm losing my grip.

I make myself a coffee to give my hands something to do and settle my nerves. I relish the quiet in the house; it's rare I get a moment to myself. Caleb is a wonderful baby, but is into everything. I need eyes in the back of my head to ensure he's not doing something he shouldn't, like drawing on walls or ransacking the fridge. Only the day before, I'd caught him turning out the cupboards again. He was happily squeezing tomato puree straight from the tube into his open mouth. He looked like a baby vampire, red smeared around his mouth and on his front teeth. Still, it was good for him at least. I couldn't bring myself to tell him off.

I ponder what's left to do in the house. Caleb's bedroom is the only room that is finished. Because he is our little prince, Mo and I had started there, putting everything into making sure his room is a fitting palace. I'd studied YouTube tutorials for hours and hung wallpaper with little spaceships on. He has a bookcase and bed linen, even a spaceship canopy hanging from the ceiling. In contrast, every other room is filled with boxes and black rubbish bags. We'd abandoned unpacking the rest of the house when we'd had to go back to work.

'Can't you do one or two boxes tomorrow?' Mo had said at dinner the night before, his face creased with irritation as he'd surveyed the chaos. 'We have been here . . . what? At least four weeks, now.'

'I'm working,' I reminded him. I got used to Mo's lack of understanding about my writing years ago. Never mind the fact book eight of my DI Robyn Dallas series paid the deposit for this house.

'Yes, I know that.' Mo dropped the cutlery and flexed both his hands, as if trying to distract himself. 'I mean, between chapters or something? Or maybe get your mum round to give you a hand?'

I returned to picking at my dinner with a fork, digesting his word choice. Give *you* a hand. Like I'm the only one who lives here. I bit my tongue. I might as well be. A couple of days ago – *between chapters* – I'd calculated how many days Mo had spent in our new house. Nine. We'd been here thirty.

Despite our financial situation, Mo is a good provider and we will break even eventually, especially now we have moved. But we would also benefit from him being at home with us more. Those endless appointments, drugs, IVF cycles have taken their toll on our relationship. We were supposed to be *so happy*. At last, a child of our own; what we'd dreamt of, for so long. Now Mo and I look across the dinner table at each other like work colleagues from a job we'd long since left.

But maybe Mo is right; I'm not pulling my weight. My eighth book, still imaginatively titled *Untitled DI Robyn Dallas Project*, isn't due with the publisher for a while. I could afford to take a few weeks off and unpack the house. All the time I've spent trawling Goodreads for new reviews and taking BuzzFeed quizzes about which Disney villain I am could have been better spent making our new house a home. Who knows, maybe Mo would even want to stay here a bit more with us? An absurd vision spears through my brain: I am in a red apron, baking; Mo is on the floor with Caleb playing trains. The cliché lifts my spirits and I smile to myself as I wander through from the galley kitchen to the hall.

There's a mess of post on the doormat by the front door. I pick it up, flicking through it absent-mindedly: it's mostly bills, free newspapers and flyers. I pause as I take in a last envelope, a familiar scrawl on the front. I'd had letters like this before, passed on by my publisher. I've received fan mail in my time; mostly from old grannies, pleading with me *not* to kill off DI Robyn Dallas's hunky sergeant, Kye Thomson. But these letters were different. I'd had three, back in London, and I'd hoped that was the last of them.

The first time, I'd laughed off my unease. Like many writers working from home, I live a reclusive life, enjoying my own company. I have friends in London, but most are acquaintances or Mo's friends. I much prefer to stay home and watch movies or read books when I'm not writing myself. I am on social media, but only for work. I guard my past and even my real name, Samantha Brennan (née Russell), jealously. This had led several sites and magazines to label me as 'Author Enigma SJ Scherer'. My agent Carole had loved that, so told me to keep it up. I didn't find it difficult.

But the first letter had been fairly innocuous, talking about us writing our own book together like 'James Patterson and those other ones'. I'd waved that first envelope at Mo, joking I might run off with my 'stalker'.

Mo looked jokingly distraught at the thought of me leaving him, and it gave me a thrill. It must have hit a nerve, because later that same night, after a few cheeky vinos, we'd had sex on the sofa whilst watching one of the *Alien* movies. We'd lost ourselves to a soundtrack of fake machine-gun fire and Ripley yelling *'Get away from her, you BITCH!'*

A second letter arrived a few weeks later. That one had been sad. The writer, going by the name of 'N1Fan', made a variety of confessions. No one understood them; no one loved them; their only solace was my books. My conscience pricked, I'd thought about writing back, an email at least, only to discover there was no return address, online or otherwise. There was no Twitter handle or website URL, either. Thwarted, that letter had gone in the recycling box, too. Perhaps all N1Fan needed was to get these feelings off their chest.

The third letter had been a marked change that reinvigorated all my previous misgivings. N1Fan's previous melancholy had vanished, replaced by a petulant rage akin to a teenage girl's, replete with an overuse of exclamation marks. In the letter, NIFan accused me of being 'too stuck up' to write back. NIFan also accused me of a number of imagined transgressions, as well as stealing an idea from an episode of *The Bill*.

I'd not been overly concerned – after all, no one else had picked up on the story's similarity – but I was perturbed by the radical about-face in tone. The murders of Beatles frontman John Lennon, actress Rebecca Schaeffer and the attempt on American president Ronald Reagan's life back in the eighties loomed heavy in my mind. What if I was in danger?

I'd finally called Carole.

'Congratulations, you've arrived, darling! A crazed stalker. How exciting.' Carole sounded a little worse for wear on the other end of the line, even though it was barely two o'clock in the afternoon. She's the old-school type of agent, which has worked out well for me. A social animal, Carole's schmoozing and long, liquid lunches have done DI Robyn Dallas proud, with my last book deal cashing in a five-figure advance.

I'd smoothed the letter out on the counter top. 'Well, I'm not sure I'd say "crazed".'

I already felt as if I'd overreacted. I'd spent a lot of time in therapy for anxiety over the years and discovered sometimes, just speaking these things aloud helped quiet my fears. That said, I always try to keep my panic in check anywhere near Mo, or my mother. Despite Mo's reckless business sense, his personal life is ruled by Murphy's Law, 'whatever can go wrong, will go wrong'. It's the one thing he has in common with Lindy. I've tried reason, but neither of them can be swayed from what therapists call 'catastrophising'.

'Well, make sure you keep the letters,' Carole giggled like a schoolgirl. In her sixties, she still has a harem of younger boyfriends. I had visions of her in bed with a buff young intern, desperate to break into publishing. 'And remember, if anyone threatens you, call me first. I have a friend at the *Telegraph* who will be all over that: "*SUCCESSFUL AUTHOR IN FEAR FOR LIFE*".'

'Erm, thanks.' The sarcasm dripped off my words, but Carole had already hung up.

I turn the fourth envelope over. Sure enough, that same heart in its wobbly scrawl on the back. There had even been one on the back of the angry one, so that was no guarantee this wouldn't be ranty or weird. I might as well get it over with. Taking a deep breath, I rip it open and pull the letter out:

> Dear SJ Scherer,
> Remember, I am your number one fan! The first time I saw your books, I felt impressed. I didn't think you had it in you.
> I see you live in Ilfracombe now. We should go for a long walk on the cliffs together. I'd make you cocktails then we'd watch the sun set. Oh, say you'll be my walking partner SJ Scherer, please . . . or should I say Samantha? ;)
> N1Fan xxx

I drop the letter as if it's hot.

Two

Two hours later and Caleb is awake, bathed and break-fasted and deposited in front of CBeebies in his sitting donut. As I got him ready for the day, I'd obsessed over the supposed fan mail, wondering if I should call Mo. But Mo is old-school, at least in his mind. He's the protector, the provider. If I called him now, no amount of reassurance that I'm fine and Caleb is safe would soothe his anxiety. He would feel compelled to call my mother to come over and guard us in his absence. Feeding off his concern, Lindy in turn would want to call the police. Later, Mo would turn up from wherever he had flown off to, all panic and proc-lamations, telling me everything would be fine, like some kind of knight in a rumpled Armani suit.

When I'd received the first letters, I'd thought it was just one of those things. Writers get weird fan mail sometimes, it wasn't a big deal. I'd tamped down my anxieties, let myself be swept away by Mo's enthusiasm for the move back home. I'd been afraid of my past anxieties and inse-curities following me back to Ilfracombe, just like they had run me out of town when I was a teenager.

I won't be a victim. Not again.

Anger crackles through me, sending my limbs out in jagged shapes. I feel like picking up a cup or plate and throwing it at the wall, like a character in a TV show who's received bad news. NīFan knows my name, my real name, and I'm starting to get an idea of who might be behind this. It's just her style.

Aimee.

Her teenage glare invades my brain. I can see her so clearly, transported twenty-three years in an instant: her blue, almost translucent eyes, round face, dyed purple hair. Her fingers full of rings, spread out as she outlines her challenge. Did she really think she could pick up where she left off? I'm not a sixteen-year-old schoolgirl any more. I've lived a lot of life since that disastrous night, the last time we saw each other. She'd been a bully then, pure and simple. But I'm no longer so easily cowed.

'C'mon, or you chicken?'

The other two gathered around; we were in one of their bedrooms. Maddy played with her strings of beads, her dark brown eyes and smile as wide as a cocker spaniel's. Arms folded, Ruby brought up the rear, sulky and obstinate, but nevertheless curious.

Aimee placed one hand on my shoulder. 'There are penalties for refusing dares, you know.'

I take a deep breath, scrunching the letter up in my fist. I can't allow this nonsense to occupy any more space in my brain. It's already taken too much. I am a grown woman, I don't need to worry about this juvenile crap. Aimee had demanded that everything stopped and started with her. That curled lip, those accusing pale blue eyes. But I am an adult now; I don't have to dance to her tune any more.

I take a deep breath and remind myself of the facts. Nothing in any real terms has changed. The letter had been addressed to my publisher, just like the other three. This means that N1Fan doesn't know where I live, even if they do know I've moved back to Ilfracombe. There is no real evidence to suggest the writer is even Aimee.

I'm still perturbed N1Fan has used my real name. How could the letter-writer have discovered I am SJ Scherer? I'm absolutely certain I've never used my real name online, nor have I revealed it at the few events I've appeared at.

There has to be a simple explanation.

I smile as the answer unfurls in my brain. I'd posted my picture online; I look my age, late thirties to early forties. There's every chance N1Fan had simply guessed at a name beginning in 'S' and got the right one. A simple search online of popular girls' names from 1979 would reveal a shortlist. The language choice was quite revealing, now I re-examined it: '*OR should I say Samantha?*' I'd read that as prior knowledge, but it was far more likely it was a literal question. N1Fan could just have easily written 'Sarah' or 'Sally'.

I decide to take my mind off my remaining disquiet and keep myself occupied. I check on Caleb, who is lying on his back, bashing his baby mobile with his feet. I smile indulgently to myself, before going in search of Mo's tools. Well, I say Mo's; it's actually me who uses them. We play at traditional gender roles in our house, but it's me who does the DIY, takes the rubbish bins out and removes spiders from the bath. Mo is much more likely to be found making Victoria sponges and flapjacks in the kitchen. That is, when he is home.

I decide to start with our bed: it's still in bits on the floor, the header and footer leaning against the wall. Its many small metal parts are still in the box where we'd packed them over a month ago before transporting them from London to Ilfracombe. I roll my shoulders, feeling the painful *click* as I do so. I'm nearly thirty-nine and Mo is well into his fourth decade. We are far too old to be sleeping on the floor.

I search for nearly forty minutes. I look in all the obvious places: boxes in the garage; the potting shed in the 'deceptively large' back garden (the estate agent's words, not mine); in the storage area of the eaves. No go. I release a frustrated yell. Some self-help guru I'd seen on YouTube had said it's a good idea to acknowledge our feelings by expressing them as sounds. I'd been giving it a try but to be honest, it just makes me feel stupid. Do I express the feeling of stupidity as a sound as well? I could end up in a weird loop of crazy noises forever.

I try to think like a metrosexual business consultant who has never actually used a screwdriver in his life. But I still have no success. I'm vaguely aware I'm creating more mess as I go, but I let this irony pass me by.

As a last-ditch effort, I trudge downstairs to the coal cellar at the bottom of the property. I look around the subterranean room with its white-washed, stone walls. There's a couple of boxes of random crap, but not much else. A smile spreads across my face as an idea comes to me. Mo has always said he wanted a 'man-cave', a space which is just his. This would be perfect. I would get it ready for him, a surprise for when he came home. What does a man-cave need? A telly of course; one of those mini-fridges, obviously. Maybe I could get a mini pool table. Then Mo would need a bookcase full of his beloved business tomes and guides. I could put his desk up in the corner, lug his favourite chair down here too. Maybe Mum would help.

As I climb the steep steps back up from the coal cellar, I make a decision. I should stop wasting time and just buy a new screwdriver. It's well past nine o'clock, Dyer's hardware store on the high street will be open. I'd been avoiding the centre of town, but I should just bite the bullet.

Caleb is glued to the television screen in the living room.

I force enthusiasm into my voice. 'Hey, who wants to go out?'

Caleb claps, holding out his arms for me. He's always been more sociable than me, just like his dad.

I grab my bag, keys and Caleb.

Three

There's hardly anywhere to park in Ilfracombe, just like I remember. I'm forced to do a circuit of the high street. Caleb and I sing along with his nursery rhymes CD as I drive straight through town, an incongruous soundtrack to my old haunts. I'd been avoiding going into Ilfracombe High Street, having my groceries delivered via the internet. I watch familiar milestones sail past.

Very little has changed. A wave of nostalgia hits me. This had been our group's stomping ground. Shops might have gone, but there are the buildings and roads I recall. The Pendle Stairway cinema, now called The Embassy, flies past; we'd all crept in to see *Basic Instinct* via a side door there aged twelve. The Bunch of Grapes pub is next, where we'd gone to see local bands play, or sing on Open Mic nights. Next comes the Queens Hotel, with its famous Tardis bar; I'd had my first shot of flaming Sambuca there and set fire to my fringe. There's a Costa and a Subway now, but the Swiss Cottage café is still open, its distinctive teapot-shaped metal sign swaying in the breeze.

I remember sitting there around a table with a gingham red tablecloth, laughing with my friends, drinking hot chocolate with cream and marshmallows. In my mind's eye, Ruby is giggling, the beads in her braids tinkling softly. Maddy is in her usual Goth get-up, her dark eyes ringed by kohl pencil. Then Aimee, wearing a Bindi in the middle of her forehead, her purple tresses scraped back into two space buns. Those cold, blue eyes and the perpetual sneer on her lip. The onslaught of faces and memories settles like a weight on my chest; it feels like both yesterday and an age ago.

Travelling on down to the promenade, I notice the tide is in; waves splash upwards towards the railings and bunting flying overhead. The arcades are all still there, as well as the infamous Landmark Theatre, its weird double-conical shape leading locals to dub it 'Madonna's Bra'. I find myself following the skinny side streets in the direction of the pier without really thinking.

'Lady!' Caleb bellows from his car seat.

Verity, Damien Hirst's controversial statue, swims into view. We crane our necks through the car windows to see her. I pull into the car park and turn the ignition off. *Verity* is a 'one of a kind' sixty-five-foot work of art. Made of bronze, she is a pregnant woman that stands on books and holds a sword aloft. She'd not been welcomed by all in the art world – or indeed everyone in Ilfracombe itself – but I think she is fabulous. She was erected in 2012, long after I had left with my parents back in the nineties, so I still get a thrill when I see her. *Verity* seems like a new beginning for the town, like the one thing here not tainted with old memories. I also feel a kind of kinship with her, the archetypal 'warrior mom'. I'd always dismissed women's proclamations of doing anything for their kids as hyperbole. Since Caleb's birth, I know deep in my gut it is as real as air or the wind.

Something occurs to me as I watch the waves splash around *Verity's* base. I whip my phone off the car dashboard where it was charging and call up my Instagram feed.

I spot the offending picture immediately.

A week earlier, I'd snapped a selfie at Ilfracombe quay, captioning it 'Back to our new home'. I'd thought I'd been so clever, positioning it so the space around me took in only the water and cliff-face, so it could be 'any' harbour.

But now I can see a big green bronze and stainless-steel foot behind me.

So, it had been *Verity* who had alerted N1Fan to the fact I lived in Ilfracombe. I might as well have left my phone's GPS function on. My fears the letters had been coming from Aimee are unfounded. I relax a little more.

I quickly delete the picture from my feed, then check my other pages and profiles for anything else that might give my hometown away. Nothing. Relieved at solving the last piece of the mystery, I drive back through the pier car park. Still singing nursery rhymes, Caleb and I complete our loop and return to the high street above the promenade.

I park on the steep incline of Oxford Grove, next to the high street. Grubby net curtains at windows twitch as I shut the car door, locking it with the key fob. It's not a fancy car, just a Nissan Qashqai, but it's obviously new. Like most British coastal towns, Ilfracombe has more than its fair share of poverty and deprivation; there aren't many vehicles driven straight off the forecourt here. I fuss over Caleb and his car seat, readjusting his rumpled clothes and checking his nappy.

I'm aware of what I'm doing. I'm putting off the moment of going into Dyer's, the discount and hardware store further up the high street. Everyone knew it was just a front. The Dyer family lifestyle way exceeded what such a tin-pot outfit could bring in. Aimee and her two sisters Charmaine and Shannon had all been spoiled princesses, enjoying a private education, pony riding and all the trappings of wealth dodgy deals could provide. Bill Dyer had a finger in every dubious pie in town and more besides.

With nothing left to delay us, I hoist Caleb up on my hip and slam the car door, letting it lock automatically behind me with a *blip*.

The shop looks exactly like it did back in the nineties, with its moss-green dormer windows and drainpipes. Various goods are piled up, resting against the glass. I'd rather go just about anywhere else, but I don't know where else in town I can buy tools.

The bell on the door tinkles behind me as I walk in, the smell of damp and pet food hitting me first. In my peripheral vision, I see a flash of purple hair and I turn towards the till, half expecting to see *her* in front of me giving me the side-eye.

But it's not Aimee, of course. The young woman behind the counter would have been a baby back then. *Twenty-three years have passed*, I remind myself.

The girl becomes aware of my scrutiny. She looks up from the phone in her hand, one over-plucked eyebrow arched.

'Can I help you?'

Her tone is deadpan, completely devoid of interest. She does not recognise me. Why should she? I flush, both with embarrassment and relief.

'Just looking.'

The girl goes back to scrolling through her feed as I let my eyes take in the chaos. There are wire baskets filled to the brim with beach balls, soft toys and buckets and spades. More are filled with packets of crab bait, or craft materials, or bottles of white spirit. Beyond the baskets are shelves carrying washing powder, sanitary towels, medicines and gloss paint. To someone who has never been in Dyer's before, this place might look like there's no rhyme or reason to it. It feels like a metaphor for my day-to-day life. But I remember the logic behind the seemingly eclectic mix of goods and sundries.

'Expensive stuff at the back,' Aimee would declare, sitting where the young woman is now, her bare feet up on the counter. For some reason, it has stuck in my mind. She's painting her toes a bright neon pink: 'Cheapo stuff at the front, along with kid stuff and beach stuff to get them and their parents in through the door. That means—'

'—middlingly expensive stuff in the middle,' I say to myself now under my breath.

I wince, both at the memory and at the word 'middlingly'. I'm not sure when I became a language snob; perhaps all writers are, deep down. How expensive are tools anyway? Front, middle or back? Nothing in this place looks precious enough to make it past the front desk of the shop to me.

'Down,' mumbles Caleb, struggling in my arms.

I don't let go of him. This place is paradise for the curious child but the floor is filthy and there's a billion hazards. The last thing I need is Caleb pulling out one thing and setting everything else raining down like giant, multi-coloured Jenga.

I trek around the shop, picking my way round yet more baskets and piles of goods. Sure enough, I find a big cork-board covered in tools in the middle of the shop: saws, chisels, hammers and pliers. I grab a spanner and a screwdriver. The other thing I need – an Allen key – is nowhere to be seen. I sigh, loudly.

'What you lookin' for, maid?'

The gruff voice behind me makes me jump. I recognise it instantly, even before I see his face. Cheeks burning, my stomach dropping into my boots, I feel sixteen again as I turn to face him.

A short man stands behind me, pricing gun dangling from his left hand. Despite his stature, he'd still been an imposing man when I had seen him last, with a taste for the finer things in life: sharp suits, cigars, plenty of notes in his money clip. He's different now. I take in his reddened face; the bushy, unkempt moustache under his nose; the shirt gaping at the buttons around his rotund middle, the greying hairs on his chest visible beneath. Faded green tattoos cover his arms, nearly all of them of naked women. Bill Dyer.

Aimee's dad.

'Allen key.'

I wait for him to recognise me. I know I haven't changed much since school. I am more lined, my body a little more angular, my hair shorter . . . But I'm still me.

But there's no recognition in Bill's pale blue eyes, either. In fact, he barely seems with it at all. Though his eyes are on me, he is preoccupied. It's as if his gaze is directed somewhere inside himself. Perhaps the credit crunch, followed by a swerve into austerity and then a crash course into Brexit had killed his business for real? He would not be the only Devon small business owner to have his prospects ruined in just a decade.

'Next aisle.' He turns and wanders back the way he'd come, brandishing his price gun like a cowboy in the Wild West.

Thankful for the reprieve, I scuttle into the next aisle. Unsure what size to get, I grab a bunch of Allen keys, paying for them with cash. I tell the girl behind the counter to keep the change and run back to my car. Sitting behind the steering wheel, I manage to steady my breathing and calm my racing heartbeat as Caleb regards me curiously from his car seat again.

Calm at last, I catch myself in my rear-view mirror and shake my head at my hysteria. Why would Bill Dyer recognise me? Even if he did, why would he care? I'm just somebody who went to school with his daughter. Bill Dyer probably doesn't even have a clue what happened between me and Aimee back then. I'm being ridiculous. The lost girl of twenty-three years ago is gone now; I am a professional, a wife, a mother. I am accomplished, valued, loved. I don't need the likes of Aimee to validate me any more.

I glance at the clock on the dashboard. Past eleven. Time's racing onwards and at this rate, I'll have nothing to show for it. I turn the key in the ignition and the engine springs to life. I need to leave all of that nonsense with Aimee back in the past, where it belongs.

Four

Back at the house, tools in hand, I attack the literal making of the bed with gusto. I imagine getting into it tonight, crisp new sheets, maybe a dab of lavender oil on the pillow. I could watch Netflix on my iPad and catch up on all the shows everyone raves about. More importantly, I could get some decent sleep at last. I must have been mad not to prioritise putting the bed up. I'd had thirty days of sub-par sleep, no wonder I am feeling strung out.

My progress is limited for the first hour as Caleb tries to help me. He keeps handing me random bits and pieces, a big smile on his face.

'Clever boy, thank you.' I beam back at him.

Caleb eventually bores of 'helping' and falls asleep right where we are on the floor, thumb in his mouth. I put him to bed. I wouldn't normally do such a thing in the middle of the day but needs must. I am able to make more headway without him next to me. Listening out for him in his bedroom, I go into auto-mode. Surveying the many metal and wooden pieces of our bed, my thoughts wander as my body fits screws, slats and other fixings together.

Never Have I Ever . . .

. . . made the entire bed all by myself.

The words return to me as I step back and admire my handiwork. The flush of pride I feel at completing my task vanishes. I'd been avoiding thinking about the game. I push the memory down, but I know I can't fend it off forever. I grab the bed knob and yank on it, checking to see if it wobbles. It doesn't, so I heft up the bare mattress, pushing it forward so it lands onto the slats with a soft *whoomph*.

'*What's "Never Have I Ever"?*'

I remember being sixteen, lying with Ruby on her bed as I asked that. She was cradling her beloved *Young Guns* videotape on her lap. She'd got a TV/VCR combo for Christmas that year and spent most of her free time watching old movies. *The Breakfast Club* and *St Elmo's Fire* had been favourites of hers too. All these years later, I still see Ruby every time I see a picture of Emilio Estevez.

Aimee had rolled her eyes. Maddy had thrown an armful of beanie babies at Ruby. Giggling, the four of us had started to pelt each other with toy bears, unicorns, monkeys and elephants.

'Oh. My. God. Everybody listen!' Aimee, raising her arms in the air as if conducting an invisible orchestra.

'Right, so this is how the game works. We played it all the time at West Buckland, with the boarding kids.'

Aimee had always liked to remind us she'd previously been a private-school kid. She had joined us in Ilfracombe High in year eight, when she'd got thrown out of West Buckland, the posh school up on Exmoor, near Barnstaple. As far as we were concerned, expulsion was the kind of thing that happened in American teen movies and sitcoms, not real life. We'd thought it so cool Aimee had got herself expelled. Dark eyeliner under her eyes, tie barely knotted, skirt rolled up, Aimee had seemed dangerous, exciting. She'd regaled me, Maddy and Ruby with tales of her exploits, including missing classes; going off campus without permission; even getting into fights. Thinking back now, we'd made it easy for her to take over our close-knit group. We'd literally rolled over and let her.

'Each person, in turn, has to say something she has never done and the others have to admit whether they have or not.' Aimee had fixed us with a smirk as she came up with a demonstration. 'For example: *Never Have I Ever* . . . been afraid of the dark!'

Nobody said anything. We'd all looked to one another expectantly, until finally Ruby, shame-faced, put her hand up. We'd all laughed, Ruby included, and for a moment I smile at the memory. This had been before everything had gone too far.

The sound of rain, hard like handfuls of gravel against the window pane, rouses me from my daydream. The blue skies of earlier are gone. Black clouds have rolled in, it's dark in my bedroom up in the eaves. I'd forgotten how changeable the weather in Devon is; you can dress for a day at the beach in the morning and need your anorak and wellies by the afternoon.

On my way to the airing cupboard, I double-check on Caleb. He is still sparko in his cot. He looks so beautiful when he is asleep. I watch him for a few moments, taking in his small body and blond curls. *He is so perfect.* It's hard to believe that in fifteen or sixteen years he would be a teenager, maybe doing mad stuff like we had.

No. I would never allow it.

'This game is for kids,' I'd declared in Ruby's bedroom.

Aimee shot me a withering look. 'You *would* think that.'

'Yeah, Sam! Stick in the mud.' Maddy cackled.

That had really stung. It was bad enough Aimee was always challenging me, but Maddy always sucked up to her. The benefit of hindsight and my sensible, adult side rise to the surface. Maybe if I had told Maddy of how I'd felt so left out, always on the fringes of the group, we could have avoided what came next that summer? This doesn't mean I'm letting Aimee off the hook though. She's the one who should take responsibility for the night of the summer party. It had been her idea and all her doing, after all.

Ruby rolled her eyes and picked up more fallen beanie babies and chucked them at each of us. '*Never Have I Ever* blamed my own farts on an animal!'

Maddy sighed, theatrical, then put her hand up. We'd all guffawed again, with Ruby falling about on the floor.

'It was one time,' Maddy appealed. 'Ruby was at mine and we'd been eating one of my dad's really spicy curries, okay?'

I'd felt jealousy flood through me on hearing that Ruby and Maddy had hung out without me. Maddy was supposed to be *my* best friend.

'Okay, my turn.' Maddy slapped her hands together. '*Never Have I Ever* lied to my parents.'

Ruby, Maddy and Aimee's hands immediately shot in the air. In contrast, I was caught on the hop. I racked my brain for a time I might have lied to Lindy or Dad but came up with nothing. I'd been embarrassed back then in front of my friends, but I shared most things with Lindy when I was growing up. I eventually shook my head, shame-faced. I'd been the classic teen; I'd felt so embarrassed when I'd realised I'd always left names, addresses and telephone numbers for my neurotic mum, as requested. Teens are so strange, thinking honesty is 'uncool', with lying the pref-erable way to go.

'Okay, fine. I'll do it. *Never Have I Ever* . . .'

Aimee grabbed my wrist, making me stop. 'I've just had the *best* idea. Let's switch this up.'

We sat forward, all ears.

'Sam's right, this game is lame.' Aimee paused for effect, allowing me a moment to savour her agreeing with me for once. 'So, I propose a twist! We find *Never Have I Evers* NONE of us have done, then we nominate one of us to do it first.'

There was silence as we all digested this.

'I'm not sure I follow,' Ruby said at last.

'Okay, let me demonstrate.' Aimee glanced at each of us, a smirk playing on her lips. '*Never Have I Ever* stolen anything from a shop.'

We all looked to each other, waiting for someone to put their hand up. No one did. Aimee's smirk turned into a wide grin.

'Okay then, I nominate you, Ruby. You have to shoplift something. Tomorrow.'

Ruby's eyes had widened with horror. 'As if! Stealing's wrong.'

'Duh, of course it's wrong!' Aimee crossed her legs under her. 'That's why this game will be fun.'

Maddy looked as thrilled as Ruby did miserable. I leant over to Ruby and put a sympathetic hand on her shoulder.

'It'll be fine. It's just one time.'

Ruby nodded, steeling herself. She laced her fingers together and stretched out her arms, as if preparing for a race. 'Tomorrow, then.'

We had all raised our hands in the air for an imaginary toast, giggling at our own cleverness and daring.

'Tomorrow!'

In my own room, I grab some bed linen and start smoothing it out on the bed. I wrestle with the duvet cover. If I had spoken up back then and told Ruby she shouldn't do Aimee's stupid dare, could everything have been different? Or maybe the rot had started long before that, with Aimee herself.

But that is all over. A time that had left us all scarred and changed forever, especially me. But it would not define me. I had dragged my feet at coming back to Ilfracombe when Mo suggested it, but I have every right to return home. Mum still lives here, and I could use her support. I am giving Aimee far too much credit. She is just messing with me. She always bored easily, so it won't be long before she stops sending me stupid notes. The best thing is to just ignore her. She'll go away.

Five

Determined to make my time off writing count, the days pass in a blur of DIY and unpacking, whilst trying to keep Caleb amused at the same time. I end up buying him a plastic tool set so he can play at putting all our new flat-pack furniture together too. When he gets tired of that, I plunder Pinterest for salt dough recipes and the back of Lidl on the seafront for cardboard boxes. Using colourful poster paints and big chunky markers, we make the boxes into trains, racing cars and spaceships for his teddies and other toys. It's frazzling, but fun; a million light years away from DI Robyn Dallas and my writing's signature dark violence.

I'm able to find places for all my things quickly since I defy the usual female stereotype – I don't have much in the way of belongings. My working life is just a computer, a printer, a single desk full of envelopes, pins and Post-its. I have a bookshelf full of reference books; a single wardrobe of clothes; just three pairs of shoes; a single shelf of toiletries in the bathroom. All my photos are framed or in the Cloud. I have no knick-knacks, no ornaments, no keepsakes. The only thing I do have in abundance are notebooks and reams of paper. I have an entire box of 'notes to self', but I stash those away easily.

I discover Mo, on the other hand, has more than made up for both of us. Just like the boxes of random crap in the coal cellar, he has brought stuff with us I'd no idea even existed. This includes two boxes of cables, junk mail sent to our London flat and stuff that 'looks useful', two words he'd scrawled on top of the boxes in faded black felt-tip. None of it is. I bag it up into black rubbish bags and leave them in the garage.

Mum drops by most days, though she never likes being called that. 'Call me Lindy' she'd always say in that conspiratorial way of hers, like we were breaking the rules. She's supposed to be helping me, but instead she makes a nuisance of herself, picking her way through my belongings and filling the house full of spearmint vape steam. She alternates between telling me how wonderful it is, having me back, and bemoaning the fact she now has nowhere to stay in London for free any more when she comes up to watch a show. *Even Travelodges are so expensive, you know, Samantha!*

As she gets in my way for the umpteenth time that day, I arrest the uncharitable thoughts. I grit my teeth and remind myself everything I'd thought so weird and New Age about Lindy when I was a teenager is now pretty mainstream. Like meditation. Back then I'd laughed at her and told her it was stupid. But I shouldn't be such a bitch. It *is* nice to have Lindy around. I've spent so much time alone or with Caleb since I've gone full-time as an author. I've just forgotten what it is like, being with someone else on a daily basis.

'So, you caught up with anyone yet?' Lindy's voice is guarded as we move Mo's newly assembled desk into place down in what had been the coal cellar.

I take in her wary expression and feel a surge of shame. Lindy is always so careful around me. I'd been a monster teenager at home, so sure it was all about me. I'd dismissed my mother, told myself she never really cared back when I was younger. But Mum *had* cared. An adult myself now, I realise she'd just been battling with a deep depression in my teenage years, one that had nearly killed her. She'd had to take several years off work; Dad had had to take that job in London that paid so much more. Back then, I'd thought both of them were distant, insular. In reality they were just doing what they could to stay alive and afloat. Kids can be so selfish.

I smile at her, keeping my voice light. 'Like who?'

Lindy feigns nonchalance at my dodge. She remembers my trouble with Aimee in 1996 only too well. It had been up to her and Dad to pick up the pieces.

'I don't know, do I? I can't remember their names, it was years ago. That tall one. And the Indian girl?'

'You mean Ruby and Maddy?' I gather up plastic wrappings, chunks of polystyrene. 'And Maddy is British, you know, Lindy, just like us.'

Mum juts her chin in that way of hers. Mo says I do exactly the same when I'm annoyed, but I refuse to believe it.

'Just saying. Her family owned the Indian takeaway, that's what I remember. God, your generation are always looking to be offended.'

Oh, really! I roll my eyes, but let it go. For all Mum's hippy-dippy, New Age shit, she's stuck in her ways just like most of *her* generation.

'I haven't seen them around, no.'

I set my side of the desk down on the over-sized rug that acts as a carpet covering the old, white-washed brickwork on the floor. In the corner, Caleb lies in his donut and kicks at his baby mobile, his chubby little legs in the air.

'Well, maybe you should actually seek them out. You know, on social media or something.' Lindy says 'social media' like others might say 'snakes'. She barely suppresses a shudder.

'Maybe.'

Lindy sighs at my second dodge but doesn't push it.

I stand back and admire our handiwork. I'm pleased with how Mo's 'man-cave' is coming together. A lick of paint on the back wall, some pictures and a few pieces of furniture from Argos have really transformed the place. Mo is going to love it. The only thing that mars it is the cold, probably because the cellar is underground. I make a mental note to pick up a fan heater in town before Mo returns.

As I continue my extreme makeover of the house, Mo phones home every night. It's an unusual step for him; he never usually calls with updates from his travels. It turns out Mo is in Germany and very bored. He fills me in on his nightly bar dates with the only other British guy in his swanky hotel.

'Seriously, he is the dullest guy in the world,' Mo complains. 'He talked for twenty-seven minutes about carpeting. Twenty-seven minutes! I counted. Anyway, turns out his warehouse is in Taunton, so he's going to come and measure up at ours when we're both back. Do you want crumb, sponge or felt underlay?'

I smile. It is typical of Mo to go a thousand miles from home and not only find someone relatively local but recognise an opportunity. 'I don't even know what the difference is.'

'Nor do I. I was hoping you did!'

I hang up, feeling closer to him than I have in months, despite the physical distance between us. I realise we are finally both reaching out. Perhaps the move back to Ilfracombe is working already? Maybe Mo was right; all we'd needed was some relief from the constant pressure of the debt and life in London. Whatever the case, I'm glad I'm making more of an effort. Mo will come home to an unpacked house, with a place found for everything. I'd make our house a home and we could get our fresh start off the blocks at last.

I climb into my properly made bed, my body relaxing the moment my weary bones hit lavender-infused sheets. I scroll through my iPad looking at curtains and carpets on a homeware website. My phone beeps again: an email.

I groan. It is past ten o'clock at night. There is only one person in my contacts list who'll still be working at this time: my editor, Aisling. She's almost as obsessed with books as she is with her Maine Coon cat, Jeff. She has no OFF switch. I can always get hold of her, even when she is on holiday, no matter the time of day or night. Unfortunately, this means she expects the same from me in return.

Sighing, I open the email. Its subject line is *Tomorrow*. I stare at it, heart plummeting. It reads, *You all set, babes?*

I tap a lightning message in response: *What have I forgotten?????*

Aisling's response comes a nanosecond later: *Exeter Waterstones reading and book signing!!!! 10am, the big store. NOT the little one by the cathedral. Sending you the address now. We spoke about it last week?*

Shit! I've always hated events, but I know I have to show Aisling willing. I'd turned down just about everything else and at least Exeter is fairly local.

I'll be there, I type.

You better!!! comes the reply barely five seconds later. Finishing the house will have to wait.

Six

In Waterstones, I'm surrounded by three old ladies; a cross-eyed young man in a chequered lumberjack-style shirt; a starry-eyed teenage girl, recording me on her phone; and a willowy businesswoman who looks like a young Emma Thompson in a trouser suit. Six people. I'd raced down the North Devon Link Road and then the M5 for this?

Scratch that: seven. Another woman hovers nearby. She's about my age, though her short hair is peppered with grey. Far from making her look old, she seems distinguished with it. She's wearing one of those tunic dresses that crease and would make me look like I had rolled out of bed wearing a potato sack, yet she is able to carry it off. She doesn't sit, but stands next to a table of non-fiction titles, browsing.

The standing woman lets her attention wander over to me. She seems familiar, but I can't place her. A surge of irrational panic tells me it's Aimee. Just as quickly I notice her eyes are brown, not blue. Thank God for that.

I am being ridiculous, anyway. As if Aimee cares whether I write crime novels; she was never much of a reader back in school. Even if she's had a personality transplant in the past two decades, this is another reason I use a pseudonym. Aimee could read the entire SJ Scherer back catalogue and be none the wiser I had written them.

As agreed with the booksellers, I read from the latest DI Robyn Dallas, book number seven, *The Silent Mist*, then the floor is opened for questions.

'Where do you get all your ideas from?' One of the old ladies hoists her over-sized handbag onto her lap.

Every writer gets asked this, at every event. I fight the urge to stick a pen in my eye and fix my best smile in place. 'The world around us. Everything that's in my books is inspired by a true case.'

The young man goes next, talking in a rambling, round-about way that reveals his is not a question at all, but a veiled plea for me to check out his own book. I promise I will, forgetting the title almost immediately.

One of the other grannies cuts in to talk about Sergeant Kye Thomson. It turns out she wants to rebuke me for what I had done to him in book five, *Whisper of Silk*.

'He's such a nice boy,' she laments, 'and to do *that* to him! I was shocked!'

'Yes, I was shocked too.' I'm not lying. Even I hadn't realised my mind was quite *that* dark. 'I know it might sound strange, but sometimes I can't control my antagonists' actions. I'm just the vessel they flow through.'

'That Elodie Fitzgerald!' the old woman mutters darkly. 'She's horrid.'

'She absolutely is,' I agree, enthusiastic this time. Elodie's the first daughter of the infamous Fitzgerald crime family, into drug dealing, gun running and the sadistic, sexual torture of unsuspecting 'nice boy' sergeants. She is vile, but oh, so much fun to write.

Finally, the question and answer session is over. One of the booksellers appears next to me, all smiles. Grateful to find a shield against the young man who is still trying to tell me about his book, I attach myself to her. She escorts me to a side room where I sign copies of my books for twenty minutes. I sit there for a further five minutes, wondering if anyone is coming back for me, before realising it's my chance to scarper. I grab my bag and stride out across the shop floor without a backwards glance.

'Samantha Russell?'

My old name makes me freeze in my tracks. I took Mo's name when we married, much to my mother's chagrin. Lindy had delighted in telling me forty per cent of married women kept their own names in the noughties. *Sorry, Mum.* I'd seen it as another opportunity to distance myself from Aimee and my past. Anyway, I'd wanted the same surname as any children that came along. As a kid I'd always found it embarrassing Lindy had a different surname to mine. Everyone at the school gates called her 'Mrs Russell' anyway.

I turn and see a burly, broad man with a beard standing outside Waterstones. He lights a hand-rolled cigarette; his blue eyes squint as the breeze sends the smoke back in his face. I'm surprised; back when I knew him, he never smoked. But then a lot about him has changed. His hair is curly, bushy like his beard. He's not a hipster, but a man's man; his clothes thrown on because he doesn't give a toss, rather than considered carelessness. He looks like a stranger, not the lanky boy I once knew with the haunted eyes. Yet I still know it's him.

'Michael Huxtable!' I laugh, surprised at the response of my body as I take him in. A shiver threatens to make its way up and down my spine.

'I thought it was you.' Michael's voice suits him better now. The other kids at school used to laughingly call him

35

Barry White: the skinny, pale kid with the incongruous, deep tone. There are ingrained creases at his eyes when he smiles, like he does nothing but laugh all day. 'Wow, how long has it been . . .?'

Twenty-three years, I want to say, but for some reason I stop myself. 'Ages!'

'Yes, less said about that, or you'll make me feel old.' Michael grins. 'You live in Exeter now?'

'Oh, no.' I think about telling him I'm there to do the reading for my book, but it seems like boasting. I'm far too British for my own good. 'Just, you know, shopping.'

'Yeah, me too.' He gives up on his rollie and throws it down on the pavement, crushing it under his boot. 'Well, not me. I get to wait around, while the missus does the shopping. You know how it works.'

The missus. Suddenly real life zooms back in. I can hear the buses roar past; adults chatting; children grizzling. I force myself not to look around too much in case Michael's wife is just inside the store, walking towards us. I can't betray my curiosity.

I smile. 'I sure do.'

He grins back at me but doesn't say anything more. It seems like a whole minute passes, though it can't have been more than five seconds. We just stare at each other, searching for something, anything to say. Yet again I am reminded that everything back here in Devon is saturated in my personal history. No matter how I try and head it off at the pass, something seems to pop up and wrong-foot me.

'Well, I guess I better send out the search party,' Michael says at last, looking at his watch.

I nod, attempting to move out of his way. Instead, I block him, so we end up doing an awkward dance. We both laugh

36

and he squeezes my arm as he passes. He goes into the bookstore, vanishing behind a gaggle of Japanese tourists looking at a display of British souvenirs.

My arm tingles where he touched it.

Seven

There are hold-ups all the way back from Exeter to Ilfracombe. Being summer, there's more traffic on the roads. A jack-knifed lorry causes tailbacks on the M5, followed by a broken-down car on the North Devon Link Road. I can hear my phone ringing in my bag on the back seat and know it's Mum, demanding to know when I will be back.

When I'd glanced at the clock after Aisling's email the night before, I'd groaned. Lindy still lives on her nerves; a phone call after dark never goes down well. But I'd no choice: I needed Mum to take Caleb during my reading at Waterstones. I would need to leave early to make it for Exeter for ten. I'd dialled, bracing myself for Lindy's reaction.

'What, what is it? What's happened?'

No greeting, just her predictable panic at getting a phone call after dark. This is what it had been like every day, my entire teenage years. With Dad working away so frequently, it had been up to me to make sure Lindy didn't freak out at home. Having a parent with significant mental health issues had been a difficult responsibility to shoulder as a teenager. The anxiety that rooted itself in my belly back then has never truly unfurled. My mother's condition made day-to-day life like walking on glass, the danger underfoot every waking second.

I'd discovered, to my surprise, that state was preferable to when Lindy didn't notice me at all. Those times, she'd flit around the house like a ghost, not speaking, like I didn't exist. Sometimes I could walk right up next to her, before Lindy even realised I was there. She's been well for years now. Even though I've always known it's not her fault, resentment still surges through me when Lindy's condition rears its head. Like now.

I counted to ten. 'Everything's fine, Lindy.'

Lindy tutted on the other end of the line. 'Samantha, you know I hate phone calls in the middle of the night. You nearly gave me a heart attack!'

According to my mother, everything 'nearly' gives her a heart attack. Opening doors too quickly. Pedestrian crossings beeping. Piers Morgan on the telly, at any time of the day or night. If she ever *did* have a heart attack, I'm bound to have one straight after, due to the shock of her multiple predictions coming true at last. She might look like a laid-back hippy with her flowing grey hair, long velvet skirts and strings of beads, but she's on high alert twenty-four seven. I take a deep breath and ask her to babysit Caleb for me.

Lindy didn't congratulate me when I told her about my event. She has always been a little self-involved. She doesn't like disruptions to her routine. I suppose I am my mother's daughter.

'Well, I was going to the library tomorrow. I have a book about Ted Bundy I need to give back.'

I took this in my stride. Reading about serial killers has been an obsession of my mother's since I was a girl. By the age of ten and to the horror of my form teachers, I could recite all the major murderers from Aileen Wuornos through to the Zodiac Killer. On my author website, I list this as one of the primary reasons I became a crime novelist.

'Oh, you can take Caleb with you, he loves the library.' *Crossing my fingers*.

I was lying through my teeth. Just like I'd dodged my mother's questions about looking up old friends, I'd been avoiding Ilfracombe as much as possible, too. Caleb has not been to Ilfracombe's library on the Candar yet, a development of municipal buildings and sheltered housing. It had been opened by Princess Diana and Prince Charles, their last ever public engagement together when I was about twelve. I can still remember the endless Union Jacks fluttering in the wind every time I go down there.

Mum sighed. 'I suppose I could. Go on, then.'

'Bye, Lindy!' I ended the call before she could change her mind.

Exeter to Ilfracombe usually takes an hour and a half, but today it's two hours ten. The delays give me time to process seeing Michael so unexpectedly. I am perturbed by how easily I had been rattled by bumping into him; and how disappointed I'd been when he mentioned his wife. I wish I'd thought to ask him if he lived in Exeter now, or whether he was on holiday, visiting family or friends. Michael had been my first kiss; my first boyfriend; my first everything. If I close my eyes – not advisable on a dual carriageway – I can still see his curved half-smile, his boyish face.

I'm being ridiculous again. Never mind the fact Michael is married; I am too. I am a mother now. I am above hankering after teenage crushes.

Gripping the steering wheel between two hands, I shake my head, as if I can expel the thoughts, the memories. It's just the weirdness of being back in Devon again after all these years, messing with my head. Michael and I had parted on bad terms when I left. But he clearly didn't bear me any ill will. Why would he? We were kids back then, life has moved on.

I park the car outside the new house, then pull my phone from my bag as I approach the front door. The screen reads 9 *MISSED CALLS*, all from Mum, as I'd predicted. There's a stream of unanswered texts from her, too:

Samantha, where are the boy's nappies?
Don't worry. Found them.
Caleb has a such a dirty laugh, just like your dad's.
BBC Radio Devon says there's a crash on the link road FYI.
Hello, this is the woman who gave birth to you. Just checking you're still alive.

I find myself smiling. Lindy is eccentric, not to mention annoying as hell, but since Dad died, she's all I have from my side of the family. I think sometimes that's one of the reasons I gravitated towards Mo and his endless Irish brood of brothers and sisters, cousins, uncles and aunts. I have to keep a little book of all our nieces' and nephews' dates of birth; barely a single month goes by without needing to buy a card or present. Once a year, there's the 'Brennan Annual Shindig' and we all end up camping at one of Mo's brothers' houses over in Ireland for a bonfire and mini festival of music, whilst all the men try to outdo each other carving the hog roast. Mo has been making some noises about holding it in Ilfracombe one year. I'd pointed out we didn't have the room in the garden; our neighbours certainly wouldn't like it. He'd argued that we might get away with a BBQ on one of the more secluded coves nearby and camp on the headland. I said I would think about it, code for 'over my dead body'. The headland is one place I definitely won't be revisiting.

As I walk through the front door I fire off a text, telling Mum I'm back and she can bring Caleb home. Yet more post litters the mat and my heart sinks when I notice another envelope. I take it into the kitchen, leaving the rest on the counter. The envelope does not have my address on the front. It doesn't look like it's come via my publisher this time.

Instead, in careful, looped handwriting: *Samantha Russell*.

For the second time in one day, my old name. The letter must have been hand-delivered. I try to compare the writing in my head to the fan mail's, but I can't be sure. I try and stop my thoughts from spiralling. I take several deep breaths to calm myself.

I think briefly about screwing up the letter, shoving it in the recycling box; even burning it. But I know curiosity alone won't allow me to do that, and it could be nothing. I am probably overreacting again. I find myself muttering 'I reject fear', just like Lindy does.

There must be a logical explanation.

Perhaps someone from school has seen me in town. Or maybe they even live near my new house, have seen me coming and going? But why not come up to me, like Michael had? Maybe they were shy. Or maybe they weren't sure it's me. But if they'd recognised me from afar in the street, they could recognise me online, even with my SJ Scherer pseudonym. Why not send me a message on Facebook? Why go to the trouble of putting something through the door? It's so old-fashioned.

Unable to take it any longer, I rip the envelope open. A thin slip of paper flutters to the floor. I lean down to grab it, eager to read what it says. Once I have, I wish I'd never set eyes on it.

Never Have I Ever been punished for what I have done.

Eight

'What's the matter?'

I look up from my noodles at Mo, who's stopped slurping his across the table. He's looking at me with that vulnerable expression he wore so often as a young man, when I fell in love with him at university. He'd treated me as if I was made of glass back then, as if I could shatter any moment. But he'd been too late; by the time I met him, I had already put myself back together. If only he'd known what I had to deal with *before* we met, he would have realised I am made of sterner stuff.

'Nothing.' I force a smile, my hand on my jeans pocket under the table. In there, the *Never Have I Ever* note I'd received, neatly folded.

Mo's brow creases. 'Did you get more of that creepy fan mail when I was away?'

I'd almost forgotten Mo knew about N1Fan. Any threat I'd felt at those letters with their talk about walking in Ilfracombe, or even guessing my name correctly suddenly seems small cheese in comparison to the one I'd just got.

'No.' I release the half-truth into the air.

The Never Have I Ever note burns a hole in my pocket, making a liar of me. The scrawled message is uncomfortably familiar. I'd received an identical letter, twenty-three years ago, just before my family had left Devon. Back then

44

Never Have I Ever been punished for what I have done had seemed risible, a last resort at a Parthian shot. The pathetic bluster of someone who had just lost. That's why I'd forgotten it, until those words had crashed right back into my present. This is serious. Aimee's not going to let this go.

'We're okay, right?'

Mo gives me a watery smile, his face betraying his uncertainty at my own demeanour. I've tried to prove to him I can handle whatever life throws at us. The loss of the businesses, all those years of fertility treatment. Perhaps I've been too successful; as my position strengthens, his seems to weaken. As time has passed, every time I have had a problem in our relationship, he's become sure it's all his fault, that I am blaming him. He seems to brace himself for incoming missiles every time we speak at the moment. Maybe he is right to. I am not sure any more either; I have lost perspective.

I nod. 'Yes, of course.'

We both stare back at our lacklustre instant noodles. I know he's wondering if I am angry with him for going away again. Mo had only arrived back from Germany that evening. He'd been impressed to see the house unpacked, a place found for everything. I'd looked forward to his return all day. I'd wanted to show him his new man-cave the moment he got back. But he'd been weary from travelling and seemed disconnected, despite his smiles. The Mo of our phone calls appeared to have receded again, like the tide going out. I'd decided to wait until it came back in, bringing him with it.

I've always been able to tell what Mo is thinking; he's incapable of hiding his emotions. There was a tall, young student with floppy blond hair that Mo knew at university – his name escapes me – but they had shared a house for years. A young gay bloke, Mo's friend had made it clear he hankered after what he assumed we would have in our future without even trying: lovely house, white picket fence, two point four children, visits to the garden centre on a Sunday.

If only that had been true.

'You two are like the stereotypical couple, only opposites!' he'd declared one night in the pub. 'Mo is the neurotic one, but you? You're the strong, silent type.'

Mo's mate had no idea how right he was . . . Or what it had taken me to get to that point. I had vowed I would never go back to the scared, sad little girl Aimee had made me. I consider taking the note out of my pocket and showing Mo. But pride stops me. I don't want to be reduced in his eyes, a victim all over again.

I push my bowl away. 'These are shit. Why don't I get us some chips?'

'I'll get them.' Mo pushes his own bowl away, relieved.

'No, no. I could do with the trip out. Been stuck here, haven't I?' My smile freezes on my face when I realise how it sounds. Mo seems to deflate. 'Sorry, I didn't mean it the way it came out.'

Mo grabs the bowls to scrape them out. 'S'fine. Grab me my usual, yeah?'

I sweep out of the house before I can stick my foot in it again, picking up my keys and bag as I go. I arrive outside in the night air and gulp it in, as if I'd been holding my breath inside the stale warmth of the house. Orange street-lamps pool around the car on the driveway. As I press the key fob, I glance across the valley in the direction of the sea: I can't see it in the dark, but I can glimpse the lights of the RNLI boat, the smaller fishing boats and the MS *Oldenburg*. It's like the stars have fallen to earth.

An overweight golden retriever waddles past, followed by its owner who nods at me. It's not until I've closed the door and started the engine that I realise I didn't acknowledge him. Years in London mean I've forgotten the Devon custom of greeting strangers constantly, day or night. I turn around and peer through the back window, but he is long gone. I turn the key in the ignition. I flick the indicator at the end of my road to drive towards the high street.

As I drive past the old newsagent's I can't help remember the time we ran out of there as teenagers. We had legged it down the road, Ruby with a stolen magazine stuffed under her top, arms and legs pumping. When we had eventually stopped, gasping for breath and giddy with success, Ruby pulled out the contraband: a rolled-up copy of *Men's Health*. The choice hadn't gone down well with Aimee at the time, but Maddy and I thought it was hilarious. It would be a funny memory if it wasn't for what it symbolised; what it was the beginning of. The group's first *Never Have I Ever* dare, completed.

It had been such a small thing, stealing a magazine; but it had opened a Pandora's box for our small group. What if I'd stood up to Aimee? Would the others have followed suit, or sided with Aimee and ejected me from the group like I'd feared? I will never know. I hadn't done what I should have.

I continue driving down to the seafront. As I make my way past the Landmark Theatre to the promenade, I note it's curiously deserted for August at half ten at night. The tide licks at the railings as I pass Wildersmouth Beach.

Most of the shops are dark, some with their steel shutters down. The Admiral Collingwood, a Wetherspoon's opposite the crazy golf course, is busy, though most of the patrons have abandoned the patioed seating area. I am forced to touch the brakes as a young, drunk couple burst forth from the shadows of Capstone Hill. The young man breaks away from his girlfriend as he lands both palms on my car bonnet. He stands up straight, as if surprised I haven't run him down, then gives me an apologetic double thumbs-up. His partner cackles, almost falling from her five-inch heels. Both laughing, they stagger off in the direction of the old bus station.

I park down a side street and join the considerable queue at the chip shop in the shadow of Our Lady, Star of the Sea. As I wait my turn, I let my gaze wander around the narrow shop. A couple of teen girls sit on the bay window seat, a baby of about Caleb's age between them. They all look like siblings; large age-gap families are common in Devon. I wonder where their parents are. The baby is in his pyjamas, happily munching away on chips, but he is up far too late. My judgement must have shown on my face, because one of the girls scowls at me. If looks could kill, I'd have been blasted into outer space with hers. I'd only left the house ten minutes ago.

Determined not to alienate any more of the locals, I avert my eyes. I dig my phone out of my cardigan pocket. I call up the Facebook app and review the searches I'd already made after Mum's suggestion the other day. I hadn't been able to resist my curiosity any longer. I need to know if it could have been them, not Aimee, who had hand-delivered the *Never Have I Ever* note. They were the only other people who'd known about our game.

Ruby Talbot
Maddy Khan

Most adults born between 1975 and 1995 are on Facebook, but not *my* Ruby. Just my luck. I had found just about everyone with the same name as hers all over the world. I'd checked Twitter and Instagram as well, even Pinterest. That's the extent of my social media knowledge. Perhaps she had got married, changed her name? Then I really would have zero chance. There must be millions of surnames in the world. I keep scrolling anyway, trying to discern facial features I recognise. Perhaps I could find one of Ruby's relatives in her place. She had a chubby younger sister who was always hanging around, maybe she is worth a try. She used to sidle up to us – denim jacket, oversized Nirvana T-shirt, stripy leggings, fake Converse – and desperately ask to join in. Blobby, we called her. I cringe at the casual cruelty. Aimee used to call her fatso, tell her to go on a diet. Ruby never quite mustered enough courage to tell her to stop. None of us did.

I try various names in the search bar, but nothing looks promising and I can only remember her as Blobby, however sick and guilty it makes me feel. Blobby had an auburn-haired friend – Jane? Julie? Jess? – who used to hang around too, but I can't find her either. She was the only person I really remember standing up to Aimee. A bully and a bitch, she called her, once. The look on Aimee's face when she promised the girl would regret it had been terrifying, and I wasn't even on the receiving end. I'd been jealous as hell of her bravery that day. Even now, I wonder why I couldn't have been brave like that.

On my phone, Maddy's name and profile flashes up again on the screen as I refresh the app. I'd known it was her the moment I saw her profile picture earlier. In it, her long, lustrous black hair cascades around her face just like it had when we were teens. She's not changed at all, is just a little more lined around the eyes. She isn't a Goth any more, though in her pictures she still wears flicked, cat-like eyeliner. She holds a guinea pig, one of her favourite animals. Her mum had never let Maddy have pets, so Maddy had always said she would leave home and have an entire zoo at her house. It looks as if she'd made good on her dream: in every single picture, she's holding mammals, birds or reptiles. I smile, pleased for her.

Scrolling through, I see there are no pictures of a boyfriend, or a girlfriend. Her relationship status is listed as 'single'. Her parents had managed to make one of their wishes for her stick though: her occupation is listed as 'lawyer', at some firm up in London. I laugh when I Google the address. Maddy's been working within three or four blocks of my old house for years. I could have bumped into her at any point, had fate allowed it. Instead, I've ended up coming back to Ilfracombe to look up my old best friend.

As I wait for my turn in the queue, I work through likely explanations for the Never Have I Ever note in my mind. I hadn't heard from Ruby in years, would she really start this up again the moment I come back? It seems unlikely. Living away from Ilfracombe, it also surely means Maddy can't have hand-delivered the note? I fire off a friend request.

I am still certain it must be Aimee. I hesitate, then type her full name Aimee Louise Dyer in the app search bar as well. If I'm going to live in this town with Aimee and her huge extended family, I should know what I am dealing with. She could look very different, for all I know. Perhaps I have even walked right past her on one of my infrequent trips to Ilfracombe High Street.

The results for a stack of Dyers come back, all within the local area thanks to various mutual friends and my phone's GPS function. *Shannon Dyer, Charmaine Jenkins (née Dyer)* appear on screen: Aimee's older sisters. There's a selection of cousins and other in-laws too. Maybe Aimee has changed her surname too and not listed her old one? I flick through their mutual friends lists and photos, see if I can find an Aimee in any of them. Nope. I sigh.

Now what?

I finally get the chips and Mo's saveloy, wrapped to go. I'd forgotten too how slow the pace of life is in Devon. Every minute in London seems to take three times as long down here. Even so, I smile as I pick up the parcelled food and sweep out.

Though I make no conscious decision, I find myself driving the long way around back to the new Barnstaple road. I travel back up the promenade and past the Lidl, up Wilder Road. I slow down and park near the war memorial. As I'd suspected, Maddy's parents' restaurant is gone. In its place, a nail salon, done out in bubble-gum pink. Mrs Khan would have hated that. I wonder if they had just retired, or whether they're dead. They'd been fairly old by nineties' standards when Maddy was born, at least in their early forties. That meant they'd be eightyish now.

My phone buzzes in my bag. Sighing, I fish it out. Mo's name flashes on the screen. I'm shocked to see the time is now almost half past eleven; the chips are cold. I must have been staring at what had been the Khans' restaurant for longer than I thought.

I don't say hello. 'Yeah. I'm coming, there was a massive queue.'

'As long as you're okay.'

Mo's voice is quiet, but it feels like a slap in the face. He hadn't been checking up *on* me, but concerned *for* me. Guilt blooms in my chest. *God, I'm such a bitch.*

'I'm coming now.'

Nine

I awake with a start as usual, my head filled with darkness and falling. The chill of that long-lost July night invades my senses, following me out into the waking world. The shadows create swirling patterns on the bedroom wall. I can see myself running through the long grass, heart hammering in my chest. Teeth chattering, Nike Airs soaked, toes numb. Combats are covered in mud. Then I am plummeting backwards . . .

. . . No. That is over with, now.

I stagger from the bed and pull the blind; daylight rushes in, banishing bad dreams away. It still feels like there's a heavy weight on my chest, like someone is piling earth on top of me. I lie back on the bed, letting my heartbeat return to normal.

The house is quiet. There's a space in the bed next to me; Mo is gone. Caleb is still asleep. Could this be where his erratic sleep patterns change, at last? I enjoy the silence for a nano-second, before reaching for my phone and checking Facebook. My friend request to Maddy is still pending. Damn it.

I stretch out. I usually wear pyjamas, but today I am uncharacteristically naked. I put my phone back on the nightstand and notice a scrap of paper. On the back of a receipt Mo has scrawled *LOVE YOU xxx* in capital letters.

I smile, though I feel detached. The previous evening feels like a dream. I'd arrived back with the cold chips, but Mo had been waiting in the kitchen, a bottle of wine open. He'd greeted me with a kiss on the lips, a wide smile. The shy atmosphere of before was gone; it was like the awkward dinner over reheated noodles never happened.

I smiled. 'What was that for?'

'I saw downstairs. The man-cave. It's awesome! You should have shown me when I got back.'

I shrugged. 'Oh, it's nothing.'

My gaze dropped to the bottle. He'd drunk at least half of it himself; he had never been able to hold his alcohol. I put on a pretend-school-ma'am voice. Mo loves it when I do that.

'Mr Brennan, I am shocked. Are you drunk?'

Mo grinned. 'Maybe a little.'

I indicated the takeaway, still in the plastic bag dangling from my hand. 'I'll put these in the microwave . . .?'

'I never really wanted bloody chips.' Mo's voice was gruff, slightly slurred.

I dropped my bag and put the chips on the counter. 'It'll only take a minute—?'

As I turned back, I found him standing close behind me. He grabbed both my elbows, pulling me towards him. He dipped down, pressing his lips against mine and sliding one hand underneath my top.

He stopped, remembering himself. 'I want you . . .?'

The question hung in the air. My reply: I unzipped his fly. Mo parted my legs with one knee, pushing me backwards onto the kitchen table. I could taste the Rioja on his tongue as he slipped it into my mouth. My last thought before surrendering was, *I was saving that.*

He'd fucked me on the table, then again later upstairs, in the bedroom. The second time had been less animal, more tender, but I'd still not fully engaged with it. It was like he'd wanted to reclaim me, put his stamp on me. I felt like I was performing, watching myself with Mo. He hadn't seemed to notice. Why would he? The problem is me. As always.

I shower and dress. I go and wake Caleb, busying myself with getting him fed and clothed. That always takes a while. Since hitting a year old, he's decided it's hilarious to fight me, kicking out his legs. He is surprisingly strong. It's like trying to put trousers on a kangaroo.

I take him downstairs and turn on the television in the kitchen for him. He ignores it, wriggling on his tummy army-style to his toy box, leaning his pudgy arms on it. Mo thinks it's funny Caleb doesn't crawl properly and calls him 'Arnie', after Schwarzenegger in his favourite eighties film, *Commando*. Caleb was premature and is still small for his age, so I'd wondered if we should be concerned. According to Super Nanny though, some babies just miss out the main crawling bit. I watch him closely, just the same. Shouldn't he be walking by now? No. Let him go at his own pace.

I check the mat at the front door with trepidation. No notes, either from N1Fan, or Aimee. That's something.

But did that mean one, or both of them, are watching the house? I shudder. No, I am 'catastrophising' now. I've been around Mo and Lindy too long. N1Fan is just some sad reader, trying to give their life more meaning. As for the *Never Have I Ever* note, maybe Aimee had just sent it to mess me up, a kind of twisted 'Welcome Home' present? It's definitely her style. Once a bully, always a bully. That doesn't mean she's going to act on it again. We are grown adults now. She wouldn't dare do anything else.

Would she?

I take in the Yale lock on the door, the chain. Suddenly it seems unbearably flimsy. I try and talk myself down. I must not let Aimee get under my skin. Reading Lindy's true crime books from a young age has left me with a lasting paranoia and suspicion there's a potential serial killer around every corner. The letters were low-level harassment, if that. I probably won't even get another one. I am being way too dramatic.

Even so, there's Caleb to think about. He's already a wriggly baby. How long before he learns to pull a chair to the door and unlock it? Yale locks are easy. Too easy. We need a deadlock, for the top of the door as well. Just in case. It's good parenting, after all.

I grab my car keys.

Minutes later, we are back on Ilfracombe High Street. This time, I'm able to find a rare parking space along the road; I only need twenty minutes. I unload the pushchair from the boot. Caleb grumbles as I strap him in, but soon forgets his discontent when I produce a pack of Pom-Bears from my bag. He munches on them as I push him up the street and back towards Dyer's.

The bell over the door dingles as I shoulder it open, pulling the pushchair in after me. The girl from the other day still sits at the till, chewing gum and looking even more bored than before, if that is possible. This time, I see she is wearing a name badge: AVA. It triggers an image in my brain: a smiling toddler of about Caleb's age, on reins, walking alongside Aimee down on the seafront, back when we were teens.

'Ava, right?'

Ava taps the badge. 'That's what it says.'

I smile. Oh yeah, Aimee's blood is in Ava's veins all right. 'Your mum is Charmaine Dyer, Aimee's big sister. You're Aimee's niece.'

Ava just keeps chewing gum. 'S'right.'

I take a deep breath, preparing myself for the plunge. I can't think of anyone I would like to speak to less. Needs must.

'Is Aimee about? I'd love to speak to her.'

But Ava continues to stare at me, deadpan. 'She's not here.'

A curious mix of disappointment and relief descends on me. What would I have said to Aimee anyway, after all these years?

Oh hi, what have you been doing with yourself for twenty-three years? Oh and by the way, have you been sending me mildly threatening notes about what happened in the summer of nineteen ninety-six?

Yet I can't just leave it, it seems. I grab a pen from the counter and scrawl my name and my mobile number on the back of a paper bag for Ava.

'Could you give this to her?'

'Sure. *If* I see her.' Ava takes the paper bag from me between her thumb and forefinger, as if it's contagious. Young people are so weird.

A nice, sturdy deadlock selected and paid for, I wheel the grizzling Caleb back out into the street. I press the button at the pelican crossing outside the cinema. Opposite me, a tall, bearded man dressed in black appears out of the doors of the American diner across the street. In his hands, he holds a takeaway coffee, which he takes towards a bundle of rags under Market Arches.

Oh, wait.

The rags move as he crouches down; a homeless woman. Shame courses through me: I'd forgotten that rural communities had social problems too. I'd remembered only rolling seas and countryside, bright blue skies and sandy beaches. But it doesn't have time to take root, as I'm distracted. I'd seen this man in Exeter only a few days ago.

Michael.

I reassess his outfit. The shining black boots. The sharply pressed trousers. The vest with many pockets and belt, the curl of cables that lead to his radio.

Michael's a policeman.

Ten

I want to turn away, hide my face. But the pelican crossing starts to beep, drawing Michael's attention.

'Sam!' He gives me a cheery wave.

I am forced to give him a wide smile in return. I grab the handles of Caleb's pushchair and cross the road towards him. As he wanders out from the arches to meet me, my mind transforms him from the adult, bearded Michael in front of me to Mike, aged sixteen: thinner, rangier, his face clean-shaven. He still has that lopsided, almost bashful smile though.

'So, fancy seeing you here!' I feel off-balance, so I try and hide it by adopting a jokey, jovial tone. I sound ridiculous, like I am acting a part.

'You can say that again.' Michael holds both the straps of his vest, confident and assured, like I've seen so many police do. 'You moved back, then? I did wonder.'

I don't know why I had assumed Michael would no longer be living in Ilfracombe. He'd not said he'd moved away when I saw him outside Waterstones; he'd even confirmed he didn't live in Exeter. Just like I had. That said, I'm still not sure which is more jarring: the fact Michael is still local, or that he's with the police now. I feel strangely let down. He'd always been strait-laced, even when we were teens. Even so,

I would have put real money on him becoming something like a teacher.

'Oh, yes. Fresh start and all that.'

I am vague, on purpose. I don't want to get into the ins and outs of the debt or marriage issues that had prompted me and Mo to go looking for a better, more rewarding life.

'Back with your mum, are you?' Michael nods at Caleb, fast asleep in the pushchair and covered in Pom-Bear crumbs.

I release an awkward, girlish laugh. Being the local bobby, Michael would know Lindy had moved back years ago too. Now, thanks to my vagueness, Michael had jumped ahead and assumed I was back home because I was getting a divorce. Where else do women go but home, when their man leaves them in the lurch?

Christ, this is even more mortifying than I thought possible.

'No, *we* bought one of the properties up near the New Barnstaple Road. One of the big, high-up ones that over-look Hillsborough and the harbour?' I try and keep my voice smooth, not defensive.

Michael whistles in appreciation. 'Not short of a quid or two, then.'

I don't know why this rankles me. 'Actually, we got a low price 'cos the house needs a lot of work. We'll be changing stuff around for a good while yet.'

'Sure, but maybe you've forgotten.' Michael extends a hand towards the shabby street, the bundle of rags in the archway. 'A low price for grockles from London? It's still a lot of money for people around here.'

His blow lands. There he is, the Mike I'd known back then. He had always been condescending when he got on his high horse about an issue. I should have realised he'd go for a job with some kind of authority. Becoming a police officer is perfect for him, after all.

'I'm not a grockle.' I glower at him.

Michael shrugs, a smirk on his lip. He knows he's got to me. Perhaps I'd not changed much, either. 'Nice seeing you, Sam. Again.'

'Wait!' Before he can turn his back on me, the word bursts from my lips before I can even decide if it's a good idea. 'Is Ruby still living around here?'

Michael nods. 'She works down at the quay, last I heard.'

'Where on the quay?' I don't bother to hide the impatience in my voice.

Michael purses his lips. 'It's a new place, a fancy Indian restaurant. Near that statue.'

That statue. So, Michael doesn't like *Verity* either. Or maybe it's because her presence means the police have to check up on her. Damien Hirst had made it clear when donating *Verity* that he didn't want any activists of any kind scaling her, to make political statements. 'Thanks,' I say through gritted teeth. I steer Caleb and the push-chair away, through Market Arches, leaving Michael in my wake.

I make a good pace on the way downhill to the seafront, gathering momentum to the point I'm trotting briskly. I breathe in the sea air, letting my irritation with Michael dissipate. If I'd thought it through rather than let Michael get under my skin, I would have realised loading Caleb back into the car and driving down to the quay would have been a better idea. Now I'd need to push him back up the steep hill to the high street when I was done. But the air down in Devon feels fresher, healthier. A good walk might help me get fit. Maybe I'd even lose a little weight, like the muffin top I'd accumulated. Mo hadn't said anything; I doubted he'd even noticed. But I had.

As I make it to the promenade, I have to slow down. At the Clapping Circle I weave my way around tourists, not to mention the inevitable groups of Spanish EFL students from the Language School. As the pavement narrows and I draw closer to the harbour, I find myself having to stop and start as people and cars get in my way. It really had been a spectacularly bad idea to bring the pushchair down here.

I pass the cafés, the church and the Royal Britannia Hotel and make it onto the harbourside at last. I abandon going against the tide of people and move with the throng. It's like a shoal of fish. I follow the ebb and flow, past the chip shops, the tourist souvenir vendors and the ice-cream sellers.

The restaurant is easy to find. I wonder if this could be where Maddy's parents moved their takeaway. Mrs Khan had always had designs on the seafront, where rents were more expensive. I relax as I draw closer: there is a liquor licence. Not only would Maddy's mother have never countenanced alcohol in her beloved restaurant, the name above the door is not Khan.

People are seated outside, so I manoeuvre Caleb around them, towards the bar. Michael had not been exaggerating; it is fancy. Low lighting, lush carpeting, velvet drapes. I can see a couple of Asian cooks through the swing door to the kitchen, though the waiters are all white and under twenty-one: students. They're dressed in black trousers and maroon waistcoats, carrying overly large naan breads on hooks and piles of poppadums. Tourists and locals line up at an 'all you can eat' lunch buffet, designed to take advantage of the foot traffic outside for day trade. It's working. The place is packed.

I see another young white guy waltz past, through another door, not in uniform. His arms are full of trays of ice; inside, lobster and crab. I'd read in the *Guardian* that Ilfracombe has become known as a foodie heaven destination. It's renowned for restaurants and cafés that serve local produce, meat and fish. The young fisherman would have caught them in pots off Ilfracombe harbour.

Behind the counter, there's a mirror behind the optics, giving the impression the small bar is even bigger. I catch sight of my reflection. In my creased clothes and Mum ponytail with no make-up, I realise I seem out of place here. That's before I add the pushchair and the sleeping baby covered in crumbs.

'Can I help you?' The young bartender is only a couple of years older than Ava up at Dyer's, but the warm smile on her face makes her seem like she is in a different league.

I decide to just go for it. 'Hi, I'm Sam. Is Ruby in?'

The young bartender's smile does not waver. 'May I enquire who's asking?'

Jesus, this girl talks like one of those messenger bots online. I grit my teeth.

'I'm an old friend. Can I speak with Ruby?'

Bot-Girl flashes me that toothpaste-commercial grin again. 'Sorry, you cannot. I am afraid she quit.'

I lean against the counter, fighting the urge to massage my temples. Of course Ruby had quit. Why had I thought this could go my way? Ilfracombe has a population of less than twelve thousand, yet it couldn't be easy to find my old friends in this rural backwater. *FML*, as the kids say.

'You could try her at her new place.'

I grit my teeth. 'And where is that?'

Finally, a human reaction from Bot-Girl: her eyes widen as it dawns on her she has absolutely no idea.

I sigh theatrically, like a teenager would. 'Do you happen to have Ruby's number?'

'Sorry, that's against data protection.'

Of course.

'Never mind.'

'Have a great day!' Bot-Girl calls after me as I push Caleb out again, into the sunlight of the harbour.

Frustrated and annoyed at my investigations being blocked again, I cross the road. I stalk towards the south side of the harbour, where the commercial boats come in. I don't trust myself to not go into full pushchair-road-rage and run over pedestrians coming the other way.

Now what?

I sit down on a bench to wait for a break in the foot traffic. I'm knackered from the walk down from the high street and I'll need a rest before I tackle that epic hill, especially as I'd be pushing Caleb all the way back.

'Sam, isn't it?'

I'm so absorbed in watching the sunlight on the water, I don't notice him at first. I only look up as his shadow crosses the concrete and obscures my view.

It's the young fisherman who had been delivering the crab and lobster to the quay. He has a broad smile and floppy, sandy hair that needs a cut. About twenty-one or -two, he's not particularly tall, but thin and rangy. Even so, I can see the strength in his forearms, the scars and callouses on his weathered hands. He would have been out on the sea since his teen years. Another *man's man*, like Michael.

The young buck flashes me a grin. 'Hi, I'm Alf.'

'Hello, Alf.' I am none the wiser.

'You was askin' about Ruby back there? Only, I know her, see. She's my mum.'

An incredulous laugh escapes me. I don't know what I was expecting him to say, but it wasn't this. The lad in front of me could not possibly be Ruby's son, he is far too old. Also, there is one other glaring issue I recall, from when we were teens.

'I thought Ruby was gay?'

'Yes, she is. Doesn't mean she's not my mum.' Alf shakes his head, but with a smile. 'And to think you city types reckon us lot down here are a bunch of closed-minded, country bumpkins.'

City types. There it was again, this notion that I'm not from round here. Maybe I really am a grockle now? I'd remembered where everything used to be, but I really had forgotten everything that mattered. Like how different the men are, compared to the businessmen with their soft hands, rumpled suits and oiled hair up in London. *Like Mo.*

I raise both palms. 'You're right. I'm sorry. How is Ruby?'

Alf sniffed. 'Good, good. She left the Indian place 'cos she's setting up her own place. Over at Lynmouth. She and my step-mum Maggie live in an eco-house near there.'

A burst of warmth courses through me for my old friend. I'm glad for her. Between problems at home and initially struggling with her sexuality, Ruby had found growing up tougher than the rest of us. That didn't excuse her actions that summer, but it made them that little bit more understandable than Aimee's, or Maddy's. Or even mine.

I scrabble about in my handbag for my phone. 'Could I have Ruby's number?'

65

''Fraid not. She's into all that environmentally friendly stuff, sustainable living. She don't do phones, no tech in the house.' He laughs. 'Not even a telly!'

I think fast. 'Well, how about you tell me the name of her restaurant, over at Lynmouth? That'll have a phone, right?'

'Not yet. Won't open for a few weeks. Tell you what, you give me your number and I'll get her to call you. Okay?' Alf pulls an ancient Nokia from his pocket.

He hands it to me to key in my number. It's an absolute brick of a phone, probably circa 2003, but then it stands to reason he wouldn't take a fancy one out on a fishing boat. It has a tiny LCD screen, no internet. I stare at the little silver buttons. I would have had one of these, when they first came out. How had I forgotten how to use it already? After an uncomfortable pause, it comes flooding back and I finally press my number in.

'Getting too old to remember all this stuff.' I give the mobile back.

'You look pretty good to me.' Alf takes the phone from my outstretched hand. 'I'll get her to call you, then!'

He gives me a mock salute and saunters off, towards a small vessel called *Gipsy Girl*, piled up with crab and lobster pots.

I smile and wave, then stop. Had a twenty-two-year-old just flirted with me? He bloody had. So, I still have it. Only . . . he is Ruby's son. I shiver. Who the hell do I think I am, Mrs Bloody Robinson?

Embarrassed for the second time that day, I grab the handles of the pushchair. Caleb snores with his mouth open, oblivious to my exertion as I push the buggy up the steep incline from the seafront.

As I make it back through Market Arches, I lean on the pushchair's handlebars to catch my breath. For a moment, I let the ambient sounds of the high street circulate around me as ghosts of the past flicker through my vision. There's Aimee and Maddy running across the road, skipping up the steps of the cinema; there's Ruby leaning in the doorway of the old Liberal Club; there's all of us, piling into the funky clothes shop that had been where the sandwich place is now. A smile tugs at my lips. It wasn't always so bad. We had fun back then, too. If only we hadn't let it all go so far.

My gaze locks on something else as I look up the high street: my car. I spot something tucked behind the wind-screen wiper. Fear spears me in the chest at the sight of it; blood pounds in my ears. It has to be another *Never Have I Ever* note.

No, I am being ridiculous. Again.

I don't have a stalker. I have been a crime writer too long. I am jumping to conclusions. It will be a flyer for a festival or pub Open Mic night. It will just be another coincidence. I hadn't even known I was going out today.

Even so, on instinct I turn, looking for Michael. He is long gone. I take deep breaths and dawdle as I approach my vehicle, wanting to put off the moment I have to find out for sure. As I near the windscreen, a hiss of disappointment or perhaps dread escapes me, as my hopes for an innocent explanation evaporate.

As I feared, it's another envelope, *SAMANTHA RUSSELL* in those neat, looped letters on the front. I turn the envelope over in my hands. It is wrinkled, a little muddy. Water drops – rain, maybe? – have left marks in the curls of the 'S' and 'R' of my old name. It looks so innocent, like a child's party invitation.

Even without reading it, I know its intention is malicious.

Unable to stand the suspense any longer, I rip open the envelope and pull out the slip of paper inside. Even prepared for the worst, the words inside feel like someone has punched through my chest, rummaged inside my ribcage and torn out my heart.

Never Have I Ever had a taste of my own medicine.

Eleven

'Michael?'

I find him again by the library. He's still in uniform, standing amongst the bright hanging baskets and the yellow brick buildings of the Candar development. He's staring out towards the seafront, the lush green of Capstone Hill contrasted against the undulating blue sea of the Bay. People mill around with cameras and shopping bags, small like toys in the distance. British summertime has flip-flopped: the grey skies and harsh breeze of the day before are gone. Now it's bright sunshine again and tourists gather outside next to the railings on the seafront in T-shirts and shorts.

He blinks as he turns towards me. 'Oh, Sam. Hello again. Couldn't keep away, huh?'

The sparkle in his eye disappears as he takes in my grim expression. He knows instinctively something is wrong; that I am seeking him out as a policeman rather than an old friend. He gives me a businesslike smile.

'How can I help you?'

I open my mouth to speak but find it difficult to form the words. I don't know where to start. All I know is, this is too big for me to deal with alone. I don't want to call Mo, or even Lindy. I can't face it. The questions, the concerns, Mo's inevitable hurt when he realises he has unwittingly brought me back to the lion's den. He will ask me why I didn't trust him with this information, why we couldn't have discussed the possibility Aimee would make a reappearance and at least plan for it in advance. He won't understand that I needed to believe this was left behind me; that childish transgressions should no longer mean anything. Schoolyard bullying usually stays in the past, even if the memories still feel fresh. I'd felt certain the passage of twenty-three years would have made a difference.

I should never have underestimated Aimee.

'Here.' I push the latest note into Michael's hands.

Michael takes it in, his expression impassive. He looks out to the horizon for a moment, as if choosing his words carefully, before meeting my gaze.

'Can I buy you a coffee?' Michael checks his watch. 'I'm due a break, so can spare half an hour.'

I nod.

He leads me down the hill, straight on from the Candar. The backs of the hotels and apartment lets are piled high with rubbish bins. We weave around them, picking our way around two mangy cats fighting over scraps, emerging near the amusement arcade and wandering down the small parade of shops opposite the crazy golf course, all bakeries, coffee shops and hippy shops with crystals and pewter statues of dragons in the window. In the pushchair, Caleb shifts in his sleep, his small mouth still open and catching flies.

Michael comes to a standstill outside a window with a big purple sign that reads ON A BREAK. It boasts the best and most extensive range of roasted beans in the south-west. There are picnic tables outside, as with most tourist towns. Inside, with its muted décor and large sofa in the centre of the room, it feels familiar, like I've been here before.

Pre-lunch, it's not busy inside. A young woman looks up from a Sudoku puzzle, a beatific smile on her face as she spots Michael.

'Hey, babe,' Michael says, clearly off-duty.

'Mike.' Despite being hugely pregnant, she has the grace of a catwalk model as she crosses the café floor to him, pressing her lips to his. She has an out-of-town accent. I can't place it exactly, but it's somewhere Northern.

I stand there, awkward, waiting for Michael to present me.

'Aren't you going to introduce us?' She laughs and gives him a play-slap.

Michael rolls his eyes. 'Oh, sorry. Rude of me. Kat, this is an old school friend, Sam. Sam: Kat, my wife.'

Kat proffers one of her slim, bird-like hands for me to shake. I do so, taking her in. She is a real beauty. She has her hair piled on top of her head, two pencils sticking out of her haphazard bun. Even with the very pregnant bump, she is small, almost elfin. She's also a lot younger than both of us, by at least a decade. I would never have thought Michael would go for someone so beautiful, or so young. Perhaps he is less strait-laced than I remember. Lindy's face cuts in and looms in my thoughts, her endless cynicism about men who weren't my ever-dependable dad: *They're all dogs, hun.*

'What a great place. Looks just like the one in *Friends*.' I eye the oversized cups, all lined up on the shelves behind the counter. 'We all wanted to go there in the nineties!'

Kat gives me a tight grin. 'Yeah, me too. It was always on at our house because it was my mum's favourite sitcom when I was little.'

Ouch!

'Who's the cutie?' Kat crouches down near Caleb.

71

'This is Caleb.' I will her to touch him, just so I can tell her not to. But she doesn't stroke his sleeping face or smooth his blond curls.

'Lovely name.' Kat stands with the ease of a young girl, despite her massive bump. She hugs her rotund belly. 'We haven't decided on names yet, have we, hun?'

'*You* haven't. I told you my choices.' It's a mock telling-off Michael gives her. I get the feeling whatever Kat wants, Kat gets.

He orders for us and I park Caleb's pushchair next to one of the tiny, tall tables as we sit down. Kat busies herself at the state-of-the-art coffee machine. She blows him a kiss from behind the counter. It is sweet, in a kind of nauseating way. They've obviously been married five minutes, not yet sick of each other.

A thought swims to the top of my brain, unbidden and unwelcome: *Wait until that baby arrives and you're like ships in the night.*

Shocked at myself, I force myself to follow this up with *Of course I love Mo.* To accompany the litany inside my brain, I rearrange the salt and pepper shakers.

'Nice place.'

Michael leans both elbows on the table. 'Yes, Kat does pretty well. Popular with the tourists and the locals. We live in the flat upstairs.'

'You might regret that, with a baby on the way.' Hark at me, parenting expert all of a sudden. I've barely begun my journey as a mum and already I am giving out advice.

Michael nods. 'Yeah, we will need a garden eventually. But we have a while yet before he or she is walking. So, what's this all about, Sam?'

Down to business.

'You remember Aimee Dyer?'

Michael's brow furrows. 'Of course. Her parents still run the discount store up on the high street. Everyone knows the Dyers, around here.'

'You seen her about?' I plunge in. 'I'd really like to speak with her. But you know what the Dyers are like, they are so suspicious.'

He tuts, as if I am wasting his time. He picks up the sheet of paper with the *Never Have I Ever* threat, gives me a pointed look. 'This was her game back then.'

His words land with the force of a hammer blow. I don't recall ever sharing the group's clandestine game with him. Aimee had impressed on us this was our secret; that anyone telling someone else would be in deep trouble. But Michael had been my first love. I'd spent hundreds of hours with him back in the nineties, counted him as one of my best friends in the world. Maybe I'd let slip about it somehow, without realising.

I smile. 'You remember?'

Michael's expression darkens. 'Of course I do.'

The atmosphere between us seems to chill. I lean forwards, grab for his forearm. He moves it away. A warning siren goes off in my brain. *Why is he being so weird?* I'd been fond of him, but twenty-three years is a long time. I barely remember my boyfriends in college, or the ones that came next before I started going out with Mo at university. I hadn't thought of Michael in years before I'd returned to my hometown. Why would I? I had moved on. He has too. Michael has Kat now, a baby on the way.

'You really don't remember.' Michael sighs. 'What happened at Will Jackson's party?'

'No . . .' I arrest the words in my mouth before I can make a liar of myself. The pieces of the jigsaw click together. 'Wait. The Easter one, at the Tunnels?'

Will's brother Felix's parties had been legendary at school. We'd all heard about them. When Felix went to university, Will had taken on the role of 'The Host with the Most'. We had all been counting down the days to his first one. Will had apparently been watching a lot of old re-runs of *Beverley Hills 90210* and become obsessed with the idea of Spring Break. He'd even called his party the *Spring Break Blowout* in the badly photocopied flyer he'd circulated at school.

Michael purses his lips, confirming it for me. 'That's the one.'

Just thinking about that night makes me shiver. It had been freezing, made worse by the dark thunderclouds overhead. I'd privately thought it was a stupid idea of Will Jackson's to have a beach barbecue so early in the season, the first weekend of the Easter holiday. I'd not voiced this opinion though, obviously. None of us had; it was more than our (social) lives were worth.

The barbecue was to take place on Ilfracombe Tunnels beaches. They were locked at night, but Will's family knew the owner. Determined to make a splash with his first soirée, he'd managed to spirit away the keys and copy them, some time before. Looking at the strait-laced adult Michael, replete in his police uniform, it's hard to imagine him being party to a crime like that, or under-age drinking. But we all had been.

'I'd forgotten all about it. What happened to Will, he still live round here?'

Michael shrugs. 'They lost everything, after mad cow disease and foot-and-mouth. His da stuck a shotgun in his mouth. His mum moved back to Glasgow. Last I heard, Will was in London.'

I shudder. The nineties and early noughties had been punishing in the provinces. Will's father Jeremiah Jackson had owned Easterbrook Farm, up on the headland above Ilfracombe. Will Jackson was an It Boy at school, his notoriety bestowed on him by who his family was, just like Aimee. Unlike the Dyers, the Jacksons had been local celebrities for all the *right* reasons. Jeremiah had been one of the lifeboatmen for the town, just as his father and grandfather had been before him. The Jacksons had sponsored the local football teams and opened school fetes. It was weird to think that now they were no more.

Michael smiles. 'You'd never get in the Tunnels now. Security's much better. It's a proper little resort now, with shops and accommodation and everything. They even do weddings. Have you seen it?'

I shake my head. 'Such is progress, I guess.'

Back when I'd been a teen, the Tunnels had just been a charming leftover from the Victorian era. In the early eighteen hundreds, a local entrepreneur had seen the potential in the two sheltered coves near the harbour. The two beaches had previously been used by smugglers and had been difficult to get to. Leading onto a shale beach, hidden from the high street and adults' prying eyes. I can see it so clearly in my mind now Michael has prompted me: it was a brilliant place for our secret beach barbecue. If it hadn't been so frickin' freezing.

'It's the perfect night for dares!'

Maddy had grinned like a loon as we entered the Tunnels, a cigarette dangling from her lip. She'd seen a poster of River Phoenix in this pose and become obsessed with recreating it.

'Oh, you think so?' Aimee stopped and extended her arms, carrier bags of booze hanging off both her wrists, like an alcoholic Jesus. 'You better watch out then, Mads!'

'Shut up!' Maddy laughed. The cigarette fell from her mouth, hitting the concrete in a shower of sparks before rolling away in the dark. 'Now look what you made me do!'

I ambled behind them and watched Maddy and Aimee giggle together, left out as usual. Teens already lolled on the rocks, chugging back booze from plastic bottles and tankards. A couple of Will's mates had taken control of cooking-stroke-burning burgers and sausages on disposable barbecues. No music was playing. Despite the beach being hidden from view, the sound would have travelled to nearby residential homes. Even so, I wasn't bothered about getting busted.

Ruby glugged back MD 20/20, a cheap, fortified fruit wine. She'd been tipsy when we'd called for her. Ruby lurched a little as we trudged down the rocks, towards the cove and the shale beyond. I reached out a hand to steady her.

'I'm fine!' Ruby exclaimed, her voice shrill and irritable.

Half a dozen teens turned around, automatically. 'Sssssssssh!'

In Kat's, Michael moves the salt and pepper shakers around. 'Drinking, breaking into private property. We did it all, back then. Do you ever think we were all out of control?'

'That's just kids.' I shrug.

Michael meets my eye. 'Let me put this way, then. What would *you* do in fourteen or fifteen years if you found out Caleb was doing the same?'

I smile. I know exactly what I would do. 'I'd ground him. Probably forever. Is that why you became a policeman, penance?'

Michael laughs. 'Hell, no.'

I flick the hair out of my eyes. Michael's smile triggers another memory. Sitting across from me now: sixteen-year-old Mike. He fiddles with the toggles of his hemp baja jumper. It is in the colours of the Jamaican flag, complete with a large Ganja leaf on the front.

But it had all been teen grand-standing. Mike had never been out of control. *Not like me.*

Michael's gaze locks with mine. 'You never answered my question. Do you really not remember what happened at Will's party?'

I sigh and shake my head.

Good-natured Michael vanishes. The atmosphere between us feels weird, prickly again. I get that strange sensation of the ground shifting beneath my feet. I try and bring forth an answer, but I can't summon one; I don't know what he wants me to say.

'Why did you do it, Sam?'

Twelve

'**D**o what?'
I'm at a loss. Back when we'd been teenagers, I'd felt so strongly for Mike, but had always kept my feelings in check. I'd figured it was important to demonstrate I wasn't 'needy'. Magazines like *Just Seventeen* had said boys hated that. That night at the Tunnels, I'd acted aloof, cool. Like I was supposed to. Looking back now, I feel sorry for the young girl I had been. I'd been so worried about what others had thought of me.

'Why don't we get out of here?' Mike had indicated the teens lolling about on the Tunnels beaches. They were already drunk. 'Why don't we go back to yours, watch a movie or something? In the warm.'

I'd been very tempted to ditch my friends. By the time Will's Spring Break Blowout came around, Mike and I had been going out for about eight weeks. We were desperate to take our relationship to the next level. But Mike had two younger brothers and his parents worked from home on their jewellery business. His mum was also one of those weird parents who had to know absolutely everything about her kids. Whenever I'd gone over to his, Mike had to keep his bedroom door open. Back then I'd thought parents were the absolute worst, but I know only too well I will be demanding the same of Caleb in the future when he has girlfriends (or boyfriends) over. Teens can't be trusted.

To hammer home his point on the beach, Mike grabbed my hand, lacing his fingers through mine. I'd been delighted, my heart leaping. As every girl knows, boys only ever hold your hand in public when they are for real.

But just as swiftly, my joy had been replaced with a dark mood. That was the year everything changed, because we'd moved to London. The night before the Spring Break Blowout, Lindy and Dad had sat me down. They'd explained we would all be moving up to London after my exams. Dad already had a new job: all his 'working away' was really him getting settled in at the new firm. It had been a huge promotion for him. Lindy told me she had been looking into private schools in the capital for me.

I know now Mum and Dad were just doing what was best for our whole family. But no teenager wants to leave the place they have lived their whole lives and start again. So I'd just listened, agog. I hadn't been able to believe it. They'd never even asked me what I thought. As far as I was concerned, they'd just gone ahead and arranged it all, behind my back. I'd been filled with furious resentment. I'd also slipped into a kind of teen nihilism; everything was pointless. Including Mike. I was leaving anyway, who cared? He would move on and forget me.

I untangled my hand from his, curled my lip in a sneer. Just like Aimee's. 'Do you have to be so needy all the time?'

Mike gave me a stunned glance. Then he held both hands up, as if in surrender. I can still see him turn on his heel on the rocks and trudge towards where Will and the others were playing frisbee golf. Instant regret had pierced through me, but I hadn't called him back.

In Kat's, I averted my gaze from Michael's. 'Okay. I was a bitch to you. Is that what you want me to say? It was twenty-three years ago, Michael!'

Michael sat back in his chair. 'That wasn't what I meant.'

Aimee's voice was full of glee. 'Look at the state of that.'

I looked up glumly from my can of beer. Ruby was dancing without music in the centre of the shale. A small crowd had gathered around her, hooting and clapping. She was doing what she thought were eighties-style robotic moves. Instead, she looked like a marionette with its strings cut. She had a quarter-bottle of vodka in her hand. She was really going for it, mixing her drinks. She would end up puking her guts up.

'Time for your dare, first.' Aimee's breath was hot in my ear as she dipped closer to me. She whispered what she wanted me to do later that night.

The words didn't make sense, at first.

'No.' I found my voice at last. 'I won't do that!'

Aimee flashed that sardonic grin at me. 'Okay. That's fine. But you know, there will be penalties.'

'Like what?'

Aimee shrugged, that maddening grin still painted on her face. 'The rest of us will have to discuss it. But obviously, it would have to be a big one. We might even have to throw you out of the group. It's only fair. Everyone else has done their dares, you would be the first default, Samantha.'

I grabbed her arm. 'Anything else. Please. I will do anything else! Just name it.'

Aimee laughed, wrenching her arm away. 'Oh don't beg, sweets. It's demeaning.'

She wandered back into the throng, clapping and hooting for Ruby with the others. I stared after her, tears pricking my eyelids. My heartbeat fluttered in my chest as I struggled to breathe. I can't do it. I won't.

But I did. Aimee's dare for that night at the Tunnels beach party ricochets back to me at last: *Never Have I Ever kissed someone other than Mike Huxtable.*

I should have seen Aimee's second dare coming. I should have told her to take a running jump, but I didn't. Instead, I'd downed some Dutch Courage as I went on the prowl for a victim, willing or unwilling. I had been certain I could get the deed done, quickly, with Mike none the wiser. When he went off with some friends to play frisbee golf, I'd grabbed the very drunk Will Jackson and planted a kiss right on his slack lips. He'd cringed and pushed me away, but not before I'd managed to slip my tongue in his mouth, as Aimee had stipulated earlier. I'd proved Aimee wrong, I wasn't a loser.

Except I was. Mike was across the beach, watching everything that happened, and I lost something very important to me that night.

'Oh Michael, I'm so sorry.'

I've been so focused on my issue with Aimee and the notes. I'd forgotten that Michael had been affected by the *Never Have I Ever* game back then, too.

Michael rolls his eyes. 'Relax. It was over twenty years ago. You were a stupid kid. I was just surprised you'd forgotten, that's all. It was quite a life-defining moment for me. Back then, anyway.'

I feel embarrassed a second time, for overestimating my effect on him. Obviously, it hadn't ruined his life or anything like that.

'Aimee brought out the worst in me.' I attempt to play it down, averting my gaze from Michael's and making a show of checking Caleb in his pushchair. Still asleep. Great.

'Yes, she did. I remember. You turned into a different person around her.'

Irritation prickles through me. It's one thing to criticise myself, but I want him to disagree. Say 'girls will be girls' or something.

'Well, I wouldn't expect you to understand. You don't know what it's like for girls, at school. Sometimes you have to do stuff to fit in.'

Kat appears to the side of me with two coffees in those giant cups and saucers the size of small bowls. I note how Michael's body language changes on a sixpence. He turns his attention away from me and back to her, flashing her an adoring smile.

I turn to take one from her, trying to be helpful. 'Thank you so much—'

I'm not sure what happens next; perhaps I misjudge the distance between us. There's a crash of crockery as one of the cups falls to the floor. Kat attempts to jump back in vain, out of the range of the black coffee that splashes her rockabilly Mary Jane shoes. This topples over the other cup in her hand, which crashes to the floor as well. I stare at her in horror, not sure what to say.

'I am so sorry.' Mortification floods through me like the liquid making its way through the floor tile grout.

'It's fine.' Kat gives me a tight-lipped, automatic smile.

I eye the colourful ceramic, in pieces beneath our feet. 'Please, let me pay for the damage to the cups?'

'Absolutely not. Accidents happen,' Kat trills, grabbing a cloth, dustpan and brush.

Before she kneels on the floor, Michael jumps up from his seat and practically wrestles the cleaning items from her. 'I'll get that, babe.'

I'm relieved. There could only be one thing worse than trashing the joint: making a heavily pregnant woman clean up after me. Kat smiles and lets him, retreating behind the counter again to make us more drinks.

Moments later everything is sorted and she places a new cappuccino with reverent care in front of Michael, then a black coffee for me. I note her lipstick matches her apron. She kisses him on the cheek and wanders back towards the till, where she picks up her puzzle book again.

Michael lowers his voice. 'So, you think the note is from Aimee.'

I nod. 'Are notes like this even illegal?'

I pull at the tablecloth, a symptom of my anxiety. I feel stupid too, like I am back in school. This is surely the effect on me Aimee wants, but I can't help myself.

'Yes, under the Harassment Act of 1997,' Michael confirms. 'You need at least two incidents for it to count as such, though.'

'I have more than one note.'

Not for the first time, I wish I had taken my agent Carole's advice and not destroyed the N1Fan letters. DI Robyn Dallas would call it 'classic escalation'. She'd send the notes to her expert Forensic Document Examiner, Ms Jinny Tudor. I realise this is unlikely to happen in real life, especially in a small-town police station like Michael's.

'You want to report this?'

Until I had met with Michael, I had been certain I did. Now, I am already talking myself down. The *Never Have I*

Ever threat is non-specific; it sounds worse than it really is; I am overreacting; I am probably playing right into Aimee's hands by going to the police. Like all bullies, she'd loved to feel misunderstood. If I set the police on her, perhaps things could escalate even further? I have to live here in this town again with Aimee. Maybe she has kids now. What if they end up going to the same school as Caleb? It wouldn't be the first time in a small town that a second generation continues a vendetta set by their parents, decades before they were even born.

'I have no idea.'

I am unable to make a decision. One moment I am desperate to throw everything possible at Aimee. The next, I just want to retreat under the covers at my new home and never come out.

'Well, maybe when in doubt, do without?'

I mull it over. Michael's words do make sense. 'I don't want to make it worse. Maybe this is just a stupid joke. Maybe I should just go and talk to her?'

Michael stirs his cappuccino. 'Good luck with that.'

I am disappointed. I'd felt certain that if anyone would know where Aimee is right now, Michael would. 'Aimee doesn't live around here any more?'

Michael shakes his head.

'When was the last time you did see her?'

Michael's eyes roll back as he tries to figure out the timeline. 'I don't know, ages.'

'Five years ago? Ten? Twenty years ago?' I prompt.

Michael kicks back in his chair. 'I've no idea. I didn't go to sixth-form college with the rest of them, in the end. I joined the marines, over at Exmouth. I was in the corps for fifteen years.'

Now it all makes sense. The regimented Michael I'm seeing now is not the natural progression of the boy I'd known back then. He's been rebuilt. He's had all his smooth, easy-going parts planed off, replaced by sharp edges. He's spent another half lifetime away from his hometown, either at barracks or sent across the world. I wonder if he'd gone to Kosovo, Afghanistan, or Iraq. What kind of horrors had he seen, in the past two insane decades post nine eleven? But I don't ask. My tongue feels too big for my mouth.

Michael smirks. 'No, I wasn't shot. No, I am not suffering from post-traumatic stress disorder. I know you're dying to ask, everyone always is.'

'I'm not.' *I am.*

Michael shrugs as if to say 'Whatever', then lifts his absurdly large cup to his lips.

'I couldn't find Aimee online, either.'

'Not being on social media is not against the law, Sam.' Michael sets his cup down, there's foam on his beard. 'Anyway, that's good, isn't it? It means she can't contact you that way.'

I point to my own lip. 'I suppose so.'

Michael grabs a napkin and dabs at his face. He looks to his watch and swears under his breath. 'I have to go.'

As he stands, I do too. 'Of course. Thank you so much.'

I bob forward and give him a kiss on the cheek. I feel his bristles under my lips, so different to Mo's baby-smooth features. Kat looks up from the till, a pink pencil hanging from her mouth. Her brow furrows. I realise she's been trying to eavesdrop the whole time.

I try to save face. 'Thank you so much for the coffee.'

'You're welcome.' Kat is not looking at me, but Michael. I can tell from her expressive face that she is wondering if she should be concerned. I dither as I try and send her a telepathic *don't worry*. An expression of solidarity, of sisterhood. Then I realise I just look deranged and turn on my heel. I push Caleb out through the café door.

It's only after I leave I find myself realising that Michael had basically done everything he could to distract and dissuade me from reporting a crime.

What kind of policeman does that?

Thirteen

Mo arrives home early with flowers for me, carrying an Indian takeaway and sweets for Caleb. He sweeps in from outside and hands them straight to our boy, even though he's not had dinner yet. Caleb snatches them with a triumphant yell before I can say no. The flowers – a classic bouquet of lilies, roses, carnations, Alstroemeria and Gypsophila, probably called something like 'Perfect Pinks' – look expensive. A fifty-pound bunch if ever I'd seen one. Even after consolidating our debts, we're supposed to be taking it easy on unnecessary expenditure.

Mo freezes at the sight of my expression. 'Sorry, did I do something wrong?'

'Of course not! These are beautiful, thank you so much.'

I fill the sink with water so I can stand the flowers in there while I attend to the dinner in the oven. It's a casserole; even I can't screw that up.

Mo's face falls when he sees I've already cooked. 'I should have checked.'

'No really, it's fine. We can save it and heat it up tomorrow.' I keep my voice level, reminding myself Mo is trying (*very trying . . . God, I'm such a bitch! Where are these thoughts coming from?*).

'If you're sure . . .?' Mo says, dubious.

I nod and he goes off to grab plates and cutlery. I rescue

the casserole from the oven and leave it on a wooden cutting board on the counter to cool. Moments later we've both drawn our chairs up to the table, Caleb in his highchair. As the aromatic spices of the tandoori flood my senses, I realise how hungry I am. I don't recall eating much in the last week or so since the notes started arriving. Caleb loves rice and naans, so it was a good choice for him too. He bangs his spoon against the plastic tray, shovelling food into his mouth.

'How was your day?'

I can feel the weight of anticipation behind Mo's question. I avert my eyes and pile a large spoonful of mango chutney on my plate instead. For a microsecond I think about telling Mo everything. But that would mean explaining who Michael is and why I was able to obtain his advice 'off the record' so easily. I am not convinced Mo's fragile ego can stand me going to another man with my problems instead of him, never mind an ex-boyfriend.

'Oh, fine.'

'No more notes, then?' Mo breaks a poppadum in two. 'No.'

The lie fills the space between us. I can sense Mo's uncertainty. He is wondering if he should pursue it further. Sometimes I think relationships are like spiderwebs, woven intricately and expertly, over time. They are often strong, capable of catching large things. Sometimes bigger things might crash right through the web and destroy it. Other times, those threads simply come adrift, so the web drifts backwards and forwards in the breeze.

Mo changes tack, instead. 'How is the book going?'

Oh great, another lie.

'Oh, you know. The evidence says, wait and see.'

The words roll off my tongue; it's my go-to response whenever anyone asks about my writing and based on DI Robyn Dallas's famous catchphrase, *The evidence says*. Mo only read the first book, before I sent it off on submission years ago. He always says there's no need for him to read them, he hears all about them at home. If that was ever true (and to be fair, it probably was until at least book three or four), he hasn't in years.

Even so, he doesn't appear to notice my stock answer. How did we get here? It can't have just been Caleb, all the IVF, the debts that followed us like yapping dogs at our heels throughout our marriage. It seemed so inevitable, so *ordinary*. I never wanted to be ordinary.

The conversation limps on as we eat. I am almost relieved when we finish. As Mo takes Caleb upstairs and gives him his bath, I take the plates, condiments and cutlery through to the kitchen. I start to load the dishwasher, but then dump everything on the side. Screw this. I can load it later.

I trot upstairs and stop on the landing, feeling like an outsider in my own house. I can hear Mo and Caleb laughing together, water splashing in the family bathroom. Aimee and the past are *my* problems. Mo and Caleb are my perfect family, my little bubble. Aimee has no right to intrude on us like this.

I have to do something about her. Now.

I dither for a moment, undecided on my immediate course of action. Obviously, I need to get to the bottom of the notes, but how to tackle finding Aimee? If Michael (apparently) can't help me, then Maddy is the next candidate to ask for help. I'd already tried to Friend her on Facebook, but she hasn't replied to my request. Perhaps she had seen my pseudonym 'SJ Scherer' and rejected it, without looking at my photo. Her profile is not locked though, so I know the legal firm where she works.

I close my study door and grab my mobile from where I left it by the computer. I could use the landline, but don't want to chance it. Mo could pick it up and hear me talking. Every teen with more than one phone extension in the house back in the nineties worried about that. Kids these days don't know they're born, they have so much privacy. They think parents checking the itemised phone bill is tantamount to child abuse.

I press the button and listen to the phone ring. It's just after six o'clock; I hope Maddy is working late. My prayers are answered when someone on the other end picks up almost straight away.

'Mark Kane and Associates.' She has a quiet nasal voice like the Snuffleupagus from Caleb's beloved *Sesame Street* on YouTube.

'Hi, can I speak to Maddy Khan?'

'Putting you through.'

There's tapping at the other end of the line. A ring tone sounds, then another click as the phone is picked up.

'Maddy Khan speaking,' another jaded voice says.

I almost bottle it and ring off. I take a deep breath. 'Hi, Maddy. This is Samantha Russell.'

'Omigod, Sam!' Maddy's enthusiasm erupts like steam from a coffee machine. 'I can't believe it! How are you?'

Warmth rushes through me, obliterating my previous suspicions about my old friend. 'I'm good. You?'

'Oh, you know. Working for The Man, living out my mother's dreams of An Important Career, instead of catering for the plebs.' Maddy catches herself, 'Sorry, I'm working towards My Best Self. No bitter ranting. God, how long has it been?'

'Twenty-three years.'

'No! That's insane!' Maddy sighs. 'I missed you, y'know. When you moved.'

A smile springs to my lips. 'I missed you, too.'

I'm surprised to discover this is the truth. I'd never settled at sixth-form college upcountry or had close friends again. It's reassuring to hear Maddy hadn't written me out of her life. We'd pledged friends forever with Ruby, back at primary school. Before Aimee. Before that fateful summer. If only it had stayed just the three of us.

'I wrote you.' Maddy's voice seems less certain now.

'Oh really? Sorry, I never got any letters.'

Another lie slips from my lips like breath. I recall a letter or two arriving now, written in Maddy's neat, looped hand, like nothing had ever happened between us. I hadn't been able to believe it. Did Maddy and the others think we could just pick up where we left off, as pen pals? I was well rid of them, I decided; I'd not replied. Dad's new job in London no longer seemed like such a bad thing. It had been the perfect escape from that pack of psychos.

'I must have got the address wrong.'

'Maybe.' Shame courses through me as Maddy gives me the benefit of the doubt.

'So, tell me everything!' Maddy squeals.

Feeling awkward, I give her a quick potted history of my life in the last two decades and a bit: my writing, Mo, Caleb. Maddy's surprised I've moved back to Ilfracombe, but confirms she's not gone back herself in years. Like my dad, both her parents have been dead a good decade. She reveals she has no husband or partner, as I'd suspected from her Facebook profile and photos. She surprises *me* when she says there is unlikely to be one either.

'It's my animals and me, just the way I like it,' she declares.

As Maddy speaks, I grab a pen and a notebook from my desk drawer. It's a new one: both Lindy and Mo give me them for birthdays and Christmases, a typical present for a writer. As I scribble down everything Maddy says, I feel like DI Robyn Dallas. I decide to dedicate the notebook to my investigation and call it my casebook. I scrawl Aimee's, Michael's and Ruby's names next to Maddy's.

'Michael's a policeman, now.' I let this snippet land.

'Wow. Never saw *that* one coming.' Sarcasm drips off her words. She had seen it, even if I hadn't. 'God, he was such a boring goody-two-shoes. Whatever did you see in him? No wonder you went off with Will Jackson.'

'I *didn't* go off with Will,' I snap, then laugh, try to cover up my irritation. 'I mean, it was one of Aimee's *Never Have I Ever* dares. Remember that stupid game?'

'Yeah, course. All teenagers are dicks, aren't they? We weren't any different.' Maddy titters. 'Anyway, you see anyone else yet, from ye olden days?'

The sudden about-face jars. Maybe I am reading too much into it, but I feel like there's something tinny about Maddy's response, not quite genuine. As if she is putting on a performance or trying to deflect my interest in the game. DI Robyn Dallas would call this a hunch; she always pays attention to her gut. Half her cases hinge on them. I note Maddy's weird sea change, with a bunch of question marks and arrows: *hiding something??*

'Not yet. So, you still in touch with Ruby?' I try and keep my voice casual, like it's just occurred to me to ask.

'Gawd, I haven't spoken to Ruby in almost as long a time as you!' The phone whistles as Maddy blows air out of her cheeks, trying to figure out the timeline. 'Let's see . . . We started sixth-form college in Barnstaple, in September. But by November, Ruby had dropped out. Because she was pregnant. I saw her a couple of times around town with a buggy, but not to speak to. Dunno who the dad was. I was pretty surprised to be honest, I always thought she was gay.'

'Yup, she is,' I confirm, 'I met her son on the quay down here. Alf. He's twenty-two and a fisherman. He is also distressingly hot.'

'No way!' Maddy cackled. 'Christ, I feel like Bridget Jones or something. Just remember: *"Old Enough to Be Legal Son"*!'

Bridget Jones is better than Mrs Robinson, at least.

'You ever speak to Aimee?'

'No. Never. You?'

The warmth emanating from Maddy at the end of the phone dissipates in an instant. It's like our conversation is a balloon and I'd just pricked it with a pin.

I choose my next words carefully. 'I went to Dyer's. Her niece said she wasn't there. I left my number, but perhaps she doesn't want to talk to me.'

'Ugh, I don't know why you'd want to. Anyway, don't worry about her. You know Aimee. She always falls on her feet.' Despite working towards her 'Best Self', the bitterness of Maddy's words is unmistakable. 'Sam, look . . . I have a deadline, I have to get back to bloody work. Let's chat again. Don't be a stranger, all right?'

Maddy's accent dips suddenly into Devonian the long 'l' and 'a' sounds, the inexplicable two syllables in 'right': *allllll ri-ot.*

I match it, only half-joking. 'All right!'

We both laugh as I bid her goodbye and hang up. I'd already known Maddy couldn't have sent the hand-delivered threatening note if she was living up in London. That didn't rule out her involvement, but I couldn't work out what her motivation could be for that. She'd also sounded genuine when she'd expressed her congratulations about my writing, and seemed to have never heard of SJ Scherer. Despite her protestations to her mother, I remember that Maddy had never been much of a reader. Now I think of it, Maddy had never been much for school work or studying. She'd made school look effortless. She'd seemed naturally gifted, able to do well just from glancing at her textbooks. Or maybe she was just really good at cheating and never got caught? Looking back now, I realise how little I really knew about my friends and the people around me. I had been so naïve. No wonder I had got in over my head with Aimee.

I look down at my notes. I'm no closer to finding Aimee or Ruby. Both Michael and Maddy seemed cagey when I spoke to them. I'm struck by the fact we all seem to be talking *around* what happened before I left for London. I shouldn't have to ask outright; I am the victim here. But perhaps I will have to at this rate.

Next time.

Fourteen

I lie in bed with my casebook, consulting my notes by lamplight on my *Never Have I Ever* investigation so far. Mo snores beside me, oblivious.

I've told him I am stuck on a plot point for book eight; the reality is I've not worked on my new book for weeks. We're already well into August and my end of September deadline is around the corner, but I've barely written half of the manuscript. I can just imagine Aisling's shocked face if I miss the deadline. I have never defaulted before. It's not my thing. I'd told her I would deliver September as a last resort; I'd felt certain I would be finished long before then, as usual. *Under-promise and over-deliver* is my motto. I can catch up. I have to.

My eye is drawn back to Maddy's and Michael's names. I'd felt sure that Maddy was hiding something, though I suppose it could have just been awkwardness. We haven't spoken for over two decades and we were on the phone, so I couldn't see her face. I'm probably overthinking, as usual.

Michael is much more of an enigma. He'd made it clear he remembered the game as well as how he felt about Aimee. Not very professional, at best. He'd not been forth-coming on any information about Aimee's remaining family in town, either. Could he have been trying to divert me?

I tap my pen against my teeth as I consider this. If he is, what possible motive could he have for that? Like he said, it might have been crushing for him back then, but a long time has passed. Teenage shenanigans like kiss-cheating and stupid dares are supposed to have vanished into the ether of time. Though they obviously haven't for Aimee, if she's sending me *Never Have I Ever* notes again. But that's the operative word: 'if'.

I close my casebook and turn off the lamp, flipping through my thoughts like DI Robyn Dallas and her beloved index cards. What should my next move be? Other than Aimee, there's still another person I haven't managed to speak to: Ruby.

I grab my phone from the nightstand and scroll through Instagram in the dark. I find Alf easily enough. I discover his surname is the same as Ruby's when his picture pops up. Most of his pictures are of him and other blokes in the pub. He does have a fancier phone than the old brick he'd handed me, then.

I'm pleased to find Ruby in a couple of Alf's pictures. She's more lined than I remember with short, razored hair dyed silver. Behind her ear and snaking down her neck is an intricate, Celtic tattoo. In both pictures, her arm is around her lad's shoulders and they're both smiling, raising pints in the air. I smile, then press FOLLOW. I have heard nothing from him, despite his promises on the harbour; he must have forgotten me. *So much for making an impression, Mrs Robinson.* Maybe if I drop Alf a private message, I'll jog his memory.

Next I type *Michael Huxtable* into the search bar. A profile pops up, but all his pictures are private. *Kat Quentin*'s is the first on the list after his. Figures. She's under thirty, so practically lives on Instagram from what I can make out. There are lots of regrams of beautifully staged coffee cups and books. All of them are tagged with the On A Break insta feed and include hashtags like #coffeeporn, #coffeelover, #coffeeholic. She has also documented her pregnancy stage by stage, taking pictures of everything from her baby bump, to parenting books she's reading, to pictures of the signs at the hospital leading to obstetrics. Nearly all of her personal pictures are tagged with Michael's name.

I feel a flash of jealousy but push it down just as fast. It's because of the baby, not Kat and Michael. I would love Caleb to have a sibling, preferably a little sister. I would call her Agatha, after my favourite crime novelist. She would wear bows in her hair and little pink wellies. They could play down on Wildersmouth Beach together, collecting stones and sea glass. But Caleb had been too difficult to conceive on our own. We have no money left for any more treatment. I am lucky.

I had steeled myself to never have *any* babies, so even having just the one feels like a blessing and a miracle. As this thought surfaces, I throw the covers back and pad across to Caleb's room. I watch his little chest rise and fall, feeling more at peace for the first time in days.

My precious boy.

As I return to bed, I check my Instagram feed again, hoping Alf might have got back to me. No go. My thoughts are racing; I won't be able to sleep anytime soon. I gravitate back to Kat's timeline. Scrolling through her selfies, I marvel at how perfect she seems. She reminds me of one of those 'Girl next door'-type stars, like Taylor Swift or Ariana Grande.

Even so, I recall Kat's worried expression that afternoon in On A Break as she'd regarded me and Michael together.

But if she had cause for concern from me (*she doesn't*), wouldn't she be the doormat type and stand by her man anyway? She seems like she would.

Never Have I Ever kissed Mike Huxtable.

My first ever *NHIE* dare had been to kiss Mike. Looking back, it's so obvious what Aimee had been trying to do. She'd felt threatened by me, so wanted to embarrass me, make me back down. She'd realised how much I liked Mike and felt sure he was out of my league. It must have seemed like an opportunity for a double-whammy to her: Mike would reject me and she could think up a penalty for me. Or even better, eject me from the game and the group altogether.

Unlucky for Aimee, it hadn't worked out that way. The girls had given me a deadline: within one week of nomination I had to have kissed Mike. In those days, there were no 'check-ins' on Facebook or FourSquare. I actually had to scope out his routine in real life like a regular stalker. I started by watching his house, down near the seafront, just by the bandstand and Jubilee Gardens. Within a couple of days, I'd discovered he walked the family dog for his mum every night, between seven and eight, down on Wildersmouth Beach.

The next night, I was waiting, seemingly randomly, by the railings. The big dog had been half-dragging him; I turned and gave Mike my best 'fancy seeing you here!' fake smile.

'Hey. Didn't know you had a dog.' *I did.*

Mike looked awkward. 'His er, name is Ernie.'

I hadn't waited for him to invite me down to the beach with him and the dog. I fell into step with them, thoughts rattling through my brain. Should I just grab him, plant one on him? Is that how this worked? I feel like laughing recalling this now, but it had been deadly serious to me back then.

The tide was in, so we'd ended up sitting on Preacher's Rock. We threw a ball for the dog across the Clapping Circle, talked about this and that. Coursework. The looming GCSE exams. The end of school that summer, going on to college. Before I knew it, two hours had flown by. I hadn't felt like I was any closer to getting the dare done. I started to make my excuses and shift, my bladder uncomfortably full.

Then – surprise! Mike pressed his lips to mine.

My dare was complete, just like that.

'Well done.' Aimee had all but choked the words out, following them up with a back-handed compliment: 'I guess you're not such a loser after all?'

I'd felt so powerful, like I'd stood up to her at last. Nothing she said could take away my victory. Even better, *Mike actually liked me.* Before long, I was spending as much time as I could with him, though I was always careful to ensure Aimee and the others couldn't accuse me of being a bad friend. As Maddy always said, so earnestly, *'Sisters before misters!'* But had we been 'sisters', really? If Ruby, Maddy and I ever had been, Aimee had poisoned it all.

In contrast, being with Mike had been so much easier than the girls. I'd felt like myself with him; that there were other possibilities. As my relationship with Mike continued, I'd felt the urge to tell Aimee to get bent, once and for all. I figured that if Maddy wouldn't support me, Ruby might. It had only been a few months to exams; to the end of school. I could survive.

Why hadn't I done this? Mike had been my get-out. Instead I'd ruined everything with him on Aimee's say-so, for the sake of that stupid second dare. I'd been such a thoughtless idiot.

I shut my casebook and turn my lamp off, none the wiser about what I could do next, yet feeling the swell of anxiety in my stomach. If only I could speak to Aimee, straighten this out once and for all.

Beside me, Mo shifts in his sleep.

Fifteen

Another fitful night filled with dreams of being buried alive means I drag myself out of bed, exhausted. I butter toast and fill Caleb's beaker on auto-pilot, wincing as he slams his spoon against the plastic tray of his high-chair. My mouth feels inexplicably dry and my head throbs. No one ever tells you parenthood is sometimes like having the worst hangover in the world, every day for the rest of your life. Not that I would change it for the world.

Early morning passes in a whirlwind of activity; I feel like Madonna in the iconic nineties 'Ray of Light' video, everything rushing around me on time lapse. Mo leaves for work; Lindy arrives to pick up Caleb; I wave them both off, then stack the dishwasher and push the hoover around. Zoom, zoom. Rinse and repeat.

Finally sitting down at my desk, I check my emails, then Facebook. I update my blog and prepare some copy for my monthly author newsletter. I know I am stalling returning to DI Robyn Dallas book eight, but I just can't muster up the enthusiasm for it.

I start scrolling through my Instagram on my phone again. Looking at Kat's timeline and her pictures of Michael, I let my thoughts wander. I hadn't liked confronting my own carelessness in the way I'd treated Michael back then, but it feels good to know he bears me no lasting ill will. It had all just been kid stuff to him.

If only Aimee could feel the same way.

I can't believe I am being dragged back in time by a bully who refuses to grow up. Not for the first time, I wish I had followed my gut decades ago. I should have dumped Aimee and the group back when I started going out with Mike. Long before that fateful July night, or even the Spring Break Blowout at Ilfracombe Tunnels. Maybe it would even have altered the course of my life? Would I have ended up going to London with Mum and Dad even? Maybe I would have stayed in Devon. Perhaps Mike wouldn't have joined the marines. Perhaps we would have got our own place and got married as teenagers, just like Scott and Charlene in *Neighbours*.

I laugh. As if. I am rewriting history. The end result would have been the same, whether I stood up to Aimee or not. It probably would have been even worse. She would never have let me get away from the group; I know this deep down. It had always been about winning with Aimee.

After forcing out four or five hundred agonising words of *Untitled*, I blink and discover the day is gone. Dusk's fingers creep across the window pane. I'm surprised to see neither Mo nor Caleb is back yet, but a glance at my phone puts my mind at ease. Mo thinks he will be in at eight or nine (not unusual for him). Lindy says she took Caleb to Barnstaple but ran into an old friend and lost track of time. She's on her way back now, which means I have at least fifty minutes before any of them return.

I wander down to the kitchen. I've missed lunch so I'm hungry, but the bread bin is empty. I open the fridge to discover a manky head of iceberg lettuce, a couple of wizened courgettes and half a bottle of tomato sauce. There's nothing in the cupboard except Caleb's kiddy pasta shapes and a tin of something that looks like chickpeas, but the label is in Polish. Irritation at my own lack of organisation, or at least delegation to Mo, gives way to the usual parental guilt. I live between two large supermarkets, they're literally an eight-minute drive away in either direction. What kind of mother allows the household stocks to get this depleted?

Even so, I can't face the bright lights of a superstore, or the idle chat of the checkout operators. I decide to take my chances at the small corner shop two streets over. If nothing else, they will have dried stuff like noodles and cans. I grab my handbag and keys and sweep out the front door.

I falter as I make it onto the doorstep. The night is clear, so I can see for miles, all the way down towards the harbour. There's no haze of pollution painting the sky like there had been in London. I take a deep breath, letting the clear air fill my lungs. It is eerily still, besides the *swish* of faraway traffic in the distance. I realise with a start I haven't heard a siren in weeks. I'd got used to them, living in the capital; they'd punctuated every hour, day and night, as faithfully as an alarm clock. Here they are a novelty. Though is that a good or a bad thing? Perhaps I don't hear them very often because we are on our own out here.

Happily, the shop is exactly where I'd thought it was. A little bell tinkles as I open the door. The sound brings a bored East Asian teen of about fifteen down the stairs, to the front of the shop. Her posture and heavy feet betray that she's only watching the shop under sufferance and with acres of resentment. I smile at her, though she looks at me as if she wishes we were both dead.

'Can I help you?' she says, monotone.

I'm surprised to hear the cadence of the long vowels of a Devon accent. This is a girl who's always lived in the provinces, like Maddy had when we were teens. I'd been so holier-than-thou, telling my mother Maddy was as British as the rest of us. Now it turns out I am more like Lindy than I realise.

'Just looking,' I say brightly (*too brightly*).

The shop is well-stocked, even boasting a small freezer section at the back. I select a number of frozen ready-meals, before grabbing a pint of milk for the morning from the fridge. Next to the bread and cereal aisle, there's a good selection of wine and spirits. I've been so preoccupied lately; I need to make more time for Mo. On impulse, I grab a bottle of Pinot. We can have a drink together when Caleb is in bed.

I pay for my goods and leave the shop, the bell tinkling behind me. The air is as quiet as when I'd made the journey to the shop. The thin plastic bag bangs against my leg as I walk. Irritated, I shift the bag from one hand to the other; its weak handles cut into my palms. Car headlights swish past as a single vehicle makes its way up the road. In the orange glow of the streetlamps my shadow casts itself first on the concrete, then the white render of a house. Illuminated from behind, my shadow elongates out in front of me as I cross the road.

A second shadow emerges on the wall ahead.

I slow my steps. The second shadow slows too, growing, monster-like, as it moves forward. It's difficult to tell how far back the shadow is from me, whether it's male or female. I can feel the icy grip of anxiety; the flutter of my heart in my ribcage. I pick up my pace again, remind myself to be more logical. I am being ridiculous. It's nothing. No one is watching me. I hadn't heard any footsteps behind me. It's just someone, waiting to be picked up by their dad, boyfriend or mate. It *can't* be—

'Hey!'

The sound of a woman's voice shouting is like a starter gun. I drop the shopping bag and launch myself forwards. I perceive, rather than hear, the smash of glass as the bottle of Pinot hits the pavement behind me. I hear the clatter of footsteps after mine; she calls my name. I don't stop or look back. 'Wait!'

The air whistles behind me as I pump my arms and legs. Adrenaline buzzes through me, like it had when I played sports as a teen. Rounders had always been my favourite. I'd been in the school team; they called me the Pocket Rocket. I might have been small, but I could leg it faster than anyone else round the bases. That had been another thing I'd kept from Aimee and the others; it's not cool to excel at anything as lame as sports.

'Sam!'

The voice sounds like it's right by my ear. But still I don't look back. I'd thought I was ready to see Aimee, but tonight is a wake-up call. I've been telling myself for too long I can handle the notes, her creepy behaviour. The truth is, I am shit-scared. Aimee had been unpredictable as a teenager, when there had at least been some consequences for her behaviour. Who's to say what twenty-three years' worth of adult freedom could have done to her? She could be capable of anything.

An idle thought enters my brain as I make it onto my road: *you're drawing her home*. But Aimee already knows where I live; she has made sure I know this by hand-delivering the *NHIE* notes. This realisation is swiftly followed by something I'd read in one of Lindy's serial killer books years ago. One killer interviewed shared that he liked to murder his victims within sight of their homes. He would let them see safety, then snatch it away, leaving their butchered remains for their family and neighbours to find.

This spurs me on, giving me the last burst of energy to leave Aimee behind. I can see myself from above, as if I am a cartoon character finding its way, platform to platform, in a nineties video game. If I fall, I land on spikes: GAME OVER. Make it to home though, I get a thousand rings. A hundred thousand. A million. Whatever: the important thing is, I win. Aimee loses.

Gasping for air, I race across the front lawn of my house, grappling with my keys as I go. I am sure I can still hear Aimee's voice behind me. With shaking hands, I slide the key in the lock and somehow open the door in one fluid movement. I make it into the safety of the porch. I'd been certain she was right there; I'd expected her to reach out, grab me by the shoulder. Terror snapping at my heels, I stagger into the galley kitchen. I am intent on looking down at the front step from the kitchen window, visible under the porch light. I need my vantage point to be higher than hers, behind glass, before I look at her again.

Confusion lances its way through my brain; I lean on the worktop. Aimee is not on my front step. I cast a glance up and down the road, trying to spot her on the pavement, or maybe on one of the other house's lawns.

There's no one there.

Sixteen

'I've come calling for the young master of the house?'
I open the door to find my mother on the doorstep.
Mum again. Thank God. Not Aimee. My face crumples
with relief as I open the door.

'Hi, Lindy.'

I don't know what I'd do without her taking Caleb for
a couple of hours every weekday while I attempt to get my
draft written. They don't do anything special. Caleb will
escort Lindy on her errands instead of mine, but of course
because they're hers, he finds them so much more interesting. She also buys him more sweets.

Mum has a wide smile on her face, but it's not for me.
She has really taken to grandparenthood and relishes seeing
Caleb every day. She looks straight to my precious boy in
my arms.

'Ganma!' he yells, his face a picture of unbridled joy,
hands stretched out.

Lindy braces herself as he jumps straight into her arms
from mine. I grin, taking in the scene, though I am rueful.
Once, I could think of nothing better than being paid to
write. Now, it feels like the shackles of every other job I
have ever had. I don't want to stay in and write my stupid
book. I want to go out with Mum and Caleb. Even waiting
in the post office queue with them seems more interesting

than sitting in front of my computer screen moving commas about. It might even keep my mind off last night, too.

Mum finally notices me. Her indulgent smile falls away as she takes in my drawn, white face, the tension in my posture. 'Christ, love, you look terrible.'

I know I look rough; I don't need reminding. 'Cheers, Lindy.'

My mother softens. 'You know I don't mean it like that. I'm worried, darling.'

I sigh. I *do* know. 'I'm fine.'

Mum pulls a disbelieving face and raises a *Yeah right* eyebrow. I summon up a laugh for her benefit, to put her at ease. The last thing I need is Lindy sticking her oar in.

'Really! I'm just stressed about this damn book.'

Another lie. It prompts an unwanted flash of Aimee through my thoughts. In all my memories, I see Aimee as she was as a teenager: she'd stand by, that smug grin on her face. The puppeteer, steering us into trouble. Before her, we'd been good girls. Yes, we cheeked our parents; sometimes we copied homework, or snuck out when we weren't supposed to. Normal teen stuff. But Aimee had taken all of us to the next level. She'd been a cancer in our friendship group, sending out her hateful spores until everything exploded that dark July night. I wish none of us had ever met her.

'Kiss for Mummy,' Lindy trills.

Caleb leans forward from Mum's arms and nuts me on the nose with his forehead.

'Ow,' I laugh, pinching both his rosy cheeks lightly between my fingers. He's such a bruiser. 'Bye-bye, darling, miss you!'

Both Lindy and Caleb blow me a kiss.

From the kitchen window I watch Lindy's little car back out of my driveway and knock down one of next door's hideous garden ornaments. She doesn't stop, even when the owner appears on his lawn, his face beetroot-red. Lindy pokes her head out her side window as she turns the car, proffering him an apologetic wave, of sorts. I smile to myself. My mother really is a one-woman hurricane.

Trudging up the stairs, I feel like a condemned woman. I find no solace from the situation with Aimee in my work. I am no closer to solving a plotting problem I'd had when I was last at the keyboard. I am in the middle of a scene in which DI Robyn Dallas interrogates Mal, a minion of the 'horrid' crime boss Elodie Fitzgerald. In it, he's taunting our intrepid DI with the fact he knows where the victim, Robyn's thirteen-year-old niece Verity, is buried alive. I am pleased with my inclusion of something local. 'Verity' also means truth, which introduces a nice dramatic irony. The innocent Verity will soon run out of air, but I have quite literally lost the plot and painted myself into a corner. I have zero clue what to write next.

I stare at my laptop, no words come. Another echo from the past does, instead.

Never Have I Ever broken into school at night.

When had that game begun to escalate out of control? I close my eyes: I can see all four of us in the Clapping Circle on the seafront on a drab February day. Tourists mill about; kids jump on bouncy castles; a very drunk busker singing a mournful and very slow version of Bob Dylan's 'Knockin' On Heaven's Door', though we would have all known it as being by Axl Rose from Guns N' Roses back then.

*

'Ooooh no one. Interesting.' Aimee popped some gum in her mouth.

We all laughed uneasily; the tension in the air was palpable. If none of us had done something, there had to be a nomination for a dare. How was it going to work?

I recall my stomach twisting up in knots. I was a good girl really, naïve. But breaking and entering is criminal. If we were found out, would that mean 'juvenile hall', like Bart is so often threatened with on The Simpsons? Could it stop us going to university? I'd fast-forwarded time in my mind to the worst possible outcome: standing in a dock, in front of a judge. Poor Mum and Dad, both crying in the gallery above.

All eyes fell on Aimee.

'Why are you all looking at me?' Aimee blew a nonchalant bubble of Hubba Bubba.

'Who is it going to be?' Ruby's eyes narrowed. 'Shouldn't I get immunity from this one? I did do the first dare. And Sam did the last one.'

'That is true,' Maddy agreed, albeit grudgingly. 'I reckon that means it's you or me, Aimee, this time?'

Ruby flashed Maddy an appreciative look. Aimee's eyes bulged at Maddy standing up to her, for once. I basked in the switch in atmosphere, but then saw an opportunity to fall on my sword. Aimee had been so jealous of my success with Mike, getting a boyfriend out of the Never Have I Ever game. I could feel her resentment swirling around me, which is why she'd got between us. I could end this, today. All I needed to do was volunteer for the next dare and curry renewed favour with the group. Maddy would be extra grateful too, because it would mean she was out of the firing line. Two birds with one stone.

'I'll do it.'

But Aimee had seen through me straight away. 'Nice try, Son of Sam.'

The perfectly planned taunt landed home. The other two looked on, blank. It was for my sole benefit, given Lindy's obsession with true crime. 'Son of Sam' had been the nickname of serial killer David Berkowitz, aka 'The .44 Caliber Killer', when he terrorised New York City with shooting attacks in the summer of 1976.

'Okay, let's settle this. You and me this time, Mads.'

Maddy rolled her eyes skywards at Aimee getting her on a technicality. Aimee pretended not to notice and lifted her palm, indicating Maddy do the same. We all understood immediately. She and Maddy were going head-to-head, via the game of Paper, Scissors, Stone.

Ruby gave the countdown. 'One, two, three: go!'

At Ruby's signal, both Maddy and Aimee fashioned their hand into one of the symbols. We all whooped, though Maddy's quickly turned to a groan. Aimee's hand was still flat, whereas Maddy had made a fist: paper beats rock.

'Looks like you're breaking into school, Mads.' I couldn't deny it felt good to be let off the hook.

'Fine.' Maddy seemed rattled, though she forced a grin on her face. 'No big deal.'

Those were the days before CCTV in every corridor and playground; before big fences, locks and security systems in every school. I think every one of us secretly felt disappointed when Maddy broke into school and made it out without incident.

'If you're a bad girl and no one is there to see it, did it really happen?' Aimee's bright purple lips had curved in a wide smirk.

We were all bad girls.

In the cocoon of my study, I decide to see if I can take my mind off Aimee and stimulate my creative juices with a little research. I have several of Lindy's old true crime books to read. Within minutes, I discover I cannot concentrate. I'm tired of reading about famous British serial killers, or parents who killed their kids. Since having Caleb, I find my tolerance is much lower for the latter in particular. I only need to think about Caleb and my heart swells twice its size. To actually harm him seems unthinkable. How could you kill your own child?

I check my phone for the fiftieth time that morning, hoping to see an Insta private message or text from Alf. None. Keeping myself busy is not working. If anything, the unease pooling in my stomach since last night is growing. My eyes flicker to a cross stitch in a frame on the wall Lindy made me to celebrate the publication of my second book in the series. It reads, *What would DI Dallas do?* in blue. Ah, Mum. My number one fan.

That said, it's not bad advice. I don't like researching police protocols much, which means Dallas has become more and more a maverick cop who's alienated half the police force going after bent coppers. This means that Dallas is not always so fastidious about following the letter of the law. Lines have started to blur in her quest to nail Elodie Fitzgerald, once and for all. Like Jack Reacher or Jason Bourne, DI Robyn Dallas has become a lone wolf. Sometimes she consults with civilians, some of them not quite law-abiding themselves. In book six, *Control-Alt-DEATH*, Dallas is forced to enlist the help of an enigmatic hacker known only as 'K' when Elodie Fitzgerald tries to take out the whole of London's power and hold the city to ransom. The *Mirror* called it 'a tired rehash of *Die Hard 4.0*', but the journalist responsible for that tripe is just jealous.

If an internet search is good enough for DI Robyn Dallas though, it's good enough for me. I wouldn't know how to access the dark web if you put a gun to my head, but Google surely has all the answers I need. It's not like my old friends are criminal masterminds on Elodie Fitzgerald's scale. I just need to find the right search terms.

I sit down at my computer and turn my laptop on. The homepage springs to life and I Google Ruby's full name, adding 'Lynmouth restaurant'. I am hoping to find out the name of her new place, at least. Surely there would be an announcement somewhere, or even just a website in construction? But just as Alf had told me, Ruby's digital footprint is zero.

Next, I find myself on psychology websites. I scroll through the various article headlines on teenage behaviour. I realise what I am doing: I am searching for information about our own actions and the *Never Have I Ever* game. Nothing jumps out at me. Peer pressure is a well-documented phenomenon generally, but insights and advice on how it actually works are surprisingly scant online. Had we been attention-seeking? If so, we were shockingly bad at it. Most of our exploits had sailed under our parents' radar.

Perhaps it had been the recklessness that enthralled us. After Maddy breaking into school, we'd been desperate to prove how dangerous we were. Michael's words at On A Break boomeranged back: *Do you think we were all out of control?* He might not have been, but our little friendship group definitely were. At Aimee's insistence, we'd all agreed we needed to up the ante for the next dare. We didn't have to wait long.

Aimee's next offering: *Never Have I Ever shown my tits to the boys at school.*

I remember the horror of the words, but also the feeling of gleeful anticipation. Aimee had known the rest of us had done nothing more than kiss a boy. She'd outlawed immunity. I guess Aimee must have figured she only had a twenty-five per cent chance of getting caught out by her own dare.

But she had.

We'd all jeered and laughed as Aimee took a deep breath and flashed the boys in the lunch queue one rainy Friday. We were sure she could handle it. But now, thinking back with the eyes of a grown-up, I can see how shaken she had been. Or I am just making it up?

After that, we'd doubled down. More dares posed. Soon it wasn't just Aimee, either. We all got into the swing of things, dreaming up creative tortures for one another.

Never Have I Ever . . .

. . . had a stranger slap me in the face.

This one ended up being Maddy's dare. She got into an argument with a drunk woman in the Bunch of Grapes pub on the high street. We were all a little suss that she *asked* her to hit her; they'd been in the toilets together about an hour before it happened. But Maddy swore she hadn't.

. . . gone to third base with a boy.

We'd all argued about what this meant before the dare was posed. This was before the internet, so our knowledge was limited to the pages of *Cosmopolitan*. With bulging eyes, we'd set the parameters, then all sworn no immunity as we did Paper, Scissors, Stone. Secretly, I had hoped it would be me. *Never Have I Ever* could be an excuse to get over my paralysing fear of sex, of getting it 'wrong'. Mike had never pressurised me; he was not that type of boy. It was all my problem, just like always.

But Aimee must have cheated somehow, because the third base dare had gone to Ruby, the one person in the group who didn't even like boys. How could we have done that to her? I marvel at our casual cruelty. I recall Ruby appearing from the Pendle Stairway cinema one evening, cheeks burning, reporting what she'd done in glorious technicolour for us. I'd mistaken her smile as one of triumphant excitement back then, but now I wonder if it had been embarrassment, or worse – self-loathing. Were her eyes dead with the horror of it, or am I just adding that? Christ, maybe that boy she'd gone to the cinema with ended up as Alf's father. Did we do that? No, I am overthinking it. I must be.

I'd woken this morning with a new part of me that regretted running from Aimee last night. Perhaps I should have just faced up to her, got it over with. But Aimee had held all the cards, surprising me like that. I had been alone, too. Anything could have happened. I had been right to run.

My thoughts return to DI Robyn Dallas. What would she do in this situation, next? She would have her hacker associate, K, search social media for information about Aimee, but I'd already done that. Dallas would probably dispatch him to look through local newspaper editions on microfilm too at the local library, but before that she would have him search online editions. As this thought flowers in my mind, I type in 'Aimee Dyer, Ilfracombe' into Google with little hope.

I get a fair few hits thanks to Aimee's large and lawless family, though most of the results return with *Aimee* slashed through. My dad used to call them 'The Dyer Mafia' as a joke, though he hadn't been far wrong. The newest articles, mostly local news stories, are at the top. In one picture, a fresh-faced tween girl Elinor Dyer holds a certificate and a medal for winning a local short story competition. Good for her. Directly underneath, twins Simone and Ashley Dyer, 18, have recently been jailed at Exeter Crown Court for repeatedly pelting eggs at doggers. Only in Devon.

Further down, there are even more articles from the *North Devon Journal* about court appearances for members of the Dyer family. Aimee's dad, Bill, appeared giving evidence against a variety of shoplifters who'd tried to rip off the store. He had also been fined himself over a Health and Safety violation; something to do with blocking fire exits. I'm only surprised he'd not been caught more often. Like the rest of them, Bill Dyer had always played fast and loose with the law. He's dodgy, through and through. Everyone in Ilfracombe knew it back in the nineties and I doubt he's changed that much in the last twenty-three years.

In another article, a man I don't recognise, Francis Dyer, had been accused of grievous bodily harm in 1995. This piques my interest right away. I don't think I'd ever met him, but I had certainly heard of him. Everyone had. Who could have been brave enough to take on Frankie Dyer, Bill's legend of a brother? You did not want him calling at your door at two o'clock in the morning. It was said he broke fingers and burned people with cigarettes as easy as winking.

Frankie has the same bushy moustache as Bill's, though he looks tall and positively skeletal, with prominent cheekbones. 'A thin streak of piss' as my dad would have put it. Bill is all round edges, short and squat. I scroll through the other articles, but I don't find the outcome of the trial. Not all articles ended up online before the internet became really widespread. I wonder if Frankie's in jail, or whether he managed to wriggle off the hook.

I carry on clicking, to no avail. I change my search terms, adding inverted commas this time so only results including Aimee's name can be returned. Immediately, an old headline jumps to the top of the results:

PARENTS TO MISSING ILFRACOMBE SCHOOLGIRL: 'PLEASE COME HOME'.
Aimee Dyer, 16, did not return home following a party last weekend 'after a row with friends'.

I sit back in my chair. There's a sharp pain in my chest and the nausea from earlier rushes back with a vengeance. I become aware I am gulping in air, helpless like one of the fish landed down on the quay. I close my eyes and lean over, placing my head on my desk.

Aimee went missing after the party. How had I not known this?

As the first burst of panic recedes, I know why I had missed it. I'd left the same week, before this news had hit the paper. There was no Facebook or Twitter then, asking for shares and retweets to find people. I hadn't even had a mobile.

Speaking from their family home in the Torrs Park area of the town, Mrs Dyer, 43, said: 'This is not like Aimee. She has loads of friends, she is very trusting. She will do anything for anyone.'

Mrs Dyer explained Aimee had posted a note for her family through the letterbox Sunday a.m. saying she'd had a row with friends at a party the night before. The pretty teen dropped the bombshell that she didn't know when she would be back.

*'She takes everything to heart, that girl,' Mrs Dyer said,
'I expect she just wants to curl up somewhere. She's
done it before.'*

Despite my burgeoning anxiety, I snort as I skim-read
this ridiculous paragraph. Trusting? Caring? Aimee's
parents clearly hadn't known the real girl. I am intrigued
that she'd run off before, however. Aimee had never
mentioned needing to get out of the house. She'd obviously
never stayed with me and I felt fairly certain I would
remember if she'd stayed with Maddy or Ruby for any
period of time. So where had she gone? Whatever the case,
she can't have been gone long and, like her mother said,
she'd turned up again. I am overthinking. Again.

As I calm myself, a thought occurs. Aimee can't have
made the national news: I would have seen that at least.
I'd also received that very first *NHIE* note, back in the
nineties, *Never Have I Ever been punished for what I have
done.* Aimee had sent her family their own note too, to say
she was safe. Also, hadn't Ava said, 'She's not here,' when
I'd gone to Dyer's? She'd taken my mobile number, too.
That suggested Aimee had come back to the family fold,
just as Mrs Dyer had pleaded:

*In a direct plea to Aimee, Mrs Dyer added, 'We love
you so much. Please come back home, sweetheart.
Our arms are always open, we will never give up on
you. Mum loves you. Dad loves you. Your sisters are
in bits. Your nanny, your friends, everybody is just
rallying around wanting to know how you are. We want
to be able to tell them you are OK. We cannot carry
on like this.'*

I glance at the date of the article. The newspaper report had been almost a week after the party. Admittedly, Aimee's absence had been longer than any other she'd pulled, which would have been why her parents reported her missing. But then, after what had happened at the party on the headland, maybe Aimee really did need to be alone that time?

I scroll quickly through the other search results but find no other reference to Aimee going missing. But I know someone who could confirm that my old frenemy had come back.

I press PRINT.

Seventeen

That stupid bell tinkles again as I trail out of the light summer rain and into Dyer's. Behind the till, Ava hunches over, scrolling through her phone. She does not look up until my shadow falls right across the counter.

'You again.' Today, Ava's hair is green.

I don't say anything. I toss a print-out of the article about Aimee going missing down in front of her.

'Look, where's Aimee to, eh?'

The Devonian phrasing jumps out of me against my will. I clamp my lips together to stop any other colloquialisms escaping. I hate the soft, long vowels of my home town. When I'd gone to London, the others at my new school had all called me *yokel* and *country bumpkin*. A Dyer like Ava wouldn't have given a toss, though. She would have been strong, like Aimee. Told them it was their problem, not hers.

Ava doesn't reply. She gives the print-out a cursory glance and goes straight back to her phone. She seems one hundred per cent uninterested.

I try again, shaping my words as standard English this time. 'Is Aimee here or not?'

Ava continues scrolling. 'Not.'

'Where is she?'

Ava glances in my direction at last, looking me up and down with those pale blue eyes of hers, so like Aimee's.

'Can't tell you.'

My hands clench at my sides. 'You can't tell me, or you won't?'

'Bit of both, really.'

Ava stretches like a cat. Her top rides up, exposing her pierced navel. I feel impotent rage pool in my chest. God, this girl is the spitting image of Aimee in every way. It is like being transported back twenty-three years in a single moment.

I count to ten. 'She came home though, right . . . Back then?'

Ava nods.

Relief settles over me.

'I really need to speak to Aimee. Can you put us in touch? *Please.*'

The conviction behind my polite request disarms Ava's juvenile belligerence at last. She sighs.

'Look, she hásn't been home in years. As far as I know, she and my mum don't speak. I was a little kid when all this happened. I barely remember her.'

'But you took my number?'

I swallow down my exasperation as Ava's eyebrows knit together in irritation.

'Sorry, sorry. I mean, why did you take my number if you don't know where she lives? Why didn't you just tell me?'

'Because you're a stranger.' Ava's words seem weirdly childish. 'Anyway, you could be a rozzer for all I know.'

Rozzer. A local word for police. Of course. Ava would have grown up with a suspicion of people asking questions, with her family background. It's the Dyer way.

I bid goodbye to Ava and stalk back out of the shop to my car. I dither as I approach the vehicle, expecting to see an envelope stashed behind the windscreen wiper. I'm almost disappointed when I see it's clear. But maybe Aimee is following me again, watching from afar? I do a quick sweep with my eyes up and down the high street, but it's quiet as ever. A couple of young delivery lads carry boxes as they jump down from the tailgate of a large van as they help stock a new shop. A small cluster of old people stand idly in another doorway chatting. They're oblivious of the young teen mum with a buggy who waits patiently for them to move, before giving a deliberate cough to catch their attention. I can't see anyone else my age, never mind anyone who might resemble Aimee, twenty-three years on. I sigh and open my car door, sliding behind the wheel.

I work through what I have discovered this morning as the high street falls away and the car climbs the New Barnstaple Road. If none of the Dyers know where Aimee is right now, she can't be in the local area. Aimee can't have been the one who had hand-delivered the note with my maiden name on. She has so many family members, someone would have seen her. Aimee had always been the free spirit type, prone to wandering off. She'd always talked about travelling the globe, doing her own thing. She reckoned there were Dyers all over the world. I could well believe it. It makes sense that she'd abandon her family once she'd finally left home. She must be out in the wind, somewhere. What was it that Maddy had said? *Don't worry about her. You know Aimee. She always falls on her feet.*

If Aimee is not as close by as I'd previously feared, is this better or worse? I am undecided. Aimee not being in Ilfracombe itself doesn't mean she is not behind the *Never Have I Ever* notes. They might have both been hand-delivered, but perhaps she is sending them to one of her many relatives to leave them for me? That would mean one of the clan is watching the house, not Aimee herself. Perhaps, if I'd turned around last night, I would have seen Ava or one of the others chasing me. Aimee had always had a touch of the flamboyant. I have no doubt she would decide making me think she is nearby is much creepier than sending through the Royal Mail. Though I am not comforted by this, at least it means Aimee's mad behaviour cannot escalate any further. The Dyers might be dodgy, but it's not personal for them. They're just doing Aimee a favour. As dysfunctional as that might be, I can't be in direct danger from them. I decide to make a note of my morning's findings in my casebook when I get back to the house.

As I turn on the lights in the kitchen to chase away the gloom of the wet weather outside I check my phone. Still no message from Alf, or from Ruby. Has he even passed my message on? I'm getting sick of waiting. Perhaps I should go back down the quay and ask him to ring her for me. Maybe I could persuade him to phone her in front of me, pass me his mobile? But it looks like it's going to rain again. British bloody summertime. I will send another reminder via private message.

Before I can type in Alf's name on Instagram, I see a shadow pass over the kitchen window. For a nanosecond, I think it's dark low-moving clouds. Then my brain unpicks its speed is much too solid and too fast. I see a blur of limbs, the whites of eyes through the pane. I flinch, my body reacting before my conscious mind knows what's happening. The glass crashes inwards. I feel the bite of shards on my cheek. A projectile hurls through the kitchen window, landing in the sink.

A large fist-sized rock, covered in moss.

Eighteen

Imust have been writing detective novels for too long, because I'd assumed the police presence at the house would be a lot bigger. But the reality has far less fanfare, thanks to austerity cuts and the fact we live in the provinces now.

A single police vehicle had turned up to investigate, with two female police officers. One is very young, straight out of training; the other is about twenty-five years older and looks like her mum, or aunt. The familial resemblance may not be coincidence. I had heard them having a muttered argument on the doorstep when I'd gone to open the front door. Perhaps, like the Dyers had taken over much of the crime rate in Ilfracombe, the police were in the control of a single family too.

Lindy had arrived back with Caleb, moments after the rock had come through the window. She'd stopped me from my first reflex of clearing up the glass. Thank God Caleb was asleep in his car seat, he could have cut his little hands. I'd been so scared, I was grateful to see Lindy even though, like me, she had jumped to the natural conclusion.

'This is that Aimee one again, isn't it?' My mother's mouth was a grim line.

I'd hesitated, then nodded. Though I'd already accepted this to be the case, hearing the assertion aloud from someone else's lips made it real somehow. Before, it had all been just a theory. Even the letters hadn't seemed as serious. But a rock is a weapon, the broken glass a hint of Aimee's intention towards me and my family. Mum had been insistent on calling the authorities at once.

'You're to take this seriously, you hear?' Lindy barks at the two officers.

'We will take it very seriously.' The older police officer rebuffs my mother with the kind of officious air that suggests she gets this all the time.

As I watch the police pick over my kitchen, I already regret letting Lindy call them. I feel inexplicably embarrassed, like this is all my fault somehow. Obviously this makes no sense, I never asked for any of this. It's my right to return to Ilfracombe; it's Aimee who won't let this go. I know how far Aimee can take this. I'd been grateful it wasn't Michael who'd turned up at the house at least.

The older officer looks over her glasses at me. 'Can you think of anyone who might wish you harm?'

Wish you harm. Oh, yes. Try a whole backwater crime family. All bets were off. Even though earlier I'd felt certain I was not in any immediate danger, from Aimee or her weirdo family, this had obviously changed now. Moments after the rock had hurtled through my window, I'd finally processed the rubber band wrapped around it, the piece of paper tucked underneath. With shaking hands, I grabbed it up out of the sink, nicking my thumb on the glass. The adrenaline coursing through my veins meant I didn't even notice until my bright-red blood spotted through the piece of white paper I'd unfolded. On it, scrawled with those big, looped letters:

Don't change the habit of a lifetime, Samantha.
Keep your mouth shut.

Aimee had made me stay silent before. The rock is supposed to scare me, ensure I keep silent. Well, it's working. What can the police do, anyway? I've already discovered from Ava that Aimee is apparently not in the local area. Though she would say this, Michael has confirmed it too. If he is lying, does that mean he is in on all of this? Maybe I can't trust any of them.

I just shrug.

The older police officer gives nothing away in her expression. She notes something down.

Lindy hisses her disappointment in me. 'Samantha, tell them.'

'About what?' I turn my innocent eyes on, sending telepathic messages to Mum: *Let me handle it.*

If Lindy receives them, she doesn't let on. 'My daughter just moved back here. Back at school, she was very badly bullied—'

Mum is interrupted by a crash in the porch as the front door opens. Mo trips on the steps in his rush to enter the house. He races inside, dishevelled and wild-eyed.

'Where is she?'

Mo drops his briefcase as he makes it into the kitchen. He falls to his knees beside me, hands on my lap, his face in mine like I am a small child.

He kisses me on the forehead. 'Darling, are you okay?'

An absurd laugh bubbles up in my throat. It is like he is taking all his moves from the Concerned Husband Handbook.

I choke it down. 'Yes, I'm fine.'

127

'Is this about the letters?' Mo demands.

He means the N1Fan letters. I groan inside.

'What letters?' The older police officer looks much more interested now.

'Oh, they were nothing. Just fan mail.' I am anxious they don't follow this thread. I don't want them uncovering the *Never Have I Ever* notes.

Mo tells her everything he knows anyway, which is not much. The police officer becomes a little less interested when I confirm I have destroyed the letters from N1Fan that Mo saw. I am extra thankful now I had not shared either of the *NHIE* notes with him, or my investigations into where Aimee could be. The last thing I need now is the police tracking Aimee down. She really would make me pay for that.

The young police officer appears from the back door. 'No one lurking outside.'

'Obviously not now!' Lindy's frustration explodes outwards. 'I was trying to tell you.'

'It's fine, Mum.' I stand, my boots crunching on the glass on the kitchen tiles. 'It will just be a misunderstanding. Something to do with the previous occupants, probably.'

Mum regards me with shining eyes. She doesn't understand my behaviour. She wants to protect me. My heart aches for her. She doesn't understand. She can't protect me. I am the only one who can deal with Aimee.

Lindy opens her mouth to counter me, then shakes her head.

'We need a glazier,' Mo frets, his gaze on the broken glass. He grabs his phone, already Googling. 'Hello? Yes, I need someone to come out immediately.'

Half an hour later and the police and my mother finally leave. The police take pictures and put the offending rock in a clear plastic bag. They hand over a business card, asking me to call them if anything else occurs to me. I know I won't.

As soon as the door finally shuts after them and then my mother, Mo turns to me. Angry fear pours out of him. 'What the hell is really going on, Sam?'

I raise a finger to my lips, as Caleb shifts in his sleep in the car seat.

'You know as much as me. I got those weird letters you saw. Then this.' My voice cracks a little. I am exhausted by all of this pretence.

'But why the hell would anyone do this?' Stressed, Mo combs a hand through his hair, exposing his receding hairline. He looks all of his forty-three years. 'A quiet life, you said. We lived in London for years, never once had any crime. We're here for five minutes and someone chucks a rock through the window?'

'How the hell am I supposed to know?' The lie feels as tangible as cigarette smoke in the air.

Before Mo can reply, the inexplicable ring tone of 'Every Breath You Take' sounds through the kitchen. I raise an eyebrow, as if to say *Seriously?* But Mo just shrugs. It's not his. Exasperated, I make a grab for my phone on the kitchen table, certain it's not mine playing the song. I hate novelty ring tones; I always set mine to a plain *ring-ring*. Yet the handset lights up in my hand, with AISLING and her picture on the screen. I see there's a number of missed calls from her. Carole, too. Quiet fury invades my chest with the speed of a freight train.

'What the hell have you done, Mo?' I spit through clenched teeth. 'Tell me you haven't called Aisling or Carole about all this.'

But of course he has. Mo meets my gaze, defiant as the Police's bass notes continue on a loop. It's a weird soundtrack to our disagreement.

'Carole's not even worried,' I point out. 'She even thinks it might be good for my career.'

'Screw your career, Sam! This family is in the shitter!'

'What the hell is this, nineteen fifty-two!' I yell back. 'Things don't go the way you want, because little wifey has too much work on? You want me back in the kitchen, making dinner and pouring you mojitos? Fuck you!'

The stupid phone goes silent just as I swear. I turn the handset off before it can start up again.

'You know it's not like that.' Mo collapses in a chair. 'One of your readers has turned rogue, a full-blown stalker. This is serious.'

'It's not a stalker.' I force authority into my tone.

Mo meets my stare. 'You don't know that, for sure.'

I double down. 'Every writer gets weird stuff from time to time.'

Mo interrupts with a derisive snort. He doesn't believe me.

'I'm sorry. I just couldn't bear it, if anything happened to you or Caleb.' He holds both his arms out to me. 'Maybe we should never have come back here?'

I'm thinking exactly the same thing. But we are here now, and it's not fair for Aimee to try and run me out of town. Mine and Mo's fresh start could be the only thing still keeping us together. I need to get to the bottom of this, or I will lose everything. I just have to try and ensure Mo isn't dragged into this any further.

'It's okay,' I say.

Mo throws his hands in the air. 'Listen to me, making it all about me. I'm such an arsehole.'

'You are *not*.' We're back on more familiar ground now: a flashpoint, then Mo blames himself, I disagree. Rinse and repeat.

'I am. I'm stressed, but you are too. Even though you were the one who wanted to come back, it still must be difficult for you, being here.'

Irritation prickles through me. Mo had been the one who wanted to come back to Ilfracombe, not me. But I let it go.

Mo proffers a wan smile. 'New book, old place. Flashbacks with it, I'd imagine.'

Relief surges through me next. He has no clue just how right he is.

'It's just weird. I'll get used to it.'

For a moment I reconsider my decision not to tell Mo about the two threatening *Never Have I Ever* notes. Maybe I should just tell him what happened that night? Or even what we were doing before that, with that stupid game? It's probably not as big a deal as I remember. We were just kids. Mo had a chaotic childhood back in Northern Ireland, with his multiple siblings and crazy cousins. Teenagers push things too far all the time. He's probably done stupid stuff, too. *It's good to talk*, as they say.

Just as I am about to form the words, Mo's expression changes. He tips me a wink, attempting to lighten the mood. 'As long as you don't take up with any old boyfriends, eh?'

Michael's face bursts into my mind. No, not Michael's. He is the adult and broad, hairy policeman. *Mike's*, pale and thin, like he was when he was just a lad. Guilt blooms in my belly as I think about how I still haven't mentioned seeing him to Mo.

It doesn't mean anything.

131

I have to contain this. Mine and Mo's position is too precarious. Regardless who pushed for coming back, I have to admit we desperately needed to consolidate our debts, take the pressure off. We even need the slower pace of life here. Mo and I have sailed too close to the edge of our marriage in the past few years, we're finally beginning to get back on track. If I tell him about what really happened back then and how Aimee is after me again now, Mo will freak out and drag us straight back to London. It won't just finish us financially, but emotionally too.

I can't risk it.

I go to Mo. I kneel next to him, rest my head on his shoulder. 'It will be okay. I promise. But you have to let me handle it. Don't get Carole or Aisling involved. Just . . . trust me, okay?'

His arms close around me, in a desperate embrace. I can hear the quickening thud of his heartbeat. His anxiety is infectious, but I force myself to stay calm. I still have options. I can make this go away. If Aimee is behind the notes and the rock like I'm sure she is, I need to get her to realise I will keep my mouth shut.

First, I have to speak to Ruby.

Nineteen

Mo is not keen on me leaving the house, especially alone. I manage to swing it by saying I am going for a drive. I assure him I will keep to well-populated areas in town and that I won't be getting out of my car. He wants to come with me, but someone has to stay in for the glazier. He tells me to 'check in' via text and that I should keep the doors locked. I agree. Anything to get out, away from his loving but oppressive influence.

I wait near the harbour, feeling ridiculous in shades, hat and coat. But despite it being high season, the poor weather has continued. It feels like October. A biting wind rattles across the quay. I shiver in my layers, even though the sun peeks out from behind grey clouds above.

I see him before he sees me. As I stalk across the harbour towards him, I watch him load empty lobster pots into his boat. Despite the cold, he's just in a T-shirt, the knots of his shoulders visible under the greying material.

'Hello again.' Alf hops down from the stone steps, onto the deck of *Gipsy Girl*. 'What can I do you for?'

'I have been sending you messages on Instagram?'

The younger man smirks. 'Lucky me. Been at sea, haven't I? Wanna go down?'

The second double entendre jumps into the space between us. He pats the seat next to him, one eyebrow raised. He is not subtle, at all. His boyish charms might impress drunk girls in the pub piers at night, but they don't work on me.

'I really need to speak to your mum.'

He seems to register my disinterest. He winds up rope between his gnarled hands. 'I told her. Maybe she don't want to talk to you?'

He shrugs, throwing the coil of rope into a pile with some other supplies.

I sigh. I'd been afraid of this. So, Ruby *has* been dodging me on purpose. With Maddy in London and Ava all but refusing to help me connect with Aimee, I have no choice but to reveal one of my cards, to get Ruby to call me back.

'So, can you give Ruby a message?'

Alf flicks his fringe out of his eyes. 'Okay.'

'Tell her Aimee's back.'

'Sam?'

The voice at the end of the line feels so familiar, yet so alien all at once. I am transported to her bedroom: the smell of patchouli incense, a million beanie babies on the bed, a bottle of vodka hidden under it.

'Ruby.' A smile springs to my lips, despite everything.

Ruby's voice is cold. 'My boy said he saw you. What do you want?'

Wow, no introductions or *how-you-beens* whatsoever. Crushing disappointment surges through me. So, the passage of time has done nothing to whittle the hard edges off that summer for Ruby, like it has for Maddy. But that figures. Maddy might have been easily led, but it meant she was easy to forgive, too. Ruby had always held grudges. I should have expected this.

'I need to talk to you. About—'

Ruby interrupts. '—About Aimee. Right, Alf said. I haven't seen her.'

'When was the last time you did see her?' I grit my teeth.

Ruby sighs, her breath causing a small whirlwind down the receiver. 'I don't know, same time as you last did, I guess?'

My interest is piqued. 'Wait . . . wait. You didn't see her after the summer party at Easterbook Farm at all? Not even at sixth-form college?'

'I only went for like, five minutes,' Ruby reminds me.

I hear the tell-tale *beep-beep-beep* on the line. She is on a payphone. I hear her swear as she tries to find more cash. 'Look, I'll call you back, Ruby . . .?'

Dial tone.

I swear myself, then redial. Ruby must know something I don't. She had still been here in Devon, the whole time. Maybe she doesn't even know she knows some important tidbit of information that will help me. I have to speak to her in more depth.

The pay phone rings and rings. No answer. I look at the screen of my phone, it's a Lynmouth landline number. So, she must be in the small village right now, like Alf said. I look up at the clock: it is barely midday. I can get to Lynmouth in half an hour if I go via Blackmoor Gate. It would be hours before Mo would be home from work; Lindy had taken Caleb to a soft-play place over at Barnstaple. No one would know I hadn't been at my desk this afternoon.

I grab my car keys.

Twenty

I normally enjoy the scenery on the way to Exmoor, but I barely register the lush, green fields either side of me as my car cuts through the countryside. In what feels like a blink, I am outside the big pub at Blackmoor Gate and the crossroads. I turn at the large coach park and tourist public toilets, pushing onwards past the old Lynton and Barnstaple Railway and Parracombe.

I'd forgotten the sheer, 'edge of the world' beauty in the depths of Exmoor. The car crests over the road leading to the twin villages, I can see its breath-taking beauty up ahead: the deep coombes on the left, the sea on the right. As I pass the petrol station at the top of Barbrook and coast the car towards the village below, I forget what has brought me here. I can see the rush of the gorge. Sheep are dotted about, like clouds fallen to earth. With its steep inclines and verdant forestry, it's known locally as 'Little Switzerland'. Literature has a long association with the area, Mary and Percy Shelley had holidayed here, and R.D. Blackmore's *Lorna Doone* was partly set in Brendon, a small hamlet above the twin villages of Lynton and Lynmouth. I take deep breaths, feeling a little less anxious for the first time in days.

The car makes an unhealthy grinding noise, but it eventually limps its way into the small village at the bottom of the hill, driving past the shooting jets of the Glen Lyn Gorge. I see a car park on Watersmeet Road, so park there. As I get out of my car, my sights are drawn to the village green, the children's play park and the pebble beach beyond. It's a clear day; I can see Wales. I search my brain for any clues Alf might have let slip on where Ruby's new place could be. I'd only been here a couple of times as a child. I remember sheepskin shops, ice cream and a cliff railway, a water-powered Victorian feat of engineering that takes tourists up the cliff to Lynton at the top.

I don't get that far. As I meander towards the village high street, I find myself in the shadow of a hotel called Shelley's. Next to the miniature railway exhibition on Watersmeet Road there's a wide café shopfront that has UNDER NEW MANAGEMENT taped to the glass. It's a deep burgundy, with a similar colour scheme inside. What's more convincing I'm in the right place is the fact it's called Ruby's.

I cross the road and try the door. It is not open yet. A man in overalls on a stepladder adds an apostrophe to the sign as I watch. Sunshine makes the windows opaque, so I raise two hands to the glass to peer inside.

'Maid's out back.'

The man on the stepladder descends, holding his paint can like it's precious. He's old, at least seventy, with crazed white hair sticking in all directions like a mad scientist. But I get the sense this is a man who would have never set foot in a university lab, or any place of higher learning. He still moves with the sinewed, knotted muscles of someone who has spent a lifetime outside. I'm reminded of Alf, then notice a strong resemblance. Could this be his grandfather? He has to be. Ruby's mother Wendy had been a single mum, so I'd assumed back then her dad was not on the scene at all. Teens were always so self-involved. But perhaps he'd always been there, helping out like he is now.

Ruby's dad does not ask me who I am, or what I am doing here. He gestures for me to follow him. 'C'mon then.'

He says nothing as he leads me down a dark side alley, into a little courtyard beyond. It's a sun trap: white metal tables are set up, bunting overhead. My old friend is there too, kneeling next to a chair, painting it. She looks up as her father arrives, though her smile falls when she sees me.

Ruby's dad looks from her to me, realising his mistake in not asking who I am. Surprise, confusion, hurt flicker across my old friend's features. The assured, silver-haired woman in front of me is replaced by a gangly, thin teen who cuts her own hair jagged-short over the sink with a pair of nail scissors. For a moment, I think she is going to turn on her heel and run like she did that March night from the Tunnels, laughter chasing after her.

'Surprise.' I don't know why I say this. I sound like I am on some stupid, dated American sitcom.

Ruby purses her lips. Any trace of vulnerability is erased. I can see a dark anger bubbling underneath her features. She was not just dodging me, she really did not want to see me. Hurt blossoms in my chest. Despite everything, I had still wanted to see her. Had she really washed her hands of me? I steel myself. Fine, screw her. I will ask her about Aimee, then be on my way.

'I'll just go wash me hands.' Her dad scuttles towards a back door, into the café.

She turns to me, eyes flashing. 'I should have known you would turn up.'

I hold up both palms. 'I just need to ask you a couple more questions, then I'm gone. I swear.'

There's an uncomfortable pause, but then Ruby sighs. 'Let's do this.'

Ruby grabs a dry chair. She indicates I sit down too.

'I told you on the phone, I haven't seen Aimee for years.'

'I know. I just want to ask you what you remember of this.'

I pull out the print-out of the newspaper article detailing Aimee's disappearance after the party we had all gone to. Ruby makes no move to pick it up or look at it.

'Why do you care, all of a sudden?' Ruby demanded.

Now there's a question. The note with the rock – *Keep your mouth shut* – sears through my mind again. I can't risk telling Ruby the truth, especially if she is involved somehow. For all I know, she could be reporting back to Aimee.

'Call it unfinished business, I suppose.'

It sounded better in my head. Ruby just snorts in derision, then takes the piece of paper, peers at it. 'Oh yeah, I forgot she did this.' She skim-reads and laughs, just as I had. 'Aimee, "doing anything for anyone"?? That is such a crock.'

I seize Ruby's words. 'But she came back, right?'

Ruby leans back in her chair. 'I did have other problems on my mind, back then. Like being pregnant.'

I can't resist. I need to know if our dare caused it. 'How did it happen?'

Ruby raises an eyebrow, deadpan. 'Call it an experiment. You lot were always going on about lads, thought I would see what the fuss was about. Turns out, not much to write home about. Anyway, Wendy threw me out when I told her about the baby. I had to go and live with Dad. That's why I left college.'

Suitably chastised, I steer the conversation back to Aimee. 'Her niece at Dyer's said Aimee did come back, but she was just a baby herself, so she couldn't be sure.'

Ruby shakes her head. 'You think I was keeping tabs on Aimee? I didn't care if I never saw that cow again. Luckily, that was exactly how it turned out. I hadn't even given her a thought until you turned up, going on about it.'

This is too much. Am I really supposed to believe this rubbish? My mother's face flashes through my mind again. She would say it's time for Ruby to take responsibility.

'I don't believe you. If you'd really not thought about her, or what happened, you wouldn't have dodged my calls. Or be this angry when I mention Aimee.'

Ruby jumps to her feet, fists clenched. 'Do you know what it's like, growing up a queer girl, trying to fit in with your "normal" friends?'

I'm not having this. It had been me who was bullied non-stop. It didn't matter what I said or did, her barbed tongue lashed at me every day. Ruby and Maddy hung onto Aimee's words like saps. They did nothing to stop it.

'You were just gay, Ruby. It's not a big deal.'

Pervert. Lezza. Freak!

The insults echo to me from nowhere. I'm shocked at the intrusion: I have no problem with gay people; I never have. Growing up with the bohemian Lindy, I'd seen many of her 'alternative' friends at the house. One, Elaine, had come over most weeks before Lindy's lengthy depression had meant she'd driven away most people she knew. My memory of Elaine is patchy, just a collection of clichés: dungarees, short hair, a bare face with no make-up. I couldn't be certain if she had really presented this way, or if my juvenile brain had exaggerated these details to remind me I had perceived her difference, even then. Whatever the case, as a small child I had known Elaine was a lesbian even though none of us had ever discussed it.

'Back then it was a big deal though, don't you remember?' Ruby shakes her head as she takes in my blank stare. 'Things might have changed in the last twenty years, but when we were growing up being a lesbian meant social death. Even if you were just *suspected* of being gay. Why do you think I was so keen to be Aimee's friend?'

I shift in my chair, uncomfortable. I don't like recalling this. 'For protection, I guess.'

'Bingo. Remember Penny Jordan?'

It takes me a moment to place the name. Then a thin girl in just her bra and pants pops up in my brain. Why would I remember her that way? Then another connection fires and it comes to me.

I recall Aimee pushing a snivelling, semi-naked teen out of the school changing rooms. She was grabbing for her clothes as Aimee threw a balled-up white shirt at her. The rest of us looked on, wide-eyed. None of us stood up to Aimee, nor attempted to help the other girl.

Penny Jordan.

'Pervert! I saw you looking at me and my friends!' Aimee shrieked, her voice echoing through my mind's eye, whether I like it or not. 'Lezza! Freak!'

It's like Penny's name dropping from Ruby's lips set a cinema projector reel in motion. I see Aimee in her sports kit; the grey-white tiles of a school changing room; I can almost smell the tang of teenage body odour mixed with spray deodorant in the air.

At her restaurant, I meet Ruby's grim gaze. 'Oh, God.'

Penny scrabbled around in the corridor, trying to shield her body with her clothes. She was skittish, looking behind her, eyes wild with fear. I could guess what she was worried about: a male teacher, or worse, our other classmates, appearing from the boys' changing rooms and seeing her in a state of undress.

'Please, let me back in!'

But Aimee didn't move from the door. Arms wide, she stood feet apart, blocking the way. 'No way. I'm protecting the rest of us. From *you*.'

Now, shame crackles through me. I can't believe I had just looked on back then, done nothing. But neither had Ruby. If I am culpable, so is she. Isn't she worse, since she'd known what it was to feel like Penny Jordan? I don't say it though. I can't afford to alienate Ruby any more than I have already.

Ruby sits back down. 'That was what it was like at school. Aimee was a bitch. It was shot through her like a stick of rock. She could smell difference, she sought it out, used it to her advantage. And me being gay? Was like a gift to her. I had to keep her on side. I had no choice.'

We all have a choice. But then my words to Michael at On A Break echo back to me: *You don't know what it's like for girls, at school. Sometimes you have to do stuff to fit in.* I suppose I can't blame Ruby for my own defence.

'If you can't beat them, join them,' I confirm. Even so, I have to know if she remembers the night I broke up with Mike. 'Do you remember the Spring Break Blowout?'

'How could I forget?' Ruby sighs. 'That night was the start of it all.'

How could I have forgotten? My memories seem to glitch, like an old-style projector. Thoughts of Mike fall away.

Ruby, drunk and swaying, attempted to catch the flying disc for Frisby Golf. She missed and fell to the shale, cackling with laughter. Aimee made a big show of picking her up, like she cared. Then Ruby threw her arms around Aimee, a big smile on her face.

'Sam and I have a dare for you, Ruby. But this time it's a secret.' Aimee had a grin like the Cheshire Cat's as her gaze met mine. 'I know you like her. You've liked her all along, haven't you?'

'No.' I am vehement, reacting against the sharp glare Ruby gives me. 'I had no part in that dare. I swear. It was all Aimee.'

Ruby shrugs. 'Yeah, you said back then. I didn't believe you then and I don't believe you now.'

Maddy supporting Ruby on the Tunnels beach, laughing as her old friend sang and held on to her.

Ruby pressed her forehead against Maddy's. 'I love you, you know.'

Everyone hooted and jeered as Ruby planted a sloppy kiss on Maddy's lips.

Taken completely by surprise, Maddy let go of Ruby, who landed on her arse in a rock pool.

'That's disgusting. You're disgusting!' Maddy stood over her, angry and humiliated as other party-goers clapped. 'Shut up!'

'Don't worry, Ruby, you'll get better!' Aimee laughed, two boys next to her whooping like the gibbons over at the wildlife park in Combe Martin.

'Not funny!' Maddy wiped her mouth with her sleeve.

'You're right, it's hilarious!' Aimee cackled.

When Ruby staggered to her feet and turned, Aimee laughed even harder at the sight of her wet bum. 'Ooops, Rubes, you look like you've pissed yourself!'

Aimee turned and gave me a double thumbs-up. 'Never Have I Ever kissed a girl. Mission completed! Well done, Rubes!'

Ruby staggered to her feet, tears in her eyes. I wanted to go to her, but Aimee locked me in a triumphant embrace. I looked over my shoulder and watched Ruby disappear into the tunnel away from the beach. Away from us.

'Why didn't you stop her?' Ruby demands. 'Why didn't you stop *me*?'

I sigh. 'You're right, I should have done something. Stopped her. Somehow.'

We all should have, I add silently.

But Ruby is not looking at me now. She is staring into the distance, raking over her past hurt. 'Y'see, I saw through Aimee straight away. She was Queen Bee, but at least she knew it. She didn't pretend to be anything she wasn't. I knew she would get at me, but I figured you had my back, at least. I was wrong.'

I don't interrupt this time. Something tells me Ruby has been waiting twenty-three years for this.

'I never had a voice. Not at home, thanks to Mum. Not at school, because of you lot. I had to keep it all locked in, all the time. It was exhausting. Then she wanted to play that stupid game.'

'*Never Have I Ever*,' I interject.

'Right. I knew it would lead to trouble. But to you, I was just stupid, naïve, gay Ruby.'

'We never thought you were stupid.' We had thought she was the other two.

'I was glad, when you moved.' Ruby looks at me now, defiant. 'It meant the group disbanded. I could get on with my life, reinvent myself. I made a few mistakes, but I don't regret it, because I got Alf.'

I'm stung, but I don't let it preoccupy me. I seize Ruby's words. 'So, the group disbanded, because *I* moved? Not because Aimee ran off? Then she must have come back.'

Ruby rolls her eyes at the change of subject back to the matter in hand. 'Not to college she didn't.'

'But no one ever came to speak to you, ask what really happened that night, did they? The . . . the police, they never questioned you, right?'

Ruby shakes her head. 'There's so many Dyers, maybe they were caught up with them. I figured it was better to keep quiet, let it all blow over. Which it did. Someone said she'd called home, let her family know she was okay. She went travelling, Australia I heard. Figures, she always liked the surf bums down at Woolacombe, didn't she?'

I nod and smile, automatic. Another confirmation of what Ava remembers, along with an added detail: Australia. Ruby does not appear to notice she'd dredged this nugget of information for me though. She stands up, hands on her hips, her message clear: *just go, please.*

'It was good to see you.' I rise from my place.

Ruby just shrugs again. I feel like I want to hug her, despite myself. I don't want this to end on a sour note; I can be the bigger person. But I know this will not be well received. I move towards the narrow alleyway, so I might make my way out of the courtyard and return to my car.

'Sam.'

I turn back gladly, hoping Ruby wants to instigate the hug instead. Then we can all move on. Maybe even get past this, become friends again. Returning to Ilfracombe has been a baptism of fire, but I have spent too long alone. I need friends around me.

But Ruby's expression is still like granite. 'Stay away from Alf, you hear me?'

Embarrassment at how wrong I'd read the situation hits me full on in the face. Hot tears sting the backs of my eyes. I avert my eyes as I nod my agreement to stay away from Alf. Eager to get out of there I all but flee, hastily blundering back to where I'd left my car. I unlock the door and slide in, glad to be back in my own safe environment.

I gulp in deep breaths, exhaling slowly to calm myself. My eyes stray to the dashboard. It's getting on for three o'clock. I needed to salvage the rest of the day, get at least five hundred words done. I turn the key in the ignition, the engine fires up. I turn the wheel to go back home.

Well, that could have gone a lot better with Ruby. Perhaps I should have realised she could never take responsibility for her role. Some people just can't challenge themselves to confront harsh truths. At least I have got the information I need. Aimee might not have gone to college with Maddy and Ruby, but she had phoned home to let her family know she was okay. Australia is a new lead, too. She's probably not still there, but it means I can hopefully catch a hold of Aimee's trail again.

On the other side of the world.

Twenty-one

My heart sinks as I turn onto our little cul-de-sac. Though it is only twenty to four, Mo's car is already on the driveway, occupying one of our two parking spaces. As I clamber out of the car, I check my phone. Sure enough, a bunch of texts and missed calls have come through, all from Mo. I don't have time to check them all, so I decide to play it by ear. Maybe he had not been back long . . . Perhaps I could salvage the situation?

'Where have you been? I got back hours ago!'

Too late.

Mo rises from his vigil at the kitchen table as soon as I open the door. His hair sticks out at angles: he combs it through his fingers when he feels anxious.

'Why don't you ever check your phone!'

I proffer Mo a fixed smile. 'Sorry, I was out at Lynmouth. There's very little signal over there. How come you're home?'

Mo's mouth drops open, incredulous. 'Someone threw a rock through the window yesterday. You've been getting weird letters. I don't like leaving you or Caleb here alone. I sacked off work early, so I could come home. You know, like a normal husband would. Why have you been in Lynmouth?'

Mo's words rush together, like they always do when he's freaking out. I learned a long time ago it's best to let him pour out all of his anxiety. This means I'm caught on the hop by his question, this early in his histrionics. Normally he rants at me for at least five minutes when he gets scared about something.

I snatch a half-truth out of the air. 'Just visiting an old friend.'

'You don't have any friends.'

Mo's words land hard, because it's true. In all the time we've been together, all my socialising has been to do with work. I have no close girlfriends, no confidantes, not even other mums from baby group to have a coffee with. I would have to be part of such a group for that to be possible. Mo is the only person I've let into my inner circle in real terms in decades.

'Well, this was someone from school. Besides, I had to do a research thing down there.'

'DI Robyn Dallas is doing house calls in Devon now. From the fucking East End of London?'

Mo's swearing is a red flag. Unlike me, or even Lindy, he usually only does it when he's *very* upset. Dogged as ever, I find myself unable to back down.

'I thought it would be fun to write some local stuff in. Smugglers, you know.'

Mo stares at me, eyes wide, his face pale. 'When did lying become so second nature to you?'

My mouth gapes open. Mo never makes personal remarks to me. He hated how his father would belittle his mother when she was alive, picking at her, breaking her down. As a reaction against his family history, he'd always treated me like a princess, put me on a pedestal. Whenever we argue, it's always his fault, regardless of whether it really is. He can't help apologising, either. For Mo to call me a liar is tantamount to heresy.

My eye strays to something on the table. There's a thud in my chest as I realise what it is. An opened envelope; a piece of paper. Another letter.

'This came for you, while you were out.' He pushes it towards me. There, on the front: those distinctive, looped letters. 'I'm sorry I opened your mail, but . . . Actually, screw it. I'm not sorry. I read it because you're not telling me a damn thing.'

OhGodOhGodOhGod.

Mo stands over me, arms folded and face stern like a teacher who's caught a student in the act. I pick up the piece of paper with shaking hands. I unfold it, struggling to take in the details as I read them.

Dear SJ Scherer,

I was your number one fan. I had a stupid fantasy that one day we might be friends, but now I see I was wrong. Sorry about the other night; I didn't mean to scare you. You won't hear from me again.

N1Fan xxx

Elation crashes through my brain. Aimee had to be N1Fan after all. She was leaving me alone. She obviously felt guilty that she had upped her game with the *NHIE* notes when I moved back to Ilfracombe. She must have decided she'd gone too far when she chased me, then broke the window. I feel an unusual surge of optimism. It's all over. Thank God.

Mo's quiet voice interrupts my internal celebration. 'What happened the other night, Sam?'

I think fast. I never told Mo about what happened when I went to the corner shop. I can't bear to see the disappointment in his eyes. 'She must mean breaking the window.'

149

'You're lying.' Mo's tone is not accusatory, which somehow makes it worse. 'Why won't you let me help? Why are you shutting me out?'

Mo mistakes my silence for belligerence. There's tears in his eyes. My heart flip-flops at the sight of him. Forty-three-year-old Mo is gone and I see him as the sallow, quiet and vulnerable youth I'd met twenty years ago.

'I'm sorry,' I whisper.

Mo doesn't hear me. He looks like Ruby did at her restaurant. I keep hurting people I care about, without even realising.

'Is it me? What can I do, to fix this? Just tell me, I'll do it. Whatever it takes. You wanted to come back to Ilfracombe, I'll go to Timbuctoo if you want. Please, Sam.'

Mo's words crash through my brain. No, *he* wanted to come to Ilfracombe. Why does he keep remembering it wrong? I open my mouth to tell him so, but freeze. Mo pulls the knot of his tie up and down absent-mindedly, like it's a noose. That glitch happens in my mind again. In the tie's place now, around his shoulders: a rope.

My tongue sticks to the roof of my mouth as I take it in. This can't be happening. I blink and the rope is gone. I feel like I am losing my mind.

'It's not you.' I am vehement.

Mo's eyes lock with mine. 'Then what is it? You're keeping stuff from me. It's not fair. We're supposed to be a partnership. Just let me in.'

I lean against the counter top. My body feels heavy. The weight I feel like I have been carrying since I got that first *Never Have I Ever* note seems overwhelming. I know I can't contain this by myself any longer. I know Mo won't be letting this go anytime soon. Maybe I should change the habit of a lifetime: I can't be the strong, silent type forever. Would it be so bad, to include him?

'I'm sorry. I haven't told you everything.' I indicate for Mo to sit down. 'When we were kids, we played this game, *Never Have I Ever*.'

'Yeah. I know it.' Mo picks at a splinter in the old pine table. His body language is stressed, the air practically crackles around him. 'The guys at work, all their kids watch YouTubers playing it. But when we were kids it was mostly a drinking game.'

I can see us all in Aimee's bedroom. All four of us laughing. We grabbed our neon plastic shot glasses, full of tequila and thrust them in the air, before slugging them back. Each of us licked the salt off the backs of our hands, then sucked on the lemon, grimacing.

'*Never Have I Ever* had a tequila shot!'

I sigh. 'Sometimes it was. Anyway, we had our own twist. And this girl . . . Aimee . . . she took it too far. She always took things too far.'

'And you think what is happening now has something to do with her? All these weird notes? The rock? Is this all some juvenile game?'

'I don't know. I really don't know. But it could be her, yes.'

Mo sighs. 'So, what is this Aimee's problem with you now, exactly?'

Great question.

'Then last time we all saw one another, there was a huge row.' I choose my words carefully, keen not to be drawn too much on the details. 'I left for London, Aimee ran off, the other two – Ruby and Maddy – didn't speak much again. It was a defining moment in all our lives. Aimee must have borne a grudge. Or maybe she's just screwing with me because I've moved back. Maybe it's both.'

The falsehood feels heavy on my tongue. I feel certain Mo can see my lies, but he just looks to me, trusting as ever. I can almost taste the tequila on my tongue. It has always made me think of that night in Aimee's bedroom; it's one of the reasons I've never drunk it since.

'End of school soon, ladies,' Aimee announced in a sombre voice.

'Good.' Ruby burped. We all laughed.

'End of an era.' Maddy linked arms with me and Ruby. 'I've known these gals since primary. My entire life.'

'It's been a helluva ride,' Aimee jumped in, anxious to reassert her authority. She never liked to be reminded she had joined the group so long after our original trinity. 'How about we do something special to mark leaving school?'

Leaving school. I still hadn't told the others I was moving to London, whether I wanted to or not. I'd kicked off more than once at Lindy since the bombshell dropped the night before the Spring Break Blowout. I'd refused to speak to Dad on the phone, or even at weekends when he visited. But that was the limit of my powers. I was adrift and at sea, my life about to change irrevocably.

'Like, a super dare?' Ruby smiled, though there was trepidation in her eyes. 'Like what?'

'Don't know yet. But this is going to be the big one, ladies. It's going to knock all the other dares right out of the park. They'll be nothing in comparison to this: a DARE OF DARES!' Aimee flung out both arms, knocking over an open bottle of gin on the thirty-pounds-a-square-metre pure-wool carpet.

'Works for me.' Maddy swayed, her vision a little fuzzy.

Ruby nodded. 'Sure.'

'Depends what it is.' The words jumped out of my mouth before I had chance to think.

Dead silence reflected back at me. The other three's heads swivelled on their necks, almost in unison. I could sense the disapproval in the air. Ruby's eyes widened and she shook her head slightly, as if to say I'd made a mistake. I already knew, but it's too late to take it back. My stomach clenched in trepidation.

'You know what I think?' Aimee leant in close to me, the tang of alcohol as tangible on her breath as disgust. 'I think you think you're too good for us.'

I gasped as something wet hit me in the face. The fruity, woody aroma of tequila dripped down onto my chest, a lime stuck to my cheek. Aimee cackled with glee at my surprise as I stood there, mouth opening and closing like a goldfish.

'Jesus, so this is all school playground stuff?'

I note how Mo's body language has relaxed as I've been talking. He's gone from being a coiled spring to a flaccid, overstretched balloon that all the air has been let out of. After all his proclamations of wanting to help earlier, his change of demeanour smarts.

A thankful laugh escapes Mo. 'Makes me glad I went to a boys' school.'

'You see, this is exactly what I was afraid of.' I wrench my body away from his. 'I didn't want you thinking I was some pathetic victim.'

'Oh darling, I'm sorry. I didn't mean it the way it came out.' Mo grabs my hands. He leans his forehead against mine. 'I'm just relieved, you know? And I could never think you were pathetic. Or a victim. You're the strongest woman I know.'

I sigh. 'We're a right pair.'

Mo's brow furrows. 'So why didn't you tell the police about Aimee?'

Oh, shit.

I can't tell Mo about Michael or going to see him to ask his advice. What if Mo goes to see him, asks about it? Michael might mention our shared history, Mo will jump to conclusions . . . I can't go down that route, not now.

Before I can try and explain though, Mo fills in the gaps himself. 'You didn't want to get Aimee in trouble, did you?'

I seize on this and nod.

'She doesn't deserve your loyalty. It was a long time ago. And she's threatening you. She threw a rock through the bloody window! What if Caleb had been in the kitchen with you?'

'I know. But he wasn't. That's the main thing.' *If Aimee had hurt my baby, I would've killed her,* I add silently.

Mo goes quiet, as he mulls something over. 'Seems to me from reading the letters that N1Fan has a very boring life if you moving to Ilfracombe is the most exciting thing that's ever happened to her.'

An incredulous chuckle escapes me. 'Thanks a lot.'

Mo realises his faux pas. 'Sorry. You know what I mean. But maybe to this Aimee you're famous, writing bestsellers, going to top parties in London, meeting J.K. Rowling . . .'

Despite myself, I smile as I let out a soft snort of derision.

'I know, I know. But she doesn't know this. Maybe she never got to do what she wanted with her life. Maybe she's stuck at home with a million kids, or maybe she's still not married and wishes she was. But whatever it is, she's probably feeling like life has passed her by . . . Then you turn up, a blast from the past who's obviously done something amazing, something most people don't. And she sees an opportunity to liven things up for once?'

It does make sense. Aimee had always been the jealous type. I mull Mo's words over. Mo's theory certainly sounds like the Aimee I remember. Jealousy had powered most of her actions, that's for certain. Whenever I think of her, it's her perpetual sneer that comes to mind first.

'Ruby said she'd heard she was in Australia,' I muse.

'Who's Ruby?'

'Oh. The person I went to see this afternoon.'

Mo shrugs, lets it go. 'Well, whatever. Perhaps she needed to get it out of her system, it's done now?'

But perhaps Mo is right: she'd sent me the *NHIE* notes, with the rock through the window as her *pièce de résistance*. She could be satisfied now. It had always been about winning with Aimee. By engaging with her, I am automatically the loser in this scenario. Maybe all I had needed to do all along was refuse to be pulled into this shit? It certainly seems logical. Maybe this really is the end of it all.

Twenty-two

The kitchen fills with the smell of spices as Mo throws together one of his famous stir-fries. We chop vegetables in companionable silence, listening to old eighties hits on the radio. As the bars of 'Ghostbusters' kick off, Mo does his impression of a stereotypical dad dancing badly at a wedding. The laugh is a release and I end up abandoning the chopping board to dance with him, sticking out my knees and elbows at weird angles.

'Hello . . .!'

The front door opens and my mother calls ahead. As Lindy appears, she holds Caleb out to me like she's the baboon and he's the cub in *The Lion King*.

'Thanks, Mum. Hello, mister-man.'

I take him in my arms, trying to keep his sticky hands from grabbing my hair. His dungarees are covered in ice-cream stains, chocolate all around his mouth. *Ewww*. No one ever tells you parenthood is this gross. Or maybe they do and no one thinking of having kids ever listens. Sticky hands would never have been enough to put me off during those dark days of IVF. I pull Caleb closer to banish the memory. *He is here now.*

'All right, mate.' Mo ruffles Caleb's hair. 'Good time with Granny?'

Lindy trudges through from the porch, her movements exaggerated as if she were trekking the Himalayas. 'This little one has tired me out!'

I see Lindy eyeing our food. I know I am being selfish, especially as Lindy has had Caleb all afternoon. Even so, I don't want her to stay for dinner so soon after mine and Mo's heart-to-heart. A husband and wife need space, sometimes. Lindy can come to dinner another night.

'Thanks, Lindy, you're a star. Why don't you get home, have a bubble bath?'

Mum just leans against the counter. 'How's your day been? You finished your book yet? When can I read it?'

Lindy never got the memo about asking one question at a time when you reach adulthood. Bless her though, she has read every single one of my DI Robyn Dallas series, a couple of them twice. She has made her book group read them all, too. She's been talking about me coming to the next one to do a Q & A session, but the other ladies must be sick to the back teeth of me by now.

'Great. Got loads done. Soon, I promise.'

Mum's brow furrows. My tone must be too bright, or maybe my smile seems false. Lindy might be socially unaware generally, but she's always been fairly well tuned in to my moods. This means she does have that spooky Kung Fu of knowing exactly when Mo and I have had words.

'What's happened? Any news on that—' She stops herself from using the word 'rock' in front of Caleb. He would not be concerned; he's far too young and never saw what happened. '—*you-know-what*?'

'Yes,' Mo jumps in before I can. He shoots a pointed look at me not to argue, 'all just a big misunderstanding.

It wasn't meant for us, but the previous occupant just like Sam said. Some old row. You don't need to worry, Lindy.'

Mum is not so easy to soothe. 'But what about those weird letters?'

'Unconnected.' Mo guides her towards the door, so stealthily she barely realises they're both moving. I watch him covering up the N1Fan letter with the local paper, still on the table and in full view. Thankfully, Lindy is so intent on making her feelings known, she is oblivious to his surreptitious move.

'Well, that's worse, surely?' Mum huffs. 'That means there's a weirdo possibly watching the house, even if their target is someone else . . . And another weirdo sending poison pen letters! Two weirdos, Samantha! That's not good!'

Her voice is becoming more and more shrill. Caleb stiffens in my arms, alarmed by the sudden change in his grandmother. I am not keen on following Mum's logic, either; I'd decided to take the N1Fan letter at its word and that Aimee was backing off. Lindy's panic is a reminder it might not be as simple as that.

'Mum, calm down!' I motion at Lindy to lower her voice.

Everything is paused as I take Caleb through to the living room. With the television turned on and Caleb distracted, I return and we pick up where we left off.

'Writers get weird stuff sent to them all the time. Remember when I got that email from that man called Robin who said he was changing his surname to Dallas?'

'I still think you're fobbing me off.' She points at me, then Mo, 'Especially *you*.'

Mo shrugs, though I can see the irritation on his face. When given a fifty-fifty choice, Lindy will always choose the man as being the main perpetrator. Ten minutes of convincing later, she finally leaves, a cloud of resentment following her. It hangs over the whole of dinner. We shovel the stir-fry into our mouths as we try and change the subject.

I push my plate away. 'Lindy means well.'

'I know.' A shy smile curls Mo's lip as something occurs to him. 'Why don't you go upstairs, take a long hot shower?'

I don't need telling twice. There's a sexual frisson in the air between us. I know what Mo has in mind: Caleb has been at soft play all day. There's no way he will wake up tonight. I kiss Mo on the lips and traipse upstairs, a skip in my step.

In our en-suite bathroom, I stand under the water turned up as high as I can stand it. The water massages the tension out of my shoulders. I shave my legs, too; buff myself with the expensive shower gel and scrub left over from an old Christmas set. One positive thing about the move to Ilfracombe is that Mo and I have started to reconnect on a sexual level. Maybe if we keep on with it, the rest will follow? I'm already feeling a lot better about things, after chatting with Mo. He is right; he's a logical type of guy. I need to ignore Aimee, not let her suck me into her psycho-drama any more.

As the cubicle fills with steam, I will it to fill my mind and obscure my memories, too. Remembering how I'd stood by so many times when Aimee went on the rampage is not easy. Every time I close my eyes, I can see their faces on the backs of my eyelids. I want to try and forget Mike's, Maddy's and Ruby's hurt and confusion. I don't want to remember the rest of the dares, what we had done. If Aimee's little vendetta is done with like Mo says, I won't have to. I can close the lid on that horrible summer and lock it once again.

I pad through from the en-suite, towel-drying my hair. I spot something on the bed, a note. I'm sure it had not been there when I got in the shower. My pulse quickens for a moment, but I tamp it down. I can't let my imagination run away with me. All the bother with Aimee is over with now.

The paper is torn from a spiral notebook, a lazy scrawl at an angle. I note with irritation it's from my casebook, then smile. It will be instructions from Mo; I will let him off. When we were younger, he'd often leave me little notes like this. They would tell me to wear a particular lingerie set, or to pose on the bed in a specific way. Used to being the dominant one in the relationship, I always found it sexy when he took charge. I still do.

My smile drops as I pick the note up off the coverlet.

Never Have I Ever told my husband what I really did.

I race back into the en-suite to throw up.

Twenty-three

Our night of passion is cancelled. I tell Mo I must have eaten something dodgy when he hears me retching upstairs. Caleb safely asleep in bed and snoring his exhausted little head off, Mo turns his attentions to me. He brings me my flannel pyjamas, a cup of camomile tea and my iPad, telling me to rest and watch Netflix. Then he retires to his man-cave to watch re-runs of *American Pickers.*

There had been an intruder in our house, *while we were home.*

Tucked in bed like a child myself, I can't stop my heart hammering. So, the N1Fan letters must have been a lie, to lull me into a sense of false security. It's the only explanation that makes any sense. The hastily scribbled note, the reference to the fact I hadn't told Mo the full story this afternoon. It had to be Aimee, lurking upstairs, listening to our conversation. How the hell had she got in? Could I have left a window open? Surely not, I'd been fastidious checking everything after the instance with the rock.

I pull the covers aside and pad over to the wardrobe, wrenching the door open like I am eight years old checking for monsters. She's not in there of course, nor is she under the bed. I pad across the landing and double-check the wardrobe in Caleb's room, then the large linen cupboard on the third landing. I know my actions have little sense, but I can't get the hurried note out of my mind. It is not like the others, almost like an afterthought. I would have expected Aimee to pick the same paper, the same rounded letters as the other *NHIE* notes. Why the change? Perhaps I have been barking up the wrong tree. Maybe I should check through my notes and the other suspects, again.

I go back to my bedroom and consult the notes in my DI Robyn Dallas-style casebook: I take in the four names I've scribbled there, *Michael, Ruby, Maddy, Aimee*. All of them had been involved back then, overtly or not, in the *Never Have I Ever* game. But as DI Robyn Dallas would say, does this necessarily mean they had 'MMO' too: motive, means, opportunity? I think over what I have discovered so far, with this framework in mind.

Michael is the closest, geographically. As a policeman, he also has access to my home address. So technically, he does have the means and opportunity, but his potential motive is shaky at best. I don't think I can count on him being so resentful of me kissing another boy in front of him twenty-three years ago that he would risk his career as a police officer. No, it's absurd. It had mattered then, but the sands of time have rendered it trivial. He is a grown man now. He has a lovely wife, a new baby on the way. No way would someone as strait-laced as Michael seek revenge for something so small.

In contrast, Ruby's motive is much stronger. She'd made no secret of the fact she is still no fan of mine this afternoon. That said, I'd believed her when she'd said she wanted me to stay away. It doesn't make any sense for her to do this. As far as the means go, I don't know if Ruby has a car. Even if she does, I would have arrived back this afternoon long before she could make it back here too. Traffic had not been bad, either; she couldn't have followed me at a discreet distance from Lynmouth, it would have been too obvious on those narrow B-roads. I do wonder briefly if she could have phoned Alf and asked him to creep around my house, but I feel fairly sure he's not the type of guy to do that. If nothing else, he would want to know why. Kids don't do whatever you tell them, especially when they are adults. Even so, I add his name to my casebook, along with a balloon and a big arrow leading back to Ruby.

That leaves Maddy. But she doesn't seem to have the motive either; she'd been happy to hear from me and being up in London, she had neither the means nor the opportunity to chuck a rock through my window or creep around my house. Unless she *isn't* up in London? Maybe she only wants me to think she is.

I grab my phone from my bedside cabinet and check Facebook. Maddy has posted a million pictures from some animal show in Earls Court, at roughly the same time I was getting out of the shower. Even a private jet could not have got her to my house in time. Could she have posted to put me off the scent, though? I check the animal show's Facebook event page and discover it's been running for the past three days. Maybe she went yesterday and posted all these pics from her phone, sitting on my bed as she listened to me and Mo downstairs. She never stood up for me with Aimee, back then. She'd followed her around like a puppy dog. They could be in on it together.

No, I am overthinking this. It has to be Aimee. However she got in, it would not have been difficult to avoid us. Our new home is big, with three storeys. We'd not been expecting anyone to be waiting, above us. She could have hidden in the wardrobe in our bedroom as I'd gone into the en-suite. Then she could have crept out, written the note whilst I was in the shower. After that, all she needed to do was sneak past Mo and Caleb in the family bathroom on the second floor, then let herself out the damn front door. Easy.

Lying on all the pillows Mo has fluffed for me, I imagine her, waiting on the stairs, listening to us in the galley kitchen below. I shudder.

Never Have I Ever told my husband what I did.

It's obvious Aimee thinks I have some kind of guilty conscience. Lindy would call it classic projection; Aimee does terrible things, yet blames me for her transgressions, real or imagined. Even so, Aimee is bang on: I have *not* told Mo everything. Self-reproach prickles through me, but I have good reason. Our marriage is in the danger zone; we've spent too long disconnected. But if Aimee has been following me, as I suspect she has, she will have seen me with Michael. Someone like her would automatically think the worst of me. She'd assume there's something going on between us.

I don't care what Aimee thinks of me, but Mo is highly strung and battered by self-esteem issues. He had been right when he accused me of not letting him in. I've been trying to protect him, save us, but he would see it differently. He would say I kept him out of the loop from the start; that I even elected to keep quiet when a rock came through the window. Mo would posit the *only* reason I told him anything at all was because he literally busted me when I got back from Lynmouth. He'd say that if he hadn't come home early, he would still be none the wiser (he would be right, too).

Worst of all, who had I confided in first? My old boyfriend. Mo would be cut to the core to discover I had not gone to him straight away. If Michael gets added to the mix this late in the game, Mo is sure to put two and two together and get five. Like Aimee obviously does, he will think I am trying to hide an affair.

I can't let it happen.

Something else occurs. I leap out of bed again and creep down to my study on the second floor, so as to not alert Mo. It's the one room none of us would have gone in since Aimee's little home invasion earlier. I cross the threshold, turning the light on as I go.

I don't know what I am looking for. Had I expected to see it trashed, graffiti on the wall reading *NEVER HAVE I EVER*? I falter: nothing looks out of place. Except one thing.

My laptop is open.

I always close it and turn it off. Growing up with Lindy, she'd always impressed on me the need to conserve power, long before 'carbon neutral' was a phrase. It's a habit I'm sure I have never broken.

Perhaps I had turned it off, then got distracted before I could close the lid? That would be it. I'm overreacting again. Even if I had left the laptop on, it's nothing in the scheme of things. Even so, trepidation surges through me as I press the keypad at random.

The laptop springs to life from 'sleep' mode. I gulp as I move my fingers across the mousepad, just in case. *Untitled DI Robyn Dallas Project* springs up as my last document. I still try and calm myself. After all, it makes sense. I had been working on it before I decided to go to see Ruby in Lynmouth.

I click on it.

At first, I am not sure what I am seeing. I'd written about twenty-five thousand words, just under a third of the book. That's about one hundred pages' worth of novel, double-spaced on Microsoft Word. Now, there is only a single page. It reads:

You know he will leave you if he finds out
Leave you
Leave you
Leave you

Twenty-four

'I need you to do something for me. Please?'

On the other end of the line, Michael sighs. When he'd answered moments earlier, it had sounded like I'd woken him up.

'It's my day off. You should really go down the station, if this is about the rock?'

Of course he knows about that. It was probably the most unusual and exciting thing that had happened in Ilfracombe in years. The police's job here mostly involves peeling drunks off the pavement at closing time; moving on homeless people from tourist spots; or stopping teenagers from tomb-stoning off the pier.

'It's not.' I catch myself on the lie. 'Well, it is. But not officially.'

I outline what I need from him. It's a small thing, but there's a pause as Michael appears to think this over.

'Okay.' He sounds as if he is making the decision against his better judgement.

'I'm sorry. I wouldn't ask if it wasn't important.'

'Come to Kat's place after lunch. I'll have it for you then.'

Michael's tone is brusque, no-nonsense. He wants it known he is not sneaking around, that this is all above board. He is hiding nothing from his wife, he will only meet me standing in front of her. Irritation rankles through me. What does he think I'm going to do, jump his bones as soon as I see him? The arrogance of the man.

Even so, I try and keep my own voice neutral. 'See you then.'

I key off and sit in front of my laptop's almost-blank screen. My mouth feels dry. Everyone must realise deleting a writer's work is one of the worst things you can do to them. I feel sick. Had I backed up my files? If I had, I can't remember where I'd stored them. I'd checked my Cloud and various folders. A memory stick in a drawer revealed nothing. I'd written about a third of my book, but now I am back to square one. I hadn't had a tech failure in so long, I had become complacent. Every writers' workshop I had ever gone to had stressed the need to keep more than one copy of a manuscript. I have a flashback of a stern-looking literary agent at some event telling us the story of a writer who swore that writing on a typewriter was the secret of his debut's (multi-million-dollar) success . . . Until a flood in the apartment above had come through the ceiling and deluged his desk. It had killed off his machine and his much-anticipated sequel, which was stacked in a neat pile next to it. Readers were still anticipating that author's book, over a decade later, as he struggled through writer's block to try and kick off his follow-up again.

Lindy had picked Caleb up that morning as usual, though she at least had not barked yet more questions at me when she arrived. I don't think I could have handled it if she had. I feel wrung out. I pick up my casebook, poring over the names again. Ringing Aimee's name with my pen, I realise Ava must be lying to me. She probably does know where Aimee is. I only have her word for it that she barely remembers her aunt. I add Ava's name to my notebook, along with a big arrow leading back to my old friend. The younger woman must be an accessory, perhaps it was even she who'd gained entrance to the house? Maybe my instincts are correct and Aimee is masterminding all this from afar? I have to find proof.

Mo had been perturbed by my sudden about-face this morning. We'd sniped at each other over the breakfast table about something inconsequential. As far as he knows, I'd been more positive about the Aimee situation before getting sick last night. But now the space between us is charged again, this time with uncertainty; it's filled up with all the things we can't say to each other. Mo had that confused look on his face again as he trudged off to work.

He will leave you.

Aimee's ability to see right into my thoughts feels almost supernatural. I *do* fear Mo will leave me. He's the only person I've ever trusted since I was a teenager, apart from Lindy. Yet even then, he doesn't know the whole me. For all my bluster about being an independent woman, I've read enough of Lindy's self-help books to know it's a defence mechanism. I've spent the last twenty-three years since I left Ilfracombe creating a wall around myself. I resolved never to let anyone get under my skin like Aimee had.

Yet somehow Mo had crept under my defences, little by little. Now I have him and Caleb, my position is weakened; an opportunity for Aimee to exploit. I feel like I might crumple like a beer can. More than Mo leaving me is the fear he might take Caleb with him. The thought he could gain custody of my precious boy makes me feel sick. It's true the IVF had been a journey for both of us, but ultimately it had been me who had had to make all the real sacrifices. It had been me who had to battle nausea, headaches and the fog of my drug-addled brain. I had to deal with the pain of injections, pregnancy and birth. I carried Caleb in my mind long before I had felt him move inside me. I know Mo loves being a dad; he is a wonderful father to Caleb. But I know that deep down, he would have been just as happy in life had we remained childless. Mo created meaning in his life beyond parenthood. But me?

It would have been a disaster.

I became so consumed with the urge to have a baby, I could think of nothing else. For five years. My brain collected tales of childless, heartbroken women who killed themselves when they'd run out of options. I'd never admitted it to myself at the time, but looking back now, safe from my own baby-fever, I realise with stark clarity I would have done the same. It was even why I had begun writing the first DI Robyn Dallas book. It had been a distraction to the endless, frenzied desire that otherwise occupied my every waking moment. It's also the reason my antagonist Elodie Fitzgerald is so twisted. She'd lost her children, twin baby girls, when she was pregnant, thanks to a hostage situation and shootout with armed police. (The *Guardian* reviews section had called it 'by-the-numbers characterisation', but my readers love Elodie's tragic back-story and grudge against DI Robyn Dallas, who'd called the armed unit in the first place.)

Michael stands as I wander into On A Break. Kat looks up from her Sudoku and gives me the fakest, toothiest smile I have ever seen outside of an American sitcom.

'Sam. Lovely to see you again.' She taps her pen on the book. 'Coffee?'

'Great, thank you.' I reach into my bag for my wallet to pay, but she waves a hand at me.

'Absolutely not. Put your money away. Any friend of Michael's is a friend of mine.'

I smile my thanks. Michael gives me a pointed look. Something unspoken passes between us. He doesn't need to prompt me; I already know Kat is not happy about this. Her words might be pleasant, but the subtext is very much *Hands off my man, bitch.* It's on a frequency only women can hear.

As Kat's state-of-the-art coffee machine bursts into life, I go over to the table. I note that Michael has picked the one closest to the till. He sits down again, bidding me to do the same. He is brusque, all business, though he's dressed in jeans and a fisherman's jumper, complete with holes. Unlike Alf's, every inch of it is designer. He would have paid extra for the scruffy look. Or rather, Kat would have. I understand now she is the one behind his devil-may-care style and nearly-hipster beard. Michael may not care about fashion, but she definitely does. Michael, whether he realises or not, is *on trend*.

'So, Detective Inspector, I did what you asked and pulled the file on Aimee's "disappearance".' Michael does air quotes.

'You sound like something out of my books,' I tease.

Michael rolls his eyes. 'Yes. It was a joke, for your benefit.'

Suddenly, Kat is by the table. She holds an over-sized cup in each of her diminutive hands. She places Michael's next to him with reverent care. She practically slams mine down; coffee slops over the side, into the matching saucer. I make out I haven't noticed. I give her another beaming smile.

'Thanks, Kat,' Michael says.

He grabs her hand and kisses the back of it. Somewhat appeased, Kat retreats behind the counter again. Holy crap, these two are something else. If I were a gambling woman, I would bet real money they're the type of couple to walk down the street with hands in each other's back pockets. Ugh. Or maybe I am just cynical because of what Mo and I have been through. I need to pull myself together.

Michael pulls a bit of paper from his pocket. 'So, you're right. The Dyers came in and let us know that Aimee had turned up.'

'Good,' I breathed. 'Thanks for looking.'

'I didn't have any trouble tracking the case down, as it goes. It's what's known as an "inactive misper". This means we never officially closed the investigation down.'

'So, a cold case.'

'If you like.'

I think this over. 'Ruby said something about Aimee going to Australia?'

'She would know better than me.' Michael shrugs.

Except, Ruby doesn't know. Unless she is a liar. Could Ruby have fabricated that little detail? It sounds a little contrived, a bit too handy. Almost like it's designed to get me off the scent. The problem is, I can't work out what Ruby could be hiding, or why she would want to do Aimee's dirty work for her.

'Aimee *is* still missing, then?'

Michael strokes his beard in that way of his. 'You have to understand, hundreds, even thousands of people go missing every year. Sometimes, it's only technical, like with Aimee, but we still have to check. We went to the Dyers' and interviewed the family.'

I can't resist. 'All of them?'

'All of them,' Michael confirms. 'We checked the house, the garage and loft, the coal cellar, the wheelie bins behind the shop, you name it.'

I don't need to ask why. I shudder at the thought that Bill Dyer might have killed his own daughter. Aimee had been the apple of his eye. But she'd also been a nightmare. Stealing, drinking, even going off with boys towards the end. Could Bill have snapped? No. Bill is dodgy as hell, but he isn't a murderer. Surely.

'Obviously, without actually speaking to the person involved, we can't close the investigation down,' Michael explains. 'But whoever filled in the file was satisfied Aimee was where her parents said she was. They didn't mention whether she'd gone to Australia. Or if they did, the duty sergeant didn't note it down.'

I'd known it was unwise to pin all my hopes on someone randomly recording the information I need. Still, at least I don't have to rely on Ruby's or Ava's fragile memories. Now I have it for definite that Aimee came home. That newspaper headline is officially out of date and out of the running in my investigation.

The more I think about Australia though, the fishier it seems. 'She was sixteen years old. How could she have got the money to go all that way on her own?'

Michael rolls his eyes. 'Maybe she got one of her male friends to pay for it. You know how she was.'

I do, but I don't like Michael's tone. Even though I despise Aimee, I can hear the undertones of slut-shaming

173

in his voice. Coming from a man, this rankles twice as much. I push it down, into that dark place where I lock away all the things I cannot say.

'Perhaps Aimee only *said* she was going to Australia?'

I'm just musing, but it makes sense. Maybe Ruby is not lying at all? She just repeated a lie to me, not realising its falsehood. And it seems like something Aimee would do. With an extended family as big as hers, she could put a rumour around town as quick as a stab.

'You're sure you haven't seen Aimee recently?' I set my imploring gaze on Michael. 'Please, just cast your mind back. Not even a fleeting glimpse, or a mention? I just need something to go on, somewhere to start.'

Michael blows out his cheeks. His eyes move as he attempts to recall. Right side is memory, right? Left for lies, 'L for L'. Or is it the other way around? I will have to Google when I get back home. Maybe it is just an urban myth.

'No, I haven't seen her,' he confirms at last. 'Have you tried her family?'

Yes, though I don't count Ava. Not only is she obstructive, she can't have been more than two or three when this all kicked off. I already know from Facebook there are other Dyer family members I can track down, but I realise they will give me the same frosty reception. Once the Dyers close ranks, they're impenetrable. It's how they've hidden their dodgy antics all these years in plain sight. It's why Aimee thinks she can do whatever she wants to me, now.

Though I'd been feeling optimistic earlier, I know deleting my book is not the end of it. Aimee hasn't finished with me yet. Well, screw that. This has all gone too far; enough is enough. I will find her and get her to back off.

'What are you going to do, when you realise it's not Aimee?'

Michael's words crash through my thoughts. Is he making a confession? Before I can get excited, I see he is gathering his jacket and keys. He is one hundred per cent nonchalant; hardly the behaviour of a man making a long overdue revelation. He must sense me staring at him, because he looks up, a bewildered smile on his face.

'I'm just saying, Sam. You're quite insistent it's Aimee, that's all. What if it's not?'

I feel my stomach clench at his words. I need it to be Aimee, I realise that. At least I can understand why she is targeting me now. She'd always hated me back in school, even before what happened. There's a familiarity to her going after me now I've moved back; a kind of warped inevitability. Any alternative to Aimee is too frightening to comprehend; I have no clue why any of my other suspects would do this to me. I don't even know if I have all the right suspects. I feel my mind shut down.

'It's Aimee.' My words come out as a low growl.

Michael does not appear to notice. 'Okay.' He slides his arms into his jacket with one fluid movement. He steps forward and dips down to where Kat is lolling on the counter top. 'Bye, doll.'

Doll. Figures. A nineties manufactured pop song sears through my brain, uninvited, as I watch Michael kiss Kat on the forehead like she's a little girl. Kat closes her eyes, a beatific smile on her face.

Uncomfortable at potentially being left alone with Kat, I grab my own things. As the bell above the door jingles and Michael leaves, her eyes snap open again as I move towards the door.

''Bye then,' I say, my voice small. 'Thanks again.'

She fixes me with a cold stare. Just as abruptly, her face cracks in a wide smile, a parody of a hostess. Kat Quentin is a *Stepford Wife*, through and through.

'Have a nice day,' she says.

Twenty-five

I can hear the smoke detector inside the house from the driveway, the moment I get out of my car. Panic lances through me as my brain struggles to make sense of the situation. Smoke alarms go off so often, everyone has become so *laissez-faire* about them: only the slight whiff of burned toast provokes the newer models. But Mo's car is not on the drive and I have been out meeting Michael.

The fire must be real.

I emit a frustrated shriek as I grapple with my keys, dropping them on the tarmac. *Less haste, more speed.* But I have no time for that. I snatch the keys up and sprint towards the house, somehow sliding my front door key in the lock with shaking hands. I yank the door open and race into the porch, then the hallway. I flinch, expecting the burst of heat and crackling of flames, but to my relief only black smoke spirals up towards the ceiling. It can't be as bad as I'd feared. (*Thank God.*)

Still buzzed on adrenaline, I try and discern where it's coming from. The kitchen? The living room? No, the doorways are both clear. My thoughts sharpen enough for me to realise I need to track the smoke back towards its source. I follow it with my eyes to the side stairs off the hall, down towards the coal cellar.

The man-cave.

My body reacts before my mind catches up. I race towards the fire, clattering down the cellar steps, almost pitching head-first down them. A tiny, more logical part of my mind politely enquires, *What are you playing at?* in Lindy's voice. But it's eclipsed by the pulsating beat in my head and the relentless tattoo of my heartbeat ricocheting in my chest.

Both my feet land on the stone floor of the man-cave as black smoke envelops me, making my eyes stream and my throat close up. I bring an impotent hand to my mouth, fighting against the poisonous plumes that constrict my airways.

Mo's desk is on fire. His OUT tray is a mass of curling papers; a collection of hardback books stacked neatly beside it is a pyramid of flames. A box of tissues and a framed family picture have gone up too: our faces smile demon-like as the fire takes its toll. The printer and computer monitor bubble next to the conflagration.

A stream of fire bursts out across the room.

I flinch, but nothing touches my skin. The fire is still confined to the desk, the image that had felt so real is just memory. In my mind's eye I see Felix Jackson, Will's brother, the bonfire and headland behind him. He's performing his party trick, 'dragon's breath'. He snaps back the lid of a zippo lighter, creating a precise mist of alcohol over its open flame. That jet of fire cuts the darkness in two again, illuminating two younger girls next to him who scream with delight. I don't see their faces, though I perceive a tubby middle in denim shorts on the first girl; a flash of auburn hair on the second. Heat dances around Felix, like a devil.

The memory blinks away and I'm back in the man-cave. I hear the *pfft-pfft-pfft* of plastic tubing and metal components as they succumb to the heat. Is the fire electrical? For some reason, I know water doesn't work on electrical fires. I've never written a fire into any of my DI Robyn Dallas books. Are you supposed to beat out fires? Or will that feed the flames? I don't know. I just don't know!

I cough, drawing toxic fumes into my lungs, making me splutter even more. I force myself to focus, noting for the first time the computer monitor and printer are not actually *on* fire, just melting. That means it can't be an electrical fire. Good. My eyes instinctively trace the flames back to their source, coming from the left-hand side of the desk, the only side where the legs burn.

They're coming from Mo's wastepaper can.

Made of tin, the papers inside are alight like a torch. I have no time to consider how this could have happened, or my actions. With a primeval yell, I race over to the desk and tip the burning books and picture frame into the can as well. There's a *whoomph* of flames as they land, making me take a step back. Already the flames on the desk are greatly reduced. I grab a throw from Mo's chair, bunching it up and smothering the fire on the legs, jumping as the computer monitor emits another *pfffft*, louder this time as its flat screen disappears inwards on itself.

The fire on the desk out, I turn my attention back to the wastepaper can. It is still on fire, though the larger books landing in it have deprived the papers at the bottom of oxygen. Still operating on instinct, I make the ridiculous mistake of grabbing for it. I scream in pain and tears spring up in my eyes as the skin on my right palm comes away, sealed instantly to the tin. The wastepaper can goes over, throwing its fiery contents onto the rug Lindy and I had put down for Mo. I kick up the rug under one boot, deftly folding it over on top of itself. Then I jump up and down on it, swearing my way through the agony in my hand and the raging fury of the situation.

I seem to zone out for a few seconds, maybe as long as a minute. I come to. I can see my reflection in the little mirror over Mo's bookcase: my face is blackened, sooty. The acrid tang of melted plastic and burned paper makes my nostrils flare. I can taste it at the back of my throat and somehow right up my nose and under my red, watering eyes.

Still feeling outside my own body, I peer at my face like it's the first time I have seen it. Something about me is off, which seems appropriate. Realisation floods through me: I have no eyebrows. When I had tipped the books into the can and caused the momentary flare-up, they must have melted straight off my face. This strikes me as ludicrously funny, or maybe it's just the shock, because a laugh bursts out of me. Moments later I am doubled over, convulsing like a hysterical hyena.

'Sam?'

My laughter dies away abruptly. I freeze as I see Mo appear on the bottom of the man-cave steps, eyes wide. He takes in the destruction of his desk, the state of me. He gasps as he takes in my raw, burned hand.

Mo's eyes fill with tears. 'Oh Christ, what have you done?'

His horror makes the adrenaline recede and starts my hand off throbbing all over again. I look at ragged, burned flesh as if seeing it for the first time. Sensing my detachment, Mo ushers me towards him. He places a hand in the small of my back and guides me towards the stairs, like a parent intercepting a sleepwalking child.

'Let's get you seen to, love.'

His tone is soothing. It makes me want to close my eyes, rest my head on his shoulder. Suddenly I am tired. So very tired. I just want all of this to stop.

'Yes, let's.'

Twenty-six

Mo takes me to the small local Accident and Emergency department over at Barnstaple. After a bored receptionist takes my details, I join a triage queue of sun-burned tourists; middle-aged men with gardening and DIY accidents and children with bumps on their heads. Mo calls Lindy who promises to look after Caleb for as long as it takes for me to be seen. She wants to drive over straight away, but she is pacified when Mo reminds her hospitals are hotbeds of MRSA. Now that Lindy has hit sixty-five, she is paranoid about what she calls 'premature death by avoidable means'.

Thankfully, a young male nurse appears within the first hour of our wait with some painkillers for me. I gulp them gratefully, chasing the pills with water down my parched throat. I'd thought the burns were bad when I did them, but now my palm is really starting to hurt. It feels as if there are still flames, caught deep beneath my skin, entombed in my flesh. If my life were a cartoon, there would be big wavy lines and giant red arrows pointing at my hand.

The stench of bleach permeates the hospital, masking the scent of body odour, panic and death. Mo chatters incessantly as we wait; I answer only to punctuate his various random points. Two hours in and he brings coffee from the machine in small cups. The beverage inside tastes of plastic, milk powder and tedium. Mo struggles to keep everything 'normal' as he helps me sip it, holding it like I would for Caleb.

'So, what happened down in the man-cave?'

'I was hoping you could tell me.' I've been brooding for the past two hours and it shows in my tone. 'Have you started smoking again?'

I don't know if it's the travel, or maybe it's the adult version of peer pressure hanging out with businessmen all day, but Mo takes his filthy habit back up every two or three years. It drives me crazy, though it seems weird to think this was one of our biggest problems before Aimee, before we moved back here. But Mo throwing a match or fag-end into his wastepaper can would explain the fire today.

Mo grimaces, like he's expected this. He breathes in through his nose and out through his mouth. He reminds me of Lindy, forcing out the 'bad vibes'. He tries to keep his tone light, non-accusatory. It doesn't work.

'I wasn't home, was I?'

I open my mouth to retort, just as a connection fires in my brain. Mo is right. His car had *not* been on the driveway when I'd arrived home. Yet the smoke alarm had already been going off. The fire had also barely spread across the desk from the wastepaper can. That means it can't have been going for long. If it wasn't Mo and it definitely wasn't me, there's only one person it could be.

Aimee.

Ice-cold fingers of fear stab me in the belly as I work over what this could mean. I'd already been sure Aimee had been in the house, leaving me the note on the bed and deleting my book. I'd thought she must have slipped through an open window, or I'd left the back door open. But today I had checked the security before I'd left to go and see Michael at On A Break. How the hell could Aimee have got in? Maybe she has a key. Perhaps a Dyer in town works at the estate agent we bought the house from. I resolve to check when I get home.

Mo shoots me a sympathetic look. 'Is it the book?'

I don't know what he means. 'What the hell are you going on about?'

If Mo notices my irritation, he gives no indication. 'Look, I know you've been struggling. All writers go through this. But to set fire to the desk—!'

'Whoa, wait a minute,' I interrupt, letting an incredulous laugh escape my lips. 'You think I did this?'

'I'm not blaming you,' Mo says. He has that maddening 'Concerned Husband' face on again. It makes me want to punch him in the face (or at least it would if my hand didn't hurt so damn much). 'You've always been impulsive. I love that about you. But you hurt yourself. And it was *my* desk, Sam. Come on.'

'Exactly!' The word bursts out of me too loud. Heads crane round to look at us. After a few seconds, we are satisfied potential eavesdroppers have lost interest. Even so, we both drop a few decibels, just in case. 'I'm not going to burn your desk, am I?'

'What if Caleb had been in the house?'

I'm shocked and hurt. 'I would never hurt Caleb!'

Mo acknowledges the unlikelihood of this, shame-faced. 'You're right. I'm sorry. You're an excellent mother. But you have to admit, you have been struggling lately.'

I sigh. Mo is not wrong there. Before I can answer though, a short, round nurse appears from a side door. 'Samantha Brennan?'

I stand up, grateful to be seen at last. Mo rises with me, his expression grim. 'We'll finish this conversation, later.'

An hour later, my wound is cleaned and dressed and we are on our way again. I call Lindy from the car to tell her we will be back soon. It's very late; Caleb is already in bed at hers. She tells me she will keep him overnight, to enjoy some time alone with Mo for once. I keep my voice bright as I thank her for being so thoughtful.

Despite what he said earlier, Mo won't be drawn on the journey back. My many omissions and outright lies feel heavy in my chest. I should have told Mo about the notes; about Michael; about being chased the other night. I should have been open with Mo from the start about all of this. Now it's like we are both actors in a bad play, a sadistic puppeteer pulling our strings, just because she can.

We pull up outside the house. I look at the clock on the dashboard: it's nearly midnight. Behind the wheel, Mo turns off the ignition. He gives a heavy sigh.

'This can't go on.'

His volume is small, barely a mutter. He does not seem wound up, or ready to go on the offensive. I chance a look at him from the passenger's side. He seems weary, his skin grey with fatigue. I note he hasn't shaved, which is not like him at all. There's a coffee stain on his shirt cuff and his hair is not smoothed into place with his usual pomade.

'I've been thinking. Why don't we go to Ireland, see the family?'

He taps his fingers on the dashboard, anxious. I want to snap at him, make him stop. I don't.

'You, me and Caleb. Change of scenery will do us good. You can have a rest?'

My mouth drops wide open. I can't believe it. A few hours ago, Mo literally thought I'd torched his man-cave because I am stressed out about writing. Now he wants to go off on some jaunt back to his homeland.

'I told you. I have to finish this arsehole book.'

'Change is as good as a rest, they say.'

I shake my head. A trip away is the very last thing I need. I have to begin writing my book again, from scratch. Besides, going to stay with Mo's family is the very opposite of rest. Mo's dad spends all his time yelling at the television and ranting about the Orange Order. Mo's twin younger brothers Kevin and Darren are both mechanics and still live at home. They spend all their spare time souping up cars, sending plumes of black smoke and the *bang*s of back-firing engines back up into the air. Mo's idle older brother Simon married well. His trust-fund-baby wife Essie's parents shower them with money, so we would have to put up with hearing about their latest holiday, car and/or home renovation (*delete as appropriate*). Mo's only sister Kelly doesn't live at home but might as well do. She's taken it upon herself to visit every single day now old Mrs Brennan has died. Kelly has five children, all of whom seem completely feral and into everything. She drags them with her everywhere like a group of snot-nosed mini infantrymen. Only Mo has truly escaped the nest and his roots, reinventing himself all the way. It's one of the (*only?*) things we have in common.

I grit my teeth. 'I said no.'

'Christ. It was just a suggestion, Sam. I don't know if you've noticed, but this marriage is in the shit right now. I am doing all I can to get it back on track.'

This is all it takes for the flood-gates to open. 'Oh really? Could have fooled me. A bunch of flowers and a takeaway aren't going to cut it. *Mate.*'

I'm baiting him and know it. Mo's face twists in rage in the rear-view mirror. For a single moment, I think he's going to lean across the gearstick and grab me by my arm, shake some sense into me. But he stops himself. He does not touch me. Furious Mo is gone, replaced by my mild-mannered, anguished, very confused husband of almost twenty years.

'I don't know why you want to go through whatever this is by yourself,' he whispers. 'I thought we were supposed to be a team?'

Shame replaces my own anger now. I don't trust myself to speak. Even if I could, I don't know where to start. I feel like I am looking at Mo through the wrong end of a telescope: he seems so small, so far away.

Mo sighs as he realises I am not going to answer. 'Get out.'

I do as I am told, clambering out of the car. 'Aren't you coming in, too?'

'I need to clear my head. Don't wait up.'

In answer, I slam the car door shut.

For the second time in twelve hours, I struggle with my key in the front door, though this time it's thanks to the bandages wrapped around my hand. Behind me, I hear Mo's car back out of the driveway, though I don't turn my head and watch. Instead I kick the front door shut.

Eyes stinging with my own angry tears, I clamber the stairs to the second floor. Entering my study, I open my computer and Google the name of the estate agent we bought the house from. No Dyers are listed in the 'About

Us' section, nor do any have a familial resemblance in the company photo. So Aimee can't have been getting into my house thanks to any of them. Back to square one. I grab my casebook from my desk and pore over the names within.

What are you going to do, when you realise it's not Aimee?

Michael's words from that afternoon echo back to me. I mull them over, trying to work out if he'd been trying to give me some kind of conscious signal. No, he couldn't be. Ultimately, I mean nothing to him, he has made that clear since I returned (*good*). But maybe, like Ruby with the Australia lie, he hadn't realised he was doing it?

Aimee. Maddy. Ruby.

Michael. Ava. Alf.

I've forgotten a name. One so obvious, I can't believe it hasn't occurred to me before. It would certainly explain a lot.

I grab my phone, tap out a message on Instagram. The answer fires back straight away, just like I knew it would.

Drop by tomorrow.

Twenty-seven

'So, you didn't bottle it, then. Interesting.'
Kat Quentin looks up from a crossword puzzle in
On A Break. Her manner is casual. She does not smile,
but she does not seem concerned either, continuing to
lounge on the counter. Behind her, chalkboards advertise
all the various drinks, cakes and meals in beautiful, looped
handwriting.

'I needed to talk to you.' I slam the notes down on the
counter, next to the glass display cabinets full of homemade
cupcakes, Viennese whirls and flapjacks.

She sniffs. 'Say whatever it is you need to say, then go.'

Kat has had her hair done since I last saw her, which
was only yesterday. Now she has red-purple streaks that
match her lipstick and her long, flowing maternity top with
cartoon blackberries. Her purple dangly earrings complete
the ensemble. This is a woman who takes accessorising to
the max. I am exhausted just looking at her, thinking about
the effort she must go to.

I tap the notes with one finger. 'You sent these, didn't
you?'

A nervous titter falls from Kat's purple lips. 'You what?'

So, she's going to play it this way. I sigh, feeling sorry
for her. Kat is so young. She probably feels fat, unattractive.
She probably worries he will go looking elsewhere. It's

classic. Perhaps she'd been reading one of my books, then Michael had mentioned he used to know me. Maybe she'd started following me online, seen that I was moving back to Ilfracombe. Then her worst fears end up confirmed when I turn up in the shop with Michael, looking all cosy. *Poor girl.*

'Me and Michael go way back. Jealous, are you? That's why you sent the letters.'

'You're mad.' Kat taps her pencil on her teeth, eyes wide. 'I legit have no clue what you're talking about.'

Legit. Such a Millennial thing to say. The age gap is brought home to me again, along with her perfect porcelain skin, the lack of lines around her eyes, on her brow.

'What I don't understand is how you know about this.' I tap the notes again, to the words *Never Have I Ever.* 'Did Michael tell you?'

Just then, the door tinkles behind me. Instinctively, I look over my shoulder in tandem with Kat. It's the homeless woman, trailing her long dirty coat and a couple of laundry bags full of her worldly possessions. Her hair is lank and greasy, tied in its salt-and-pepper ponytail. Her toothless maw hangs open as she pants, like she has been walking for miles. She probably has. Her eyes look as weary as her body.

Kat's voice is maternal, like she is the elder one of the two, though it is impossible to tell how old the bag lady is. 'You take a seat outside, darlin', I'll be right with you.'

The homeless woman nods, then goes back outside. I understand this is a long-standing arrangement. Small towns often take the old saying 'charity begins at home' to heart. A lack of resources and funding from Westminster for the provinces means this woman is on her own otherwise. Through the window, I watch her collapse onto a picnic table bench out on the promenade. She starts rolling a very thin, small cigarette from a near-empty pouch of tobacco.

Kat grabs my attention again. 'I'll be straight with you, Sam. I don't like you.'

I turn back to the counter. Kat's baby-doll smile and mild manner have gone. Now, her expression has a harder edge, accompanied by a much stronger Northern twang in her accent as she looks me up and down.

'You're right. You and Michael have got history, so what woman would? And no, he told me nowt about what went on before between you two, which makes me think it was something big.' The younger woman slaps butter on a roll, adds cheese and cucumber. 'I bet you think it was some big romance, reminiscing about first loves. All that senti-mental shit.'

Wow. I'm on the back foot, again. I don't like it. I am floundering. I realise I have underestimated Kat Quentin. Her baby-doll act really is only skin deep. Does Michael know? I squash this thought down. It's not my concern.

'It was nothing. We were kids . . .'

Kat holds up a finger, like a teacher in kindergarten telling a child to be quiet. To my own surprised chagrin, I obey. Kat pours some milk into a tall tumbler, to accompany the sandwich she's made the homeless woman.

'I seen the way you look at him. I might be young, but I ain't stupid. Lucky for me, I know being possessive don't work. The more jealous you are, the more you push them in the direction you don't want. So no, I didn't write any bloody letter and I haven't got a scooby what *Never Have I Ever* refers to, other than YouTubers playing it on their sodding videos. Okay?'

191

With that, Kat sweeps out of the café. I watch her through the window. Her face softens as she approaches the homeless woman, giving her the food with no sign of the vitriol she'd just poured on me. She makes no move to come back inside and finish our conversation. Instead she leans against one of the ornate Victorian balustrades, picking at her pinafore and chatting idly, like she doesn't have a care in the world.

Rage floods through me. It's a burning urge that pours forth from my chest, down my arms and through my finger-tips. I'm desperate to do some damage to Kat's ridiculous little shop. I grab the cash register, lift it above my head and chuck it through the glass cake counter. The tinkling of glass feels so satisfying as tiny shards shower down on cupcakes, cinnamon swirls and croissants. I pull down the stupid bunting, kick over the over-stuffed armchairs, up-end the tall tables.

The bell above the door rings as an oblivious customer wanders in, breaking my reverie. I blink.

The destruction is gone; the shop is restored to its former glory. I've imagined it all. The only movement is my clenching and unclenching of my fists. Shock comes next. *Where the hell had all that come from?*

I live my whole life in my head. I have never been a particularly physical person. Day-to-day manual tasks in my life are limited to driving, cooking and going for the odd walk. I have never even set foot in a gym, never mind gone to a spin class or touched a weights machine. Yet had my mind allowed it, my body would have surrendered to a tsunami of demolition just a moment ago.

What is happening to me?

I push past the new customer and stagger outside into the sea air, taking deep lungfuls as I go. I don't look back to see if Kat is watching me leave.

I know she is.

It's stress, that's all it is. No one can live with what I have had to put up with since I got that first *Never Have I Ever* note. Not for the first time, I regret not having any friends to share theories with, or at least sympathise. It is exhausting being strong for both Mo and Lindy. I feel like I have nowhere left to turn, my heart batters against my chest like a caged animal. Is this how you feel before you have a full-on breakdown?

I am in such a flap, my thoughts racing, I can't remember where I left the car. I end up wandering the whole length of the seafront, past the Landmark and the Tunnels beaches. I see the car parked on Wilder Road and almost cry with relief. I clamber in, shutting out the sound of the gulls and relishing the silence inside. I take deep breaths, another one of Lindy's mantras falling from my lips unbidden.

'Peace is within my reach.' I repeat the phrase over and over, feeling its balm with every word as it soothes my anxiety. After two or three minutes, I can finally control my breathing. *Thanks, Mum.*

Still feeling a little light-headed, I don't trust myself to drive yet. I pull my casebook from my bag. I'd added Kat's name last night and ringed it with pink highlighter, my favourite colour. It had all seemed so obvious then: *of course* Kat was behind the notes, breaking my window. I'd known she would deny it; she was hardly going to admit it to me, like criminals spill their guts to DI Robyn Dallas in my books. It couldn't be that easy.

Other than Aimee, Kat is the only one with a real motive. People have done terrible things out of jealousy for less. But Kat had unnerved me in On A Break. I had not expected her to be so self-assured in the face of my accusations. I had been naïve and superior enough to think I would have the upper hand. She is clearly either a better actress than I thought possible, or she's telling the truth. I grab a pen and hover it over her name, wondering if I should cross it out or not. Am I playing into her hands?

I can't decide.

I don't know how to find out, for sure.

An involuntary yell of frustration escapes me as I chuck my casebook at the windscreen. It slides down the glass, onto the dashboard with a flop.

I have let Michael get under my skin. It was him who made me doubt this is all Aimee's work. That's why I have jumped to the conclusion Kat is behind it all. She would have been about seven when it all kicked off.

I am jumping at shadows, seeing things that aren't there.

Twenty-eight

I dream I am being buried alive.

The air is still, humid. Even so, I shiver in just combat trousers and short sleeves. I am underground, standing in water, my feet sodden and frozen with cold through my shoes. I can't lean against the cold, furry walls. Unable to sit down, I can barely turn around either. I can see no light at the top: I'm perhaps eight to ten feet down. Beyond the hole, the trees swish their creaking arms in the air. The night shadows create swirling patterns before my eyes.

My eyes open, my brain awake before the rest of my body. I can't move. Anxiety clouds my thoughts for a moment before I realise it's just sleep paralysis. It's common, affecting people when they wake before REM sleep is finished. I'd seen articles shared on Facebook, suggesting wiggling your toes to combat it. I try and concentrate on my feet, just as something in the corner of the room catches my eye.

A shadow.

Fear lances me straight in the chest. Momentarily, the shadow changes shape. For a moment, it is Kat Quentin, complete with pregnant belly. Then she shimmers and fades, like a ghost.

The dark shape becomes Aimee. In that split second, she is sixteen again, dressed the way she was the night of the party after the School Leavers' Ceremony. Black flared jeans, purple Doc Martens. A T-shirt with the *Jurassic Park* logo. Her long hair in two space buns, a string of plastic beads around her neck. Homemade friendship bracelets loop around her wrists.

In the corner of the room, she raises a finger to her lips, *Sssssh.*

I wake for real, gasping. I jump from the bed, both fists raised, ready to defend myself and my home from the invader. But Aimee is not in the corner of the room. Even if she had been, she is no longer sixteen. I realise it can't have been sleep paralysis after all. It must have been a 'False Awakening'; a dream within a dream.

Or was it . . .

Could Aimee have somehow got in again? Perhaps she had been standing over my bed in reality, only for my unconscious, almost-awake brain to turn her into a teenager again.

I pad quickly across the hallway, checking on Caleb. He's thrown all his covers off, both arms raised above his head. I tuck him back in, then make my way down to the second floor. I find Mo lying on the guest bed, fully clothed, mouth open and catching flies. There's a bottle of whiskey on the bedside cabinet and one of our best crystal glasses. I sigh, upset he'd opted not to come to bed with me. Again.

I check each of the other rooms on the second storey, finishing with my study. I see a piece of paper on top of my laptop. I snatch it up, certain it will be another *NHIE* note. But it's only a hastily scribbled note to myself, about a DI Robyn Dallas plot hole for book eight, still called *Untitled*. I smile, relieved, then turn to leave.

And scream.

'Christ, Sam!'

Mo jumps back from the study threshold, almost comical in his exaggeration.

Adrenaline floods through me, making my hands shake. I'm aware I've grabbed a pair of scissors from the desk. I'm holding them above my head, like Norman Bates's mother in *Psycho*.

'Don't creep up on me!' I hiss.

Obviously it had not been Aimee behind me, but my husband. Which makes a lot more sense, given he lives here and Aimee is a product of my imagination (*at least tonight*). I listen out for Caleb, but he must still be out for the count in his room. We can't have been as loud as it had felt.

'I didn't. I woke up and heard *you* creeping about in here.' Mo's eyes alight on me, the various things in the study. He's searching for what brought me in here. His brow furrows. 'What's going on?'

'Just had a bad dream, that's all.' Not a lie, for once.

Mo is still dressed. I had gone to bed alone; I can't have been asleep long before I woke again. Maybe it had been the front door closing when he came back in downstairs that had woken me.

Mo stalks into the study, snatching up the note to self to see for himself. He reads it, then shoves it back on the desk.

'Why didn't you come to bed?' I demand. Hurt at his decision fuels my anger. I can feel the distance between us lengthening by the day.

Mo seems preoccupied with my desk. 'You've been so strung out lately, I wanted to ensure you got a good sleep, that's all.'

My anger evaporates; shame fills the space where it had been. *God, I am such a bitch.*

Mo collapses in my chair. Wild-eyed and sickly-looking, he looks even more rumpled if that's possible. 'This place is poison.'

'You wanted to come here.'

'What?' Mo lets out an incredulous chuckle, like he can't believe his ears. 'No, no I didn't. This was all you. Sea air for Caleb. Smaller class sizes, you said. Better standard of life. I wanted to stay in London, near our friends.'

'*Your* friends, you mean.'

My tone is wretched, like a schoolgirl's. But I am not having Mo rewrite history like this. I had not wanted to come back. We could have down-sized in London. We could have made it, somehow. We're both clever, educated, blessed with entrepreneurial spirit. We would have figured it out eventually.

Mo combs his hair with his fingers. It's a nervous habit he's had since I met him. His thinning hair looks like Christopher Lloyd's in *Back To The Future*.

'All right, yes, my friends. Another reason I wanted to stay in London. Being by yourself all the time, it's not good for you, Sam. I am really worried.'

The tenderness in Mo's voice sucks the defiance out of me, makes me back down.

'I'm sorry. We just keep missing each other.'

The admission leaps out of me, filling the space between us. For once, the pause it creates feels peaceful, not spiky. I'd read a lot about relationships in trouble: how every attempt at communication feels like an assault; that everything feels like sharp edges, misunderstandings around every corner. I'd dismissed it all as hyperbole. I know better, now.

Mo is in an earnest mood. He moves forward, grabs my good hand in his. 'Sam. I know it's hard, coming home. You must be expecting to see your dad on every corner.'

Guilt lances me in the chest. I'd barely thought of Dad at all since I'd come back to Ilfracombe. What kind of daughter am I? But I've had no time to. Thanks to Aimee.

'You don't understand,' I mumble.

Mo lifts my chin, makes me look into his eyes. I can see my reflection in the black of his pupils. 'So, tell me,' he whispers. 'Trust me? *Please*, Sam.'

Immediately, my mind's eye flips back to that large, round, fist-sized rock flying through the kitchen window, glass shards falling like deadly diamonds on the worktop and floor. The note that had come with it, reminding me of what had happened last time I spoke out. I can't say anything. Not when Aimee is still out there, watching.

Mo shakes his head, realising I am not going to answer. The sadness of his eyes is matched by the angry curl of his lip. 'If that's the way you want it.'

He turns his back on me and strides back down the corridor, into the guest bedroom. He slams the door after himself. I wince in anticipation. The sound travels up the stairs and sure enough, Caleb's grizzling cries filter back down.

Sighing with tiredness, I trudge upstairs to see to our son. He's angry, his face tomato-red, his skin hot to touch. He's in that half-awake, half-asleep state, restless and in desperate need of soothing. I can relate.

I press the button on his red projector lamp. The chimes of the nursery rhyme begin as it turns around and around, sending shadows of little spaceships onto the wall as it spins. I coo to him, stroking his hair away from his face, resting my weary body on the floor next to his cot. Suddenly Caleb sends an arm out through the bars, crashing into his nightstand. The lamp falls to the floor, along with his beaker.

As I reach out to retrieve the lamp from the floor, I stop. At an angle, the spaceship patterns have lengthened, throwing their shapes across the ceiling. They're no longer recognisable as what they're meant to be. Now they look like dancing flames as they shimmer round and round. They make the burns on my hand throb, sending prickles through my mind and a shiver down my spine. I feel like I am on the verge of remembering something, like a word on the tip of my tongue.

There's a large gap in the curtains. I pick my way around Caleb's abandoned toys towards the window, intent on closing them. As I draw close to the window, I spot a movement of shadows. It's a young girl's silhouette, the light behind her. I freeze. Like the other night, it grows to monster-like proportions as she crosses the road, towards my home. Towards me. My baby.

(*Get back.*)

Then the shadows recede and the girl is illuminated in the orange glow of the streetlamps as she walks straight past the house. I realise I am not used to seeing kids out after dark; I rarely saw them in the suburbs in London. She's about fourteen or fifteen and carries an open bag of chips. She wears cut-off jeans, a Bart Simpson T-shirt. There's a choker around her throat and she has two buns of hair piled up on her head. I smile; she looks like something out of the nineties. It's true what they say: *what goes around, comes around.*

As I watch her disappear around the corner, a name comes to my lips.

'Blobby.'

Twenty-nine

'**W**ho?' Maddy sounds as tired on the end of the line as I feel.

I'm still in my pyjamas, even though it's well past two o'clock in the afternoon. I've retreated into my casebook, DI Robyn Dallas-style. As I flick through the names listed there, it triggers another memory of flames. A bonfire. Music rumbles across the headland. In my mind's eye I can see all of us spinning round and round.

'Blobby. She was always hanging around. Remember?'

We are holding plastic battles of cider aloft and laughing: me, Ruby, Maddy and another young, tubby girl of about fourteen, hair tucked behind her ears, dressed in denim shorts and jacket, a neon-pink Global Hypercolor T-shirt on. A flower garland on her head, she spins around and around drunkenly on the headland. The bonfire serves as a ferocious backdrop, like a warning. Maddeningly, her face is blank.

'Don't quit on me now.' I am testier than I have any right to be. This is only the second time I've called Maddy in twenty-three years. 'Can you remember her real name?'

Caleb throws some bricks at the wall. He is not dressed either; he shuffles around the living room on his bottom in a foul temper. Lindy is not taking him out today, she has a migraine. I know I ought to put Caleb in the bath, get him dressed, put him in the buggy and take him for a walk on the beach or along the pier or *something*. A change of scenery would benefit both of us. But I just can't face leaving the house. The anxiety attack of the night before has left a long-lasting sense of unease. I can feel everything threatening to unravel, inside me. It will pass. I just have to batten down the hatches and keep myself occupied.

'No,' Maddy says airily. 'Are you sure you're not thinking of Becky Gillespie? The one who reckoned she was engaged to the PE teacher?'

Despite myself I smile, remembering the scandal that never was. Becky had very much *not* been going out with poor Mr Granger. She'd bought herself a cheap engagement ring made of Cubic Zirconium from Argos for twenty quid and told everyone he'd given it to her. Mr Granger had been suspended, pending an investigation. Even Becky's parents had backed him up, saying Becky was a known fantasist. Not long after, Becky had disappeared from school. We'd all heard she had ended up going to a unit for pupils with emotional problems.

'Nope, not her.'

I'm exhausted, having been up with Caleb most of the night since the early hours. Caleb has been sustained by ten-minute cat naps. When I'd slept, it had just been hazy, snatched moments.

Maddy sighs, causing crackles down the line. 'This was all ages ago, Sam. It doesn't matter any more. Let sleeping dogs lie.'

I ignore this. 'Oh come on, Mads . . . you remember Blobby. She was Ruby's kid sister.'

I cringe as I recognise the pleading in my voice. I push it down; I don't want Maddy to recognise how important this is to me. She could still be involved with sending the *Never Have I Ever* notes, for all I know. I don't think she is, but I don't want to chance it.

'She tagged along to the summer party at Will Jackson's, Ruby was furious. But she said she'd tell their mum if Ruby didn't let her come too.'

Maddy just grunts at the end of the line, non-committal.

I grasp for another fact that could spark a connection. 'She was really fat?'

'Oh, yes!' Maddy laughs. 'Christ. That's a blast from the past. Was she always hanging around? I don't remember.'

I bite my lip. I'd forgotten Blobby too, I could hardly rebuke Maddy for it. I'd airbrushed her out of my life, treated her like she was nothing. We'd all ignored Ruby's sister when we were kids. We'd never paid her any attention; she was just Ruby's kid sister. Of no consequence. We'd all rendered her invisible, as teen girls are wont to do.

I prompt her again. 'What was Blobby's real name?'

I've already spent hours combing through Facebook. I already know Ruby isn't on there, so without a first name for her younger sister, it's like looking for a needle in a haystack. I've scrolled aimlessly through Alf's photos on Instagram too, but nothing has jumped out at me, either in names, comments or tagged pics. That's when I'd decided to call Maddy; fat lot of good it seems to be doing me.

'I'm seeing the letter "L",' Maddy says in a 'Mystic Meg'-style voice, chuckling softly. When I don't laugh as well, she tuts and switches to serious. 'Lucy?'

'No, that's not it.' I sigh, though a second later something clicks. Sometimes talking these things through with a real person acts as a powerful trigger. 'Actually, yes. There's definitely an "L" in the name. Lily? No. Ellie?'

'Holly!' we both say in unison.

Maddy's confirmation fills in the space where Holly's face had been in my mind. Instantly, I can see her features: her dark brown eyes; her full, red mouth, the dimple in her chin. She'd been a pretty girl, just like Ruby. Teenage girls can be so vile.

Maddy's voice cuts through my thoughts. 'Why are you asking about her?'

I hesitate. Going through my DI Robyn Dallas-style casebook, I'd already decided it's unlikely Maddy is involved, being so far away in London. She's so obsessed with social media I can see her movements not only checking in on Facebook, but Google Timeline as well. So far this month she's spent fifteen hours in a vehicle, walked thirty-two kilometres and visited forty-one places, none of which are Ilfracombe. I take the plunge.

'Remember *Never Have I Ever*?'

Maddy's distaste is instant. 'I'd rather not.'

There it is again, that sudden change in her. There's a sharp edge to Maddy's voice. I feel an alarm bell ring in the back of my mind. Maybe I am being reckless, sharing this information with her? She had been there that night, and she'd done exactly zero to help me. But on the other hand, Maddy may know something. The more pragmatic DI Robyn Dallas would tell me to put my misgivings aside and just get on with it.

I fill Maddy in on the *Never Have I Ever* notes; how I think it could be Aimee behind it all. I don't mention the Kat Quentin debacle, or how there's still a question mark over her head. I only tell Maddy I want to speak to Holly. Aimee is still the mostly likely suspect.

There's silence at the end of the line.

'Maddy?' I think the phone might have cut out.

'I'm thinking.' Maddy's voice is all business now, typical lawyer. 'You think Holly could have seen something that night, at the summer party? Seen what happened at the, *y'know*?'

It's the closest we have come to discussing what happened. I grab the opportunity with both hands.

'She might have, yes. She's the only one I haven't tracked down.'

'I thought you hadn't tracked Aimee down yet?'

Damn, she's good.

'Right, I mean apart from Aimee. I just need to eliminate her from my enquiries.'

But Maddy kills this line of enquiry stone-dead. 'No. She was pissed as a fart that night. She passed out near the bonfire. Don't you remember?'

I'd always prided myself on my memory, yet I keep finding blank spots. I read on WebMD that memory loss is a symptom of post-traumatic stress disorder. I'd given it to Sergeant Kye Thomson when Elodie Fitzgerald tortured him in *Whisper of Silk*. Maybe my subconscious has been trying to send me cries for help all this time? That would make sense.

'Maybe she noticed we'd gone. Followed a bit after . . .'

I trail off. I can't bear to describe what had happened at the summer party. The horror of it feels like a warm shower of liquid shit settling over me, even after all these years.

Maddy sighs heavily. 'I know. I can't bear it either.'

There's an awkward pause as we both acknowledge the horror of what happened.

Maddy breaks the silence at last. 'You know it's not Holly, sending the *Never Have I Ever* notes. Or creeping around your house.'

'And the rock through the window.'

Maddy sucks in a breath, as she makes the connection too. Another memory sears through my mind. I can see us all, raising our hands: Paper, Scissors, Stone. How we'd nominated someone to take the dare, so many times.

'Sam, you did keep your word, didn't you?'

'Yes, of course I did!'

My answer comes too fast. I watch Caleb play innocently across the room, the sinking feeling in my stomach goes into full-on freefall. Perhaps I am making a big mistake. Maybe we should just put the house back on the market, get out of here.

'Only I keep thinking . . .' Maddy's voice peters out, as if she thinks better of saying what she wants. She emits a deep sigh on the end of the line.

'About what?' I clench my teeth. I don't want to hear it. Except I have to.

Maddy sighs. 'It was just a game, Sam. A stupid, juvenile game that got out of hand. Not even Aimee would go to these lengths to pay you back.'

'What are you trying to say?' My grip tightens on the phone.

Maddy's voice is cold. 'You broke your word.'

Before I can reply, the line goes dead. She's hung up. With a cry of frustration, I press redial, but only get the engaged tone. I slam the receiver in the cradle and punch in the number again.

Dial tone.

Thirty

I'd spent the rest of the afternoon trying to call Maddy back. She must have told the switchboard she wasn't taking calls, because I kept being put through to a young man with a reedy voice who became more and more irritated as our game of phone tag wore on. I'd gone back to Facebook and discovered myself blocked: I could no longer see Maddy in the platform, nor send her a private message. I ended up scrolling through Instagram, but if Maddy was ever on that site, she's blocked me now.

In contrast, 'Blobby' was not hard to track down, now I had her name. The private Instagram message I receive is bald, to the point.

What do you want?

She doesn't ask who I am, but then she already knows. I had been the one at a disadvantage last time we'd been in each other's presence.

It had been Holly who had come to see me at Waterstones. She hadn't been seated in the audience, she'd been the woman who hovered nearby, by a table laden with non-fiction titles. Prematurely grey like Ruby. Distinguished-looking, eminently middle-class, lithe body. One of those sack dresses that cost about a hundred quid that only yummy mummies who do yoga and drink kale smoothies every day can carry off. It's no wonder I hadn't recognised her: she could not have looked more different to the cruel nickname of her childhood.

I'd found Holly via Ruby's boy's account. Like most young people Alf has a lot of followers and comments on his pictures, so I hadn't noticed Holly on his timeline before. Now I had a name, I noticed the number of comments, going back weeks:

Tell your mum that . . .
Alf, can you get your mum to ring me . . .
Stop ignoring me, Alf! I know you're not at sea! I need
to speak to your mum!

There's only one reason young people ignore people on social media without blocking them. They're either 'making a statement without saying a word' (like the perfume); or they are being careless as hell with family members. Given Holly's interest in Ruby and the fact she appears to know Alf's timetable, I'd deduced it had to be the 'right' Holly, *aka* Blobby. I clicked on Holly's Instagram profile name. Sure enough, I was transported to a profile filled with her selfies; pictures of beaches and sunsets; memes about spirituality, parenthood and telling people to Fuck Right Off; not to mention photos of her doing sports. I'm wrong, she's not a yoga enthusiast, but a triathlete.

I noted that Holly is not a Talbot any longer, like Ruby or Alf. She must have got married; *Holly Greengage* was listed on her Instagram profile. Her name sounded like a Dickens character, or a cartoon mouse that lives in a teacup. I imagined someone who had reinvented herself like Holly would now expect perfection in all facets of her life. I could picture Mr Greengage in my head: a male model type, with sharp cheekbones and a big smile. On weekends he'd go mountain biking and walk a large dog through the forest.

Despite Ruby's assertion at her restaurant that I had always thought she was an idiot, I *had* loved her as a kid, just like I had Maddy. Some of my favourite memories included them both when we were children, before everything went wrong when we were teenagers. The epic Halloween discos in the school hall, dancing to Michael Jackson's 'Thriller' and buying glo-bands. Singing Christmas carols at the old folks' home, then pelting each other with snowballs the one time it snowed heavily down here in Devon when we were about ten. The body spray fights we had after PE in the school changing rooms when we were tweens, full-on chemical warfare of Charlie Red, So . . .? and Exclamation. It had been so much fun.

Until Aimee.

I'd fired off a message to Holly right away, but now find myself hesitating before replying to her Insta PM. Should I match Holly's forthright message? All I remember is an overweight child who was nearly always in pyjamas at home, even in the middle of the day. I remember her being needy, always wanting our attention, but little else about her. Maddy hadn't remembered her at all. God, teens are so self-involved.

I type a message and press SEND: *Why didn't you come and say hello at Waterstones?*

The reply is almost instant: *Didn't think you would remember me.*

Well, she's not wrong there. I try another tack: *Do you live in Exeter?*

No, I do a class there. Buggy Fitness in Northernhay Gardens. You should come ;)

Buggy Fitness is all the rage with middle-class mums: go for a workout in the park, take the kid with you. There will be a generation of adults who associate exercise with being pushed at speed across green spaces. I don't recall Holly having a baby with her at Waterstones. But maybe she'd parked the pushchair nearby. Or perhaps she's the instructor of the class. Or maybe she goes anyway, pushing an empty buggy? Though that strikes me as being a little sad.

The last part of her message registers. She knows about Caleb. I'd been careful not to put pictures of him online on my SJ Scherer pages and profiles. For the first time, I wonder if I'm wrong about Aimee. Maybe it's been Holly all along? Has she been watching the house? My mouth feels dry. But I can't think of any reason why Holly would have a beef with me to the point she would throw a rock through my window or delete my book. I must be over-thinking it all again.

So, you're in Ilfracombe too?

For my sins. Same old dump, brand-new Holly.

I smile. She would want to point that out.

You look great! I type.

I looked great before.

That's me told. It's in keeping with the memes on her profile, all about personal validation starting 'on the inside' and rejecting what others think of you. Fair enough.

Holly hasn't finished. More words appear on the screen: *I grew up, got fit and made a career of it, for me. No one else.*

Her last words conjure an image of Holly and Ruby's mum Wendy into my brain. Wendy had seemed impossibly glam to me as a teenager. She got her nails done every week and wore expensive perfume and full make-up every day, even when she was just lounging around the house.

She'd worked as a teacher, which always struck me as weird because she seemed to hate kids. Wendy had been a severe and brooding presence. I'd only ever seen her laugh when she was grabbing at Holly's rotund middle, or chubby biceps. She'd been a bully, pure and simple.

Ruby had told me Wendy had thrown her out when she was pregnant; that she'd had to go and live with her dad over at Lynmouth. Maybe Holly had gone with her. I hoped so. Wendy must be in her early to mid-sixties now, like Lindy. Did she still live in Ilfracombe? If she did, it must be hard for her to see Holly around town yet be unable to speak to her. But, serves her right, the narky, abusive old cow.

Maddy's warning about letting sleeping dogs lie flutters through my brain. Maddy might have something to hide, but I don't. I need to meet with Holly, check it's not her behind the *Never Have I Ever* notes. She may even know something about Aimee and where she is now. Since she clearly remembers me vividly, she might recall something Ruby and Maddy couldn't (or wouldn't). I decide to go for it.

I'd love to meet up for a coffee?

I don't think so.

I don't allow the instant knock-back to dent my confidence. *Please?*

I've left all that behind me.

Now I am intrigued. Does Holly mean she avoids talking to people who knew her 'before'? If so, what's happened to not needing anyone else's validation? I've seen this kind of behaviour in New Age types before – 'methinks they doth protest too much'. Perhaps I could bait her to meet me.

I understand. If you change your mind, I will be in Costa tomorrow on the high street, between 11am and midday.

No reply comes. But I know Holly has seen the message. She will come and see me tomorrow, I just know it.

She has to.

Thirty-one

Lindy arrives to pick Caleb up at ten. She gives my burned, bandaged hand a sorrowful look, before grabbing me by the elbow and steering me into the kitchen. 'Okay, missy, what's really going on?'

I feign a yawn. 'Just worried about this book, that's all.' (*It's the truth, for once.*)

Lindy's eyes narrow. Ironically, she doesn't believe me. 'You look terrible.'

'Oh thanks, Mum!'

My sarcasm is not enough to divert her unwanted attentions, though. As if psychic, my editor Aisling had texted me the night before, straight after Holly: *How's things going with the new book, babes?*

For a microsecond I'd thought about confessing all to Aisling. How Mo had been right to call her and Carole the other day. How I am stressed out; I've burned my hand; my stalker appears to have bigger issues than we thought; how she even deleted my entire manuscript.

But I know Aisling would be delighted by this news. She'd want me to write a piece about my 'stalker hell' in the *Guardian*, the *Daily Beast* or the *Atlantic*. Carole had already said her friend at the *Telegraph* would be interested, too. Besides the irritation they'd inevitably not take me seriously, I have neither the inclination, nor, it seems, the ability to write any more words today. I just can't face it.

Great! I tap out on my phone to Aisling. *Couldn't be going better.*

Another bare-faced lie. They are adding up. Though can lies be 'bare-faced' via text? I don't even know or care any more. But Lindy is my mum, not my employer. I sigh, leaning against the kitchen counter top. I want to cry. I let a tear roll down my cheek.

'I'm just really stressed.'

Mum's face softens. 'Oh, darling.'

She envelops me in her bony embrace. I let her. It's like hugging an ironing board, but there's still comfort in it. She wipes a tear from my cheek with her thumb like I am a small child again.

'It's the price of success, sweetheart. They always want more where that came from.' Lindy gives me a smile. 'Well, don't you worry. If you need more time, I can take Caleb for longer next time. How do you like that?'

I don't like it at all. I hate that I am hardly seeing Caleb – or Mo – at the moment. We'd moved to Ilfracombe for a quiet life, with less work, but so far it has been nothing but stress. Even so, I nod, grateful Lindy is so willing to try and help.

Twenty minutes of pep talk from Lindy later, I wave them both off again. I moon around the house for ten minutes, then decide to go out as well. I take my laptop with me. I figure I need the change of scenery. I might as well get some words done while I wait for Holly.

It's a new Costa, dark but clean, shining posters of coffee beans in extreme close-up on the wall. My sweet tooth makes me buy a Salted Caramel Crunch Frostino from the summer menu, which I carry like a sports trophy to a dark corner of the café. I set up my laptop near the toilets. I'm seated opposite a big leather sofa where two mums have dumped the Lego box on the floor. Two robust toddlers keep trying to give them multi-coloured bricks, to gain their attention. It doesn't work. The mums accept them absent-mindedly, talking over the kids' heads, desperate for adult conversation.

Through sheer desperation, I have decided to rewrite DI Robyn Dallas book eight for Aisling based on my own casebook and experiences. It's not the book I am contracted for, but the fact it's essentially a true story might sweeten the deal with my publisher. Better still, somehow I have managed to write nearly twelve thousand words in the past four days already, meaning I am close to the wordcount I lost when Aimee broke in and deleted the original, so I am feeling fairly upbeat about the new book. I think I can get it finished for my end of September deadline after all. I have a title, *Stalker From Hell*. In it, DI Robyn Dallas is forced to go into protection in Devon when she becomes the star witness in a big trial. During her exile, someone discovers her secret and tries to blackmail her, which of course alerts Elodie Fitzgerald and her minions to Dallas's secret location. Write what you know and all that.

Of course, this time I have backed it up in my Dropbox and on various USB sticks, dotting them about the house in random places. I have been checking all the locks every night, and every room when I come home. I've even woken in the night and patrolled, just in case Aimee breaks in again. Whether I can write anything *today* is another matter.

I tell myself I will only allow myself tiny sips of my Frostino every time I make it to one hundred and fifty words. In reality, I slurp half of it up before I even get to fifty. As half eleven rolls around, I have managed to scrape a paltry three hundred words together. A sorrowful amount in ninety minutes, for me. *Grrr.*

My burned hand hurts like hell. I shouldn't be typing but needs must; I swallow some paracetamol back dry, chasing them down with the dregs of my Frostino. I've always been a 'binge' writer, splurging out words in snatched increments of time. I'd written DI Robyn Dallas book one, *Death By Numbers*, in my lunch hour when I was still a legal secretary; even on the toilet, on my phone. Further books in the series had been written the same way, then around additional challenges like all those IVF injections, egg-harvesting procedures, three miscarriages, then eventual pregnancy and breastfeeding. Now I've hours of uninterrupted time: Mo is at work and Caleb is happy and content to spend time with my mother, yet I've dried up. Despite my earlier optimism, anxiety flaps around in my belly like a dying fish. It's already the middle of August. I've worked out I needed to write approximately fifteen thousand words per week to hit my target. It feels like a gargantuan task, even with the inspiration flowing. I don't even have an ending yet. It feels like a horrible reflection of my real life.

A shadow casts over my computer, making me look up. Holly stands in front of me. She's in designer workout clothes this time, a sports bag over her shoulder. State-of-the-art headphones around her neck. iPhone strapped in her little arm-holder thing. Purple headband with *GODDESS* embroidered on it. Because, obviously.

My eyes stray to the clock. Eleven fifty-five. 'You made it.'

Holly seats herself, daintily like she is at a queen's tea party. She doesn't smile or make any pretence at social norms. Her face is completely deadpan.

I'm caught on the back foot. 'Okay. Can I get you a drink?'

'No, thank you.'

Holly's elocution is more rounded, particular than Ruby's. She's had lessons. I note the engagement ring on her left hand. It's a rock, a good three grand's worth. Now I've got her here, I don't know where to start. I dive straight in.

'How are you?'

'What do you care?'

I grit my teeth. No one has told Holly answering a question with a question is rude. Or maybe she does know, but just doesn't care. That seems quite likely, actually.

'Fine. If that's the way you want to play it.'

Holly shrugs. 'Why did you really want to see me?'

Now there's a question. Why had 'Blobby' returned to my memory at last, when I'd seen the young girl from Caleb's window the other night? I'm not entirely sure yet, though I have a working theory. I feel like Miss Marple, or Columbo, or my own beloved DI Robyn Dallas. I take a last slurp of my Frostino, which ruins my gravitas a bit.

'Why did you *really* come to Waterstones to see me read?'

'Curiosity.' Holly does not avert her gaze from mine. 'I recognised your picture on the billboard. I realised I'd read an SJ Scherer book, so came in.'

Attention-ho that I am, I can't resist. 'Right. Did you like my book?'

'It was okay.'

'Just okay?' Finally, someone from my past who has read my book and she hadn't been struck with it. *Typical*.

'The middle dragged and the resolution felt a little rushed.' Holly picks at a napkin on the table, finally a little embarrassed. Though not enough to stop trashing my book, it seems. 'And the character tropes were a bit samey. Why do all female detectives have to have a broken heart and a drinking problem?'

'Well, thank you for your feedback.'

I soak up her criticism, attempting to look like I am not bothered by it in the slightest. But I can see my reflection in the mirror behind Holly's head; I look like I am chewing wasps. As I grope for my next question, I seize on the significance of Holly's words. She hadn't used the word 'ending', like a layperson would, but 'resolution'. She'd also used the word 'tropes' correctly. Interesting.

'You seem to know a lot about writing?'

'Gotta have a hobby.' Holly shrugs. 'All work and no play makes Holly a dull girl.'

These words spark another connection in my mind, confirming my theory at last. I'd already noted N1Fan from the original letters was a reference to Stephen King's *Misery*, a book about keeping an author hostage and torturing him. *All work and no play makes Holly a dull girl* is a bastardised version of Jack Torrance's fevered typings as he goes mad in *The Shining*.

It can't be a coincidence.

I grin. 'You sent those notes to my publisher, didn't you? The ones signed from "Number one fan".'

Holly's impassive expression wavers. 'I don't know what you're talking about.'

But I am not letting her go so easily. 'Apparently I've stolen ideas, am stuck up?'

Holly shrugs, as if to say *If the cap fits.*

I go in for the kill. 'Apparently, *you've* got no life. No one loves you and your only solace is my books?'

Finally, Holly's stony face lifts. She hesitates, unsure whether she's going to make her confession or not. Her forehead wrinkles as irritation and regret pass over her features. It's enough to answer my question.

'I knew it!' I shake my head.

'Okay, fine. I've read all your books. I started following you online. I found out it was you writing them when I saw you at some crime event in London last year . . . Where you didn't recognise me *again*, by the way.'

I know the event Holly's referring to. Besides the Waterstones event in Exeter, it's the only other appearance I've done recently. *That's* how she knew about Caleb; I would have been pregnant then. It had been at Goldsboro Books on Cecil Court, off Charing Cross Road. I am unsurprised I'd not seen Holly there: it's a labyrinthine little shop, with plenty of nooks and crannies. I hadn't been the only writer in attendance either, so had assumed most people had not come to see me when they could speak to the likes of Peter James, Paula Daly and Belinda Bauer.

'Sorry. I can't have seen you—'

Holly interrupts me, with rolled eyes. 'We talked for two or three minutes, face to face. You signed my bloody book.'

Holly chucks down a copy of my most successful and only critically acclaimed DI Robyn Dallas book, *Broken Things,* number four in the series. It's a hardback collector's edition, the spine still unbroken. Holly must've been a genuine fan. Guilt prickles through me as I open the book and discover my trademark scrawl in there, as well as DI Robyn Dallas's catchphrase, '*The Evidence says . . . happy reading! SJ xx*'.

But fury floods back just as quickly. I might have been self-involved, but I am not the criminal here. 'You've been stalking me. Watching my house, breaking the window, creeping about inside, deleting my book, chasing me . . .'

'No!' Holly falters when she realises she's not telling the whole truth. 'Well, one of those things. But just one, I swear.'

'Which one?' I demand.

Holly blows out her cheeks. 'It was me, the night you came out of the corner shop.' She raises both hands in a supplicatory gesture, before I can blow my top. 'I swear, I never meant to chase you that night. You just legged it. I ran after you, certain you would turn, see it was me. But you were off like a hare from the trap. I never got as far as your road.'

I chew over what Holly is telling me. It's true the shadow-woman had disappeared when I'd reached my house. Even so, Nı Fan's behaviour had been odd. I don't understand why she would admit to those letters, to chasing me, but not to the other things.

I quote one of the first letters, '"*We should go walking on the cliffs together*"?'

Holly shifts in her chair, embarrassed. 'Look, I'd had this fantasy, that you and I could be friends, maybe even writing partners.' She sighs. 'Then you didn't even recognise me – twice! – and I got angry. Invisible Holly, all over again. I wanted to get even, perhaps freak you out a bit. But then I saw you round here, with your kid. Then I ended up chasing you – by accident – so the fun went out of it, for me.'

Another connection fires in my brain. 'So that's why you sent me the last letter, saying I wouldn't hear from you again.'

Holly nods. Disappointment crashes through me. I'd felt so optimistic this morning, but now I am back to square one yet again. I'd assumed that last N1Fan letter was to lull me into a false sense of security, but it was real. One mystery might be solved, but the writer of the *Never Have I Ever* notes is still out there.

'I was also a bit worried sending notes was illegal or something.'

I roll my eyes. 'Technically, it is. They don't do much about it without a tangible threat though, so you're safe.'

'Yes, that's what Michael said.'

I'm stung that Holly has already gone to Michael, that he has not shared this information with me. I'd envisaged him hard at work, investigating who'd been stalking me. Instead, he must have been stringing me along, keeping me happy. Was that because of a lack of resources, or because of something more sinister? I resolve to make another note in my casebook about his strange behaviour.

'Do you remember that summer party up at Easterbrook Farm?'

Holly fixes me with that defiant glare of hers. I'm shocked to see undisguised contempt in her eyes. 'I told you, I left that behind me.'

Those words again. I clench my teeth. 'So, you do remember what happened?'

Holly seems to enjoy my frustration. 'You see, this is the thing. When you're an ignored and neglected kid, you get really good at fading into corners. I saw you, at our place. Lots of times. Daring each other with that stupid game.'

I close my eyes at this confirmation. We'd thought we were so clever, so daring. But we'd left ourselves wide open. Michael hadn't been the only witness. Holly had been, too.

'I saw what you did.'

Thirty-two

'And what was that?' Ice-cold fear lances my chest like a pick-axe; my tongue sticks to the roof of my mouth.

'I saw you hurt that defenceless animal.'

My pulse quickens. Relief spirals through me, quickly replaced by shame with the power of electricity. How could I have forgotten?

Never Have I Ever killed a living thing.

This dare had fallen to me. I'd realised I got this dare because I'd ended up going out with Mike; he had not rejected and humiliated me, as Aimee had hoped. She'd made a big deal of the dare being completely random, tossing a coin between me and Maddy for it, but she cheated. She must have.

Aimee *made* me do it.

Even more than twenty years on, I can still see Aimee's wide eyes as she presented me with the hamster. It had been two pounds sixty at the local pet shop. It's funny the things you remember.

Queasiness threatened to engulf me, but I choked it down. I looked to my friends. None of them backed down, laughed and said 'Gotcha!' Not even Ruby.

'Our dares have been just as bad,' Maddy said, though her voice wavered.

Tears in my eyes, I swallowed. I closed both my hands around the little creature. I was vaguely aware of the others gathering around, but I couldn't understand what they were saying. There was a primeval piquancy to the air. I remember feeling far away, like I was outside of my own body. Heat enveloped me as I closed my hands around the tiny creature. I could feel its tiny bones. I gagged but continued, squeezing harder.

The hamster emitted a high, keening noise as it realised what was happening. Desperate to live, it bit me. Sharp pain seared through my palms. Blood ran between my fingers, but it was my own, not the hamster's. I knew I couldn't let go. If it escaped, it would disappear into Ruby's mum's skirting board. Aimee would declare it a default and I would be out of the group: a loner, a billy-no-mates forever. I was holding on to the group by the skin of my teeth. Aimee was looking for any excuse to get rid of me. I couldn't afford a default. I just couldn't.

'Sam.' Ruby's voice brought me back to Earth.

I stopped squeezing and opened my hands. The hamster was dead. The tiny animal lay on my bloody palms, its fur slick with gore, its neck at an impossible angle.

'Savage.' Aimee grinned.

In the dark light of Costa, I look at the tiny white scar on the palm of my hand where the hamster had bitten me. It's a lasting reminder of that terrible thing I'd allowed myself to be chivvied into, for the sake of the group. All these years later, I am still disgusted with myself. I had been so weak. I should have told them no. When had we crossed the line? The very first dare? When I'd cheated on Michael by kissing Will Jackson? The flashing? The hamster? Or maybe it was everything that happened after that.

I inhale a shaky breath. 'You're right. I have no excuse, except I was just a stupid kid. We all were.'

Holly slams both palms on the table now, eyes flashing. 'Don't blame Ruby!'

I choose my next words with care. 'What do you remember about the summer party?'

Holly sucks in a breath over her teeth. 'Not much. It was the first night I'd ever got smashed. I spent a lot of the time dancing round the bonfire, thinking I was Sabrina the Teenage Witch.'

Another memory: Holly, rolled onto her side into the recovery position by Mike by the haybales. Maddy had said Holly passed out near the bonfire. Maybe Holly hadn't followed us then, like Maddy had said.

'Did Ruby say anything about the party afterwards?'

'No.' Holly slumps in her chair and crosses her arms, a display of almost teenage belligerence. 'It was after all that Ruby went off the rails, tried it on with boys, got pregnant. It's taken her years to get back on track. Now, she's happy. Anyway, this is a waste of time.'

She stands to leave. I stand too, grab her arm. 'I'm sorry about not recognising you at either of the book launches.'

Holly's lip curls in a sneer. 'Always thought you were so special, didn't you? Could always see little spoiled princesses like you a mile off, even when I was a kid. Think the world revolves around you.'

She doesn't say goodbye, just turns on her heel and heads for the door. I hang back as Holly weaves her way through the tables and chairs. Then I walk briskly after her, through the café. I make it to the big glass doors at the front, pushing them open with one hand. I look up the street, across the road. I can see Holly stop outside a red car near Market Arches. She opens the passenger door and slides in.

I stand on tiptoe, trying to catch a glimpse of the driver. But it's not Aimee, or even a woman. Holly leans across and kisses the cheek of the jowly, much older man behind the wheel waiting for her. He looks irritated, even angry. Holly shrinks back from him, towards the car door as she pulls her seatbelt on. I'd already seen their dad up at Ruby's café, so it has to be Mr Greengage, Holly's husband. Interesting. He does not look like I imagined at all, though I realise his mean mouth reminds me of Wendy's.

'Got any spare change?'

I jump as a thin, rasping voice interrupts my surveillance. I look down, to see the homeless woman. She sits on the steps of the old chapel nearby, cloaked in an over-sized coat despite the burgeoning sun overhead. Greying, salt-and-pepper hair scraped back from her forehead this time, she's skeletal, skin stretched over her bones. She's missing most of her front teeth. Whatever Kat Quentin is feeding her, it's not enough.

'How do you know Kat?' I stare at the older woman's pale blue eyes. There seems to be no recognition in them at the sound of Kat's name.

Spindly fingers point to the old ice-cream tub by her feet. It has only coppers in. I put my hand in my pocket and pull out a five-pound note. It flutters down, into her box.

'Thank you kindly.' The homeless woman coughs. It sounds hoarse, horrible, like it is ripping her up from the inside.

I grow tired of waiting for her answer, try and prompt her. My Devon accent jumps out of me, involuntarily:

'How do you know preggers, down at the café on the sea-front?'

'She's a good maid.'

The homeless woman smiles indulgently, like she's describing her own granddaughter. I finally spot the litre bottle of White Lightning at her feet by her grubby skirts, already half-empty. She's three sheets to the wind. I won't get a straight answer from her. I trudge back into Costa, to grab my laptop and bag.

The glass doors close behind me.

Thirty-three

Blocked from contacting Maddy and effectively blocked in real life by Ruby and Holly, stress and desperation consume me, pressing down on me like a lead weight. That night I close my eyes to a feeling of being trapped, in the dark and alone. In my dreams I hear the crackle of flames and Aimee's mocking laughter. I awake exhausted; I feel like I have been running all night. As I drag my weary bones from bed, I realise I only have one course of action left.

I must bring Aimee out into the open.

As I already know, Aimee has family all over Ilfracombe. Caleb off with Mum again, I resort to Googling and looking up Aimee's relatives on social media. Some I already know, such as Ava, Bill and Frankie Dyer. Within an hour I have a list of five more. I'd already found both Aimee's older sisters, thanks to Facebook; I just had to call the search back up again. One is Ava's mum, Charmaine. In her profile picture she looks exactly the same, only more lined. She is even wearing the same sort of clothes, as if noughties fashion never happened. The others must be cousins, uncles and aunts I guess. I don't recall seeing any of them before, but as I know, my overall memory can't be trusted one hundred per cent.

Fearful of losing my nerve, I set out straight away in the car for the high street. The bell tinkles as I appear across the threshold in Dyer's. Bill mopes behind the counter, whilst Ava leans over a box of plastic junk. Two for the price of one. Good start. The tattoo at the base of Ava's spine is on display. It reads, *DRAMA QUEEN.*

'I need to send a message to Aimee.' My voice sounds stronger than I feel.

'You and me both, maid.' Bill's voice is softer than I remember. He looks me up and down. 'Ava said you'd been in. Sally, innit?'

'Sam.'

Ava blows bubbles of gum behind her grandfather's head, it's very off-putting. But that is the point. The Dyers hate questions almost as much as they hate the long arm of the law. I turn back towards Bill, cutting Ava out of my line of sight.

Bill kisses his teeth behind his walrus moustache. 'Look, love. We ain't seen Aimee in years. She sodded off donkey's ago.'

But there's a tic in his eye. Does that mean he's lying? I don't want to antagonise him. If anyone can make contact with Aimee, it's surely Bill Dyer. Aimee was always a daddy's girl, underneath all her bluster.

'Police said she'd gone to Australia?' I try and keep my tone light, non-accusatory.

Bill smiles, revealing yellow tobacco-stained teeth. 'Then that's where she'll be.'

'Seems a bit far to go, expensive too.' *And a bit handy*, I want to add. I don't.

'She was always a wanderer.' Bill shrugs.

This is going nowhere. I pull a piece of paper out of my pocket, with a pre-written message on it. 'Just, if you see her. Please pass the message on?'

Bill accepts the note from my outstretched hand. I take that to mean the affirmative and leave the shop.

I'd discovered that Charmaine Dyer has a little bed and breakfast out on Capstone Parade. She answers the door with a big, fuschia-lipstick smile, which drops as soon as she sees me. She'd obviously thought I was a guest.

'Hi, I am an old friend of Aimee's?' I begin, but Charmaine cuts me off.

'No time, love. I got a party of eight arriving any minute now.'

'Just, if you see her? Please give her this.'

Charmaine rolls her eyes and takes the bit of paper, slamming the door in my face.

I hit the pubs next. One female Dyer is behind the bar of a pub near the seafront, cleaning the pipes. In the flesh I recognise Aimee's other older sister Shannon, who'd been a couple of years above us at school. She's an ageing rock chick of about forty-two, covered in tattoos and still in impeccable shape thanks to an obvious daily gym habit. She is lean and strong, carrying a huge tray of empties without breaking a sweat. She accepts the bit of paper without comment and shoves it on a bulletin board.

I find one of the male cousins on the newly built pier, fishing in *Verity's* shadow. He looks like he's around eighteen or nineteen and tells me his name is Ethan. He takes my bit of paper and tries to offer me a freshly caught mackerel in return. I find another cousin Jim in the old snooker hall on one of the back roads. He's middle-aged, a little bit lechy. He takes my number down and then texts me immediately with a selection of suggestive emojis. I don't care, if it means I flush Aimee out.

I find Frankie Dyer in the Bunch of Grapes pub opposite Costa, already half-cut before three in the afternoon. I'm shocked to see how the past two decades have changed him. He's about five stone heavier than the picture in the newspaper article I'd read about him at the start of my investigation. He's lost the bushy moustache and his head is completely bald. Had the barman not told me who he was, I would have walked back out, none the wiser.

I approach him, bringing a pint for him with me. He accepts my word and the alcohol without even asking me why. I see his hands are trembling. As I watch him gulp it back, I realise I am watching a man who has lost everything to addiction.

'I need to get a message to your niece, Aimee.'

Frankie looks me up and down. 'Niece. Good one.'

'What do you mean?'

Whatever I'd expected him to say, it wasn't this. I am intrigued. Frankie rolls his eyes, like he expects me to catch up. When I don't, he shoots me a withering glance.

'Why'd do you think I ended up in the crapper, outcast of me own family?'

'I don't know.' I try and keep my tone neutral, though exhaustion means irritation is never far away. I want to grab him, shake the truth from him.

He leans forward, as if to whisper. The smell of body odour and alcohol is overpowering, but I force myself not to cringe away. 'She ain't my niece. She's my gal too, you see.'

Pity floods through me as I watch his grimy face crumple. Aimee had never told us this scandal about her family.

'Those bastards, they didn't even tell me she'd gone, you know?' Frankie seems completely unaware of the tears making track marks down his cheeks. 'I had to find out from the paper, like any old Tom, Dick or Harry.'

I search for something to say but come up with nothing.

'I done wrong by Bill, I know that. You don't sleep with your brother's wife. But he forgave that missus of his. Why not me? All these years, left out in the cold. And Aimee don't want to know a single one of us, anyway.'

I buy Frankie another pint. I realise I shouldn't facilitate his addiction, but I figure one more won't hurt. Even if it does, his life hurts more. He seems to forget about me as the full glass is pushed towards him, so I take the opportunity to sneak away.

I make it back out onto the high street. I wander back to my car, my mind whirling with Frankie's revelation. My earlier sense of empowerment at doing something vanishes into the ether. There's zero guarantee any of the messages will even make it to Aimee. Still, I have no other choice left and I guess it's better than nothing. It has to be only a matter of time before Aimee surfaces again.

I'll be ready.

Thirty-four

'Have you been going through my desk?'

Fury flutters inside my belly. It's been twenty-four hours since I put the word around to try and flush Aimee out at long last. And here is Mo, sitting oblivious in the living room which is a pigsty as usual. Plates and cups litter the low coffee table, the television has been on for hours playing endless re-runs of *Pawn Stars*. I can still smell the smoke damage emanating from downstairs in the man-cave, like the rot in the centre of our relationship.

Mo shakes out the newspaper and looks over his reading glasses at me. 'FYI, I would never touch your desk. I know it's more than my life's worth. And I would certainly never set it on fire.'

'Ha bloody ha.'

Mo is still of the opinion I must have set his property alight during a fit of pique. It's my own fault of course, for shutting him out; I've dug my own hole. But he can be so infuriating. Who the hell says 'FYI' in real life, for God's sake? Perhaps he always has, but I just haven't noticed.

Pacing the living room, I note the little fan heater is going full blast as usual. Despite it being the end of summer, it is still ludicrously cold in this old house. There is a strong draught. Where the hell is it coming from? Maybe we should get a man in, lag the roof or change the windows or some-thing. More expense, but isn't that what you were supposed to do, to keep the heat in? I have no idea. I have always lived in modern properties before.

'Are you looking for this?' Mo pauses the TV and holds up my casebook.

I can't believe it. 'You *did* go through my things!'

'I told you, no. God, you are so paranoid.'

I'd been attempting to work after putting Caleb to bed, but I'd reached across the desk for my DI Robyn Dallas casebook, only to find it was not where I'd left it, next to the printer. I'd pulled out all the drawers of my desk, the books from the bookcase, the boxes of papers underneath. All to no avail. Mo doesn't know why I am so anxious and angry, but I am not thinking straight right now.

'You left it next to the cooker in the kitchen.' Mo opens my notes on the *Never Have I Ever* notes, flicks through the various spider-grams and names. 'So, you've told me about Ruby and Aimee. Who are Holly and Maddy?'

'Just old friends from school.'

'And Michael and Alf, who are they?'

Mo's tone is measured, but panic blooms in my chest. Alf I can explain away without problems, but I don't want to have to explain who Michael really is right now. I can still try and contain the situation. I decide going for old-fashioned outrage may serve me well.

I push anger into my voice. 'How dare you!'

'No. How dare *you*.'

Mo's voice is quiet. Usually when he's angry with me, he will turn up the decibels. I am unnerved, on the back-foot again. For a crazy second I wonder if I really had left my casebook in the kitchen; could Mo be involved in all this, somehow? No, that really is the paranoia talking. This nightmare is Aimee's doing, no one else's.

Mo clenches both fists, counting to ten. 'I'll ask you again. What the hell is this really about, Sam?'

'Why don't you tell me?' I challenge. 'You were the one who wanted to move to Ilfracombe in the first place. Maybe you had an ulterior motive?'

Mo laughs, incredulous. 'Are you for real? I cannot have this discussion again. You were the one who wanted to move to this godforsaken place. Then you have consistently cut me out of this from the start. All I ever wanted to do was help you, protect you. I have tried everything I can think of to reach you.'

The sarcasm pours out of me, on instinct. 'Oh yeah, well done. You tried really hard.'

Mo jumps up from the sofa and throws the casebook at me. It hits the wall next to my head with a *thwack*, making me flinch.

An awkward silence follows as we eyeball each other across the room.

I move towards the hallway, just in case. Sure enough, upstairs, Caleb yells 'Mama!' and we both wince. He follows it up with some garbled protestations, then is quiet again. He's just talking in his sleep. That was close.

'I can't take any more of this.' I sit down on the sofa, head in hands.

Mo slumps back on the sofa, face to the low ceiling. 'You can't? How do you think I feel? I've been on the phone to Kelly and Dad. I'm going to take Caleb and go and see them for a few days.'

There it is: my worst fear, breathed into being. Mo wants to take Caleb and exit our home, leaving me behind. I won't have it. I've spent my whole life on the sidelines. Mum and Dad couldn't be there for me, not really; they'd always been preoccupied, their thoughts elsewhere with Dad's job troubles and Mum's depression. Aimee stole Maddy and Ruby from me. Even Mo has his business ambitions; the respect of his peers is everything to him. My writing sustains me, but it doesn't complete me. If someone were to force me to choose between my books and my baby, it's no contest. I wouldn't even have to think about it.

Whatever happens between Mo and me, Caleb is *mine*. I fold my arms. 'You're not.'

Mo keeps speaking as if he hasn't heard me. 'He'll enjoy playing with his cousins. It's not good for him, being around all this drama. You can get your bloody book written, or go see this Aimee, or whatever it is you feel you have to do on your own. It's a win-win for everyone.'

'You're not taking Caleb to Ireland!'

Mo blinks as he takes in my defiant stance.

'It would just be for a few days, Sam.' He enunciates slowly, as if talking to a child. He's always underestimated me.

'And I say, *over my dead body*. Caleb belongs with me. His mother.'

An absurd smile takes over Mo's face. He cannot believe what he is hearing. 'I'd bring him back, Sam. I'm not leaving forever.'

The words race out of my mouth before I can think them through.

'Maybe I *want* you to leave forever?'

They stay there, between us, like poisonous plumes of smoke. My heart hammers in shock. Mo's mouth opens and closes in disbelief.

'You don't mean that.'

Don't I? I can't be sure. But I do know that if forced to choose between Mo and Caleb, just like with my writing, it's no contest. I can't risk Mo leaving this house with my child. The chasm between us has opened up too wide, these past two years. Back with his family, Kelly or one of the others might remind Mo he never signed up for all this. Maybe he will decide life is a lot less hassle without me. As the decision lands in my mind, weary relief makes its way through me. I can't keep up the pretence any more. I am exhausted.

It's better if he just goes.

'Samantha, you don't mean that.' There's an underlying panic to Mo's voice now. 'Not after everything we've been through. All those years, trying for Caleb. The failed businesses. We turned it all around, we can get over this. We're so close. Don't give up on us now?'

'I just can't any more,' I whisper.

Mo moves towards me, banging his shins on the coffee table. Swearing, he avoids it and grabs my hand. He falls to his knees, an unwitting parody of a marriage proposal.

'It will be okay. I swear. I'll do whatever it takes. Please! Just don't do this.'

I close my eyes. I can feel tears on my own cheeks now, but I am not in the room with my husband. I am thinking of poor, lost Frankie Dyer. Unable to take up his rightful place in his own family, thanks to his own poor decisions.

That's me, now.

I push my husband away, literally and figuratively. 'Just go.'

Thirty-five

'What are you doing here?'

Lindy stands on the doorstep, one of her big Mary Poppins-style bags in hand. 'I thought I could come and stay for a bit?'

Mo left in the early hours of this morning. He'd been unwilling to wait for the next space on a flight from Bristol. Having found a last-minute flight that left for Ireland from London, he'd taken the car and gone. Caleb is used to Mo going away for work, but he appears to have picked up on something in the air. He seems unusually tearful, wilful. I dread to think what will happen if this enforced separation drags on.

I lean my head against the door frame. 'We're fine, Lindy.'

'Just to keep you company. Come on, it's more for me than you. I'm bored.'

Lindy smiles at me, but she has a look I have not seen on her face before. With a jolt, I realise it's sympathy. But Mo leaving is not the same as my dad suddenly dying of a heart attack. Part of me had wanted Mo to go, for God's sake.

'Lindy, you live a five-minute drive away. I don't need you to stay.'

I don't invite her in. I can't think of anything worse right now than my mum staying. She'd stink up the place with her vape pen; she leaves a trail of scarves and dirty cups everywhere she goes. She makes Mo look tidy.

'I could clean up, look after Caleb while you write. Make dinner?'

Okay, that's it. Mum's not the nurturing domestic goddess type.

'What's this really about?'

Lindy's smile falters, then falls away. She's never been a good liar.

'I'm not happy about you being alone.'

'I told you, I'm fine, Mum.' Suddenly I feel incredibly lethargic, pulled down by it all. I just want to be left alone. By everybody.

Lindy might be attuned to my dark moods, but she's never been good at hearing what I really say. She attempts to push the door inwards, muscle her way inside.

'Look, darling. We'll feel so much better if you just let us help.'

'*We'll?*' I push back, propelling her back onto the step. 'Mo sent you, didn't he?'

Lindy's eyes widen as she realises her mistake. 'No. Of course not. Samantha!'

The door cuts off her voice to a muffled wail as I manage to slam it shut in her face. She bangs a fist on the door as I grab my phone from my pocket, pressing Mo's number on speed dial. I turn my back on the front door as he answers straight away.

'You sent Lindy round? Seriously?' I spit down the phone.

'You left me with no choice.'

I roll my eyes. 'What do you think she's going to be able to do, Mo? Take on a serial killer with her secret ninja skills?'

'Jesus, you think a *serial killer* is after you?'

Mo's tone is rising. I have a vison of him jumping back in the car and getting the first plane back, the last thing I need.

'No! Of course not. Just trust me, will you? I don't need babysitting!'

I ring off. Mo's name and picture immediately appear on screen as he attempts to call me back. I key the OFF switch and the handset powers down. Feeling satisfied, I jump as there's more hammering on the front door behind me. Upstairs, I hear a wail from my son as all the noise rouses him.

'Mum, for crying out loud, you've woken Caleb . . .!'

My words trail off. It's not Lindy at the front door any longer, but Michael.

He turns towards me on the doorstep. I flash him a smile, only to be met with a ferocious grimace. I'm absurdly hurt by his demeanour. It feels like I am being chastised by a parent, yet I can't put my finger on why. It's getting more and more difficult to hold all the fragments of my life together. I've shattered like china, like the cat in the old *Tom and Jerry* cartoons.

'Kat is your phantom note writer, seriously?' Michael barks.

Oh, that.

My contretemps with Kat seems like a million years ago. Since then I've tracked down Holly and about a million Dyers, but somehow managed to send my own husband away. I am reeling, yet still no closer to finding Aimee.

I burst into tears.

'Oh Jesus.' Michael sighs, his fury dissipating instantly.

I inhale his woody scent as I feel his big arms wrap around me. I don't fight him. I slump, my face resting on his chest. I'm reminded of doing this with my dad when I was just a little girl. It is comforting. No wonder Kat Quentin does the baby-doll act if this is her reward.

Life stops. We just stand on the doorstep, hugging.

A few minutes later, Michael has made me a cup of tea and I've fetched Caleb from his cot. Michael lies on the floor with him, playing cars while I pull myself together. I go up to the bathroom and wash my face, dabbing my red eyes. I brush my hair and pull it into a ponytail, so I look more presentable and less like the little girl who crawls out of the well in *The Ring*.

Coming back downstairs, I watch Michael with Caleb from the doorway. He's a natural father. He's entirely focused on my boy, his face cracked in a wide smile as they build a race track together. For a moment it feels like an alternative life; like somehow we have slipped into a parallel world, where Michael and I got married instead. But that never happened. I don't want it to have happened. A pang of pain sears its way through my chest. I've sent Mo away. My best friend, my only friend. How could I do that?

I force cheeriness into my tone. 'You know whether you're having a boy or girl yet?'

'We want the surprise.'

I proffer a wan smile. Of course they do. They'll probably be having one of those baby showers and a naming ceremony. They won't have a buggy, but a 'travel system'. Kat will buy all the baby's clothes from a catalogue and have their paediatrician on speed dial. Everything will be done by the book, the *right* way.

Michael settles back on my sofa, arms on the backrest, one foot balanced on his knee. He looks like he belongs. He watches Caleb crash all his cars into a tower he'd made. It all comes down, a rainbow of coloured wood.

'Are you okay, Sam?' Somehow his concern is worse than his anger.

'I'll apologise to Kat.'

'Yes. You will.' Michael tilts his head at me, amused as I shoot him a glance. 'Now answer my first question.'

'God, what is this? You're not a social worker, or a doctor. I'm fine.' I can't resist trying to rankle him. 'Kat know you're here?'

It doesn't work. 'Of course. We don't have any secrets.' He smiles at Caleb as my boy hands him a brick. 'What about you and your husband?'

Irritation prickles through me, making me jab back. 'You know Kat is a lot tougher than she makes out?'

'Oh, I know.'

'Then what's the deal?' I demand. 'The Mike I remember liked strong women, independent types. Not baby dolls.'

Michael stands, readying himself to leave. 'There's more than one way of being strong, you know. Weak, too.'

I don't like the sound of this. Was that a jibe? I can't decide. Michael moves to the door. I follow him through to the galley kitchen, as I show him out.

'You're always looking for trouble. You seem to think everyone is lying to everyone else, all the time. You were always lying back when we were kids, too. Why is that?'

Fury flowers in my belly. Who the hell does this guy think he is? 'I didn't lie all the time when we were kids!'

Michael says nothing. This somehow makes it worse; I can hear the wooden falseness of what I just said. Yes, I did lie all the time when I was a kid. But the others did too. The *Never Have I Ever* game was the rot that spoiled all of us. It changed us, sending us in directions we should never have gone. But that wasn't my fault. Aimee was the ringleader, not me.

Michael's brown eyes lock with mine as he turns back towards me at the front door. 'Whatever's bothering you, you need to forgive yourself.'

No words come to me. I just stare back at him, unable to speak. I can feel tears stinging the back of my eyes. My instincts had been good, all that way back when we were kids at Preacher's Rock. I should have just dumped Aimee and the group, hung out with Mike instead. Not because we were destined to be together forever; most teen romances go nowhere. But I might even have avoided what happened next. I might have had a different life. Instead I'd thrown Michael away, all for Aimee's approval. I'd ended up tainted forever.

But I can't admit this. Not now, not to Michael. Not when it's far too late and I've just sent Mo out the door.

I clear my throat. 'How do you know Kat definitely wasn't the note-sender?'

'I just know.'

Michael's certainty is gut-wrenching. I hadn't graced Mo with the same. Mo has been nothing but supportive. He has tried to help me, whilst juggling his own stuff too. I have barely taken note of his career in recent years, nor asked him how he's doing. For me, it's been all Caleb and my books. And now, these notes. Mo has been way too far down my list, for far too long.

'Kat's never even met Aimee, Sam. She would have been a little kid back then. She didn't even move to Ilfracombe

243

'til after university, anyway. Their paths would never have crossed. C'mon, you know this really.'

I do. I nod, averting my eyes.

He kisses me on the cheek; I feel the bristles on my skin. 'It will be okay.'

'I hope so.'

I close the door on him as he disappears back into the dark mouth of the night.

Thirty-six

The bell above the door tinkles.

On A Break is moderately busy. I have to pick my way over a couple of large dogs splayed between tables as two pensioners indulge in idle chitchat. A couple of lone mums drink coffees and eat croissants and scroll through their phones, their babies asleep in pushchairs beside them.

Some teenage girls gossip in the corner, breaking into hyena-like laughs. Their fashion sense is nineties, all neon colours and glitter. I feel young for noticing and old for realising the fashion has come around full cycle. One of them turns towards me and scowls, probably because I am not whom she expects. Why would I be? I am another grown-up, the enemy. All the same I feel weirdly crushed, just like I did back when I was a girl. Always the outsider.

Kat is not behind the counter; she must be out the back. I check my watch. I am conscious of the time ticking away. Lindy is bringing Caleb back for me at lunch. I've felt Mo's absence keenly in the past three days. I've realised before during his many business trips that I underestimate how much he does with Caleb: bathtimes, stories, playing, tidying and cleaning. This time it seems so much worse though. Probably because I am not sure if he will ever be coming back again.

A side door I hadn't noticed opens next to me. Kat staggers through, humming along with the radio. It's 'Crazy in Love', by Beyoncé. Seems appropriate, given how loved-up she and Michael are. This time I don't allow myself any cynical, snarky thoughts to go with my internal monologue.

'Let me get that for you.'

Before Kat can object, I wrestle it off her. It's a box of takeaway cups, so not heavy. It just would have been cumbersome with her pregnant belly in the way. Her brow furrows as she realises it's me, so I give her a reassuring smile as I take the box to the counter for her.

'What do you want?'

I plunge right in. 'I came to apologise.'

Kat stands there, like she thinks this is some kind of trap.

'Obviously you didn't send me those notes. I was stressed and acting out—' I catch myself. Lindy would not approve of me 'centring myself' in my apology. '—But that is an explanation, not an excuse. I'm sorry.'

Kat seems to mull over my words as she takes her place behind the counter.

She leans both hands on the wood, like a bartender. 'Okay, fine. You can go now.'

The symbolism of the barrier between us is not lost on me. She is in the weaker position; she's much smaller than me and hugely pregnant. She thinks I am weird, possibly unstable. Short of vaulting over the counter now though, I can't get to her.

Kat Quentin is afraid of me.

The realisation stops me in my tracks. Perhaps I have been behaving more out-of-character than I thought. No. Kat is a master manipulator, I already know that. Just because Michael likes playing daddy to her, doesn't change that. She is trying to make me doubt myself. I don't know why, but maybe she doesn't even have a reason. Perhaps it's just for sport. Aimee liked to mess with people for the thrill of it.

I can't resist. 'Just tell me one thing.'

Kat's rigid posture slumps, as if to say, *Here we go*.

'You've definitely never met Aimee Dyer?'

Kat rolls her eyes skyward. 'No. I didn't grow up round here, remember?'

I'm conscious of the one-woman queue behind me. 'But you must know the Dyers?'

Kat grits her teeth. It is clear she is counting to ten. 'Not really. I know the big shop up on the high street. Oh, and there was an Ethan Dyer living with his dad in the flat underneath mine. Before I moved in with Michael.'

That was the young lad fishing on the pier for mackerel. 'Yeah, met him. He's not seen her either.'

'Then I can't help you, Sam.'

One of the mums gets bored of waiting to pay for her coffee, so slams some change next to the till before grabbing her buggy and the child in it, muttering under her breath. Before Kat's attention can wander, I lean on the counter top. Kat takes this as a demonstration of aggression and takes a timid step back to keep the space between us. Yes, she is definitely afraid. I can use this. Before I examine the ethics of intimidating a pregnant woman with questions, I dive into the next one.

'So, why are *you* here?'

I can't believe I have never thought to look into Kat's background before now. So what if Kat had grown up in the North? It didn't mean she hadn't come here for holidays

as a child; or that she wasn't related to the Dyers somewhere. I search her face for clues. The local Dyers are
known for those pale blue eyes, the John Travolta-type cleft
so many have in their chins, male or female. I can't see a
familial resemblance, but that doesn't mean Kat doesn't
have Dyer DNA coursing through her veins.

Kat notices someone else over my shoulder, but I don't
turn. I can't allow the spell between us to break. I am
relying on other customers being far too British to queue-
jump and spirit her attention away.

'No big reason.' Kat appears to be regaining her confidence. She's irritated, bewildered. Or is she just a good
actress? I have suspected her of this previously. 'I worked
down here, during the summers at university. I liked being
by the sea. I met Michael. We got married. End of. Now,
can you please just go?'

A feeling of anti-climax seizes me as Kat turns her back
on me. Despite my reservations about Kat, something tells
me again she is telling the truth. Perhaps it's living with
the burden of others' actions in the past for so long myself.
I can't see that same heaviness in the slope of her shoulders,
or the way she holds her body. The dodgy Dyers all have
it, carrying their transgressions forward in their body
language, plain for all to see. In contrast, there had been
no secrets in Kat's eyes.

'Okay. Thanks anyway.'

Kat ignores me. Behind the counter, she grabs a bread
roll, starts buttering it. As she fills it with grated cheese
and pours a large glass of milk, déjà vu grabs me.

I've seen her do this before.

I whip around, but On A Break has the eclectic mix of
locals and tourists, young and old it had when I arrived.

My gaze strays back to the large window that faces onto the promenade. Sure enough, there is the homeless woman seated at one of the picnic tables outside. She's taken a notebook from one of her laundry bags. She writes in it with a stubby pencil, her face a picture of concentration.

Hang on.

It's not a notebook. It's an envelope.

I stalk out of On A Break, ahead of the oblivious Kat. The bell tinkles as I crash through the front door, onto the promenade. Single-minded, I slalom around the various tables in my way until I stand next to the homeless woman's. The sun behind me, she looks up blinking as my shadow falls across her.

But I can see her face clearly, including those eyes I had once known so well. In fact, everything is as clear as day now.

'Well look who it is,' I say, 'Aimee Dyer.'

Thirty-seven

'I know it's you, Aimee!'

I pinch her chin between two fingers, make her look at me. Her skin feels shockingly old, spongy. The lack of teeth in her mouth means pockets of flesh hang down, like a mastiff's. Old dirt fills her pores, creating large pimples like pinheads across her cheeks. I breathe through my mouth, trying to ignore the smell of the streets emanating from Aimee. Urine, ground-in dirt and tobacco.

'I don't know you!'

The homeless woman shrinks away from me, raising her elbows and shielding her face. But God help me, I don't stop. I grab a grimy wrist, pull her back towards me. On another table, two middle-aged women stare at us, open-mouthed, as they pour tea. The cups begin to overflow.

'You've been here all along, hiding in plain sight. Haven't you?' My fury makes way for tears, just as quickly. They track down my cheeks. 'Why have you been stalking me?'

The homeless woman stops struggling, but still says nothing. She won't look me in the eye. I'm reminded of a wild animal, playing dead. I can't connect this dirty, wretched creature with the Aimee I had known. Teenage Aimee had taken so much pride in her appearance. She'd taken good care of her body, too. Like at the chapel on the high street, I can smell the stink of booze on her, the tang of sickness. She does not seem long for this world.

'How can you do this to me?' I let go of her face, grab her by both shoulders. I fight the urge to cringe at the sensation of the fabric under my fingertips, stiff with dirt. 'Aimee, please. I just want a quiet life, a fresh start, with my family?'

As I say these words, another thought occurs to me. Aimee hadn't just been hiding from me. She must have broken off contact with her family as well. Yet she'd been here all along, under their very noses. I doubt the rest of them know she is here. They must think she is globe-trotting, just like she said; otherwise, why would every single Dyer I'd tracked down lie to me? In a family as big as theirs, you'd think at least one of them would break ranks or slip up along the way. Yet not even poor, drunk Frankie Dyer had given up the goods, yet he'd been cast out. That was some brand of clan loyalty.

Unless they really hadn't heard from Aimee in a long time.

'Why are you hiding from your family?' I try and soften my tone, in the hope she will confide in me. 'Have they done something? Maybe I can help you. Is that what you really want? Help?'

The homeless woman smiles. In her ruined face, her grin makes her look more like a witch than ever. 'Want to make yourself feel better, *Samantha*?'

I let go of her, like I've been stung. The way she says my name, I'm transported twenty-three years in a single moment. Aimee the bag lady is gone. Seated in her place is that teenager of old, twirling her long strings of beads, smirking at me.

'No.' My voice is small; I feel reduced. 'I want to help?'

Real life floods back in as the *hiss* of a double-decker bus hitting the brakes on the promenade grabs my attention. A group of Spanish students shout from the Clapping Circle. But it's not jay-walking teenagers who caused the vehicle to stop, but a small blue car. It careers around the bus and stops outside the Sunspot amusement arcade. Parking hastily, a man jumps out and comes running towards On A Break.

Michael.

I raise my hands in a supplicatory gesture, but he's not running towards me. He races straight past. I look behind me and see Kat has appeared on the threshold of the café, tears in her eyes. She must have called him. She looks angry and afraid, twisting her apron around in her well-manicured hands. I have to give it to her: she is very convincing.

Kat points straight at me. 'She just went nuts!'

Michael gives his wife a quick hug, smoothing her hair like a parent would a little girl's. She leans into him as best she can with her huge belly, closing her eyes. Though I'd tried to understand, my lip curls in distaste. Michael really does like playing the father figure. I would have wagered real money there's more to him than this. But maybe Lindy is right: maybe all men do want to play traditional roles like rescuer and hero.

'Samantha.'

My full name again. I feel a sense of alarm ripple down my spine as he lets go of Kat, advances towards me across the promenade.

I grab for the homeless woman. 'No, Michael. You don't understand. This is Aimee?'

The homeless woman leaps up from the table. She bustles about, averting her eyes from the scene and gathering up her things. There's a babble of voices all around us. The two older ladies sound off very loudly, whilst the Spanish students have made it across the road on their way to the arcade. They hoot and laugh, jostling one another as they file past us.

Michael regards me with pursed, bloodless lips. His eyes bulge with anger, but he moves aside and addresses the homeless woman instead.

'I'm so sorry.'

Michael moves very carefully towards Aimee. He helps her put the last of her things into one of her laundry bags. He reaches in his back pocket, pulling a twenty-pound note from his wallet. He proffers it to her. The homeless woman accepts the money and makes a gesture of thanks, shuffling off without a backwards glance.

Michael finally has me in his sights. 'Come with me.'

Thirty-eight

'That was Aimee back there, Michael.'

I pick at the cardboard beer mat in front of me. We're in the Admiral Collingwood pub a short distance down from the main promenade. We sit up in the impressive roof garden, surrounded by white-washed walls, bright green Astroturf under our feet. The word PEACE clearly visible on Capstone Hill opposite, its tarmac path zigzagging up towards a Union Jack flying at the top in the breeze.

Michael sighs. 'It wasn't Aimee.'

'She knew me. She called me Samantha!'

'Did she, though?'

Anger bursts through me as I hear the doubt in Michael's voice. Even so, I can feel the conviction inside me deflate. I recall the curve of the homeless woman's toothless mouth, the way she'd transformed into sixteen-year-old Aimee, right in front of my eyes. That wasn't possible, so maybe I *had* imagined her calling me 'Samantha' too? Perhaps moving back has been messing with my mind, just like Mo had said. Am I having some kind of breakdown?

Michael nurses half a Coke. 'Her name's Jaye something. She's been homeless for years, rattling around town, long before I joined the force. We've tried helping her, but you know how it is. Never enough money, or resources, or whatever. Government never gives a shit about the provinces. They think we're just a bunch of yokels.'

I'm still not quite ready to let it go. 'She's got the same eyes as Aimee.'

'That's because she's a bloody Dyer as well.' Michael raises his voice, then takes a deep breath to calm himself. 'Christ, Sam, you know how big that family is. You also know they're always at one another's throats. Frankie and Bill falling out cut the family in half. Frankie came off worse, obviously. Bill was always the brains. Anyway, Jaye likes a drink too much, just like her dad.'

'So, she's Frankie's daughter.' An image of Bill's brother, staring into his pint in the Bunch of Grapes sears through my brain. 'Why doesn't he help her? He looked down and out as well, but not as much as her.'

'Who knows? The police aren't a counselling service. The best we can do is try and ensure she doesn't come to any harm.'

Michael looks world-weary all of a sudden. I place my hand on top of his. He lets me, for all of ten seconds before removing it. He still looks irritated with me.

'Kat told me you tried to interrogate her again. Couldn't you have just apologised and be done with it?'

Embarrassment surges through me, now. 'Yeah. Not my finest hour. But did she have to make such a song and dance back there?'

I want him to smile, agree that Kat had overreacted about me accosting Jaye outside On A Break. But Michael's expression is stony.

'Kat grew up in a house with really bad domestic abuse. Her father used to scream and shout most days, throw stuff at her and her brothers. Have them walk around on eggshells, afraid of the next outburst. He never hit them, but that wasn't the point. Raised voices and verbal violence are actually really painful for her to witness.'

Verbal violence. Is there such a thing? Sounds like woke pop psychology to me. Words can't wound, only actions can. But my treacherous brain connects more dots, against my will: Wendy raging at Ruby and Holly at their home, all of us cringing as she'd bellow up the stairs at us. Wendy's endless, dark fury and mocking *had* felt like violence. I guess Kat had decided to break the mould of her own background and choose the opposite of her father in Michael. I feel ashamed, assuming Kat had been play-acting.

'I'm sorry.'

Michael gives an almost imperceptible shake of his head as he rises from his seat. 'It's not me you need to apologise to, but I think it's better if you leave Kat alone from now on. Don't go back to On A Break.'

Then there's only an empty space next to me. I watch him stride across the roof garden and trot down the stairs. I stare at my glass, watch the bubbles rise to the surface like thoughts. I am alone, just like poor, sad Frankie Dyer. His secret had torn the Dyer family apart; made him an outcast. It didn't seem fair that Aimee had wanted nothing to do with him; whether she liked it or not, he was her father. Presumably she'd rejected Jaye, too. Yet they'd been sisters. Maybe Bill had made Aimee choose. Perhaps that was why Aimee had really left? She'd cut her losses, got out of that dysfunctional family forever.

I return home, still feeling drained and tearful. After lunch, Lindy appears with Caleb as promised, full of false cheer and wary with it. I can't blame her. The last time we'd spoken in any detail, I'd slammed the front door in her face. I'd barely spoken to her this morning either, handing over Caleb with grunted instructions and a tepid goodbye.

I dive straight in, before I lose my nerve. 'I'm really sorry, Mum.'

Mum takes my apology in good humour, just as I know she will. 'That's all right, darling. You've been under a lot of stress with the move and new book. Not to mention all that stuff about the notes.'

Lindy's never been one to hold grudges, not like me. I am my father's daughter, after all. Poor Mo, he never stood a chance.

'Do you want to come in?' I take Caleb in my arms, accepting his nappy bag as well.

Mum dithers on the doorstep, fiddling with the dream-catcher around her neck. 'I'd love to, darling. But I, er, have a date tonight. Off one of those app things.'

My face must have been a picture of alarm because Lindy laughs.

'Not that sex one. One of the nice ones. I decided it was time to y'know, get back on the horse so to speak. Your dad has been gone a long time, Samantha. You're not mad, are you?'

I smile. 'Of course not.'

In all honesty, I'm more surprised Lindy is using an app. Not because she is one of those old people who doesn't understand technology. She understands it perfectly well; she just doesn't like it. She said phones 'severed human connections and fragmented society'. It took about a year of convincing to get her to send a text message.

Mum leaves, promising to tell me more about her date the next morning over a cup of tea. I am pleased for her, but close the door fretting about her getting stood up. Or worse, going out with someone selfish and unsuitable.

Like me.

I've treated Mo like crap. He is a good man, who has stood by me and my dreams, through thick and thin. In contrast, I have been self-focused and insular, at best. He doesn't deserve a wife like me.

I stare at my mobile, working up the courage to call him. But I am a coward, too; I couldn't bear it if he rejected my call. I feed Caleb his tea, then put him in the bath. As I watch him splashing with his ducks, I work through the events of the past three weeks in my mind.

I'm no closer to finding Aimee, but it's obvious that if she's going to reveal herself, she would have by now. I grasp understanding at last, better late than never.

Aimee had another endgame in mind all along. That's why I'd failed to flush her out; she'd *never* wanted to see me. She probably *was* in Australia too, on the other side of the world. Why not? Thousands of Brits emigrate there every year. As Ruby had said, the lifestyle would suit her: non-stop surf bums and barbecues on the beach. Knowing Aimee, she probably did steal the money to get there, or got one of her many beaus to pay for her, just like Michael had suggested.

Aimee's plan to mess with me would have been simple. She could have left a bunch of letters for one of those many cousins of hers to deliver. She would have directed one or more of them to break my kitchen window and creep around my house. One of them would have set the fire in the wastepaper can and set the smoke alarm off, moments before my car pulled up in the driveway. They'd all done far worse.

Now Aimee would be thousands of miles away, cocktail in hand, as one of her many relatives filled her in on her campaign of terror, orchestrated from afar. Her motive is not difficult to work out. Aimee had always been a bully. She'd wanted to drag me back into the past, get between me and my family. She would have seen me online, how I've moved back to Ilfracombe; geographical distance is not the type of barrier it once was, now we live in a globalised world.

Her plan had worked.

The past three weeks have been excruciating. I've been jumping at shadows, afraid for my own safety and my family's. I'd talked to and been rejected by Ruby and Maddy, all over again. I've been careering around town accusing innocent people like Kat Quentin, doubting my own sanity. I've even let the rot sink into my own marriage, sending Mo to Ireland with a flea in his ear.

I have to try and put all this right.

As soon as Caleb is in his bed, I pour myself a stiff drink for Dutch Courage. Ten minutes after downing two more, I dial Mo's number. I'm so anxious to speak to him, apologise. I pray it's not too late. It can't be. He'd been so desperate to not throw it all away. Unlike me. I don't deserve a man like Mo, but Caleb deserves a daddy who is a good man. I owe it to my boy to try and fix this.

The phone rings. I close my eyes in disappointment as the voicemail kicks in.

'Hi, this is Mo. Sorry I can't take your message right now but leave a message after the beep and I'll get back to you.'

I fight the urge to ring off. As predicted, the alcohol loosens my tongue. I start slow, but warm up as I go along. I begin by telling him he's absolutely right (I know he will

259

like that). I tell him I *have* been holding back. I have allowed old ghosts to come between us. I tell him that when he comes back from Ireland, I promise I will tell him everything.

Fear slices through my chest as I say these words. I would be laying bare the real Sam for Mo to see for the first time. I am quite literally changing the habit of a life-time, just like Aimee's note and rock through the window had said. Aimee had stolen my voice all those years ago and set me running. My whole life and viewpoint were warped out of shape that night. Aimee has influenced the last twenty-three years of my life, but no more. I'm tired of jumping before I am pushed; of sabotaging my life and relationships because of her. I can't flush my marriage away. I am ready at last for the real fresh start Mo has craved for ages.

I finish my message and hang up. I wait an hour, drinking more, hoping Mo will call me back right away. But perhaps he hasn't checked his phone, or maybe he's just thinking through what I've said. Words are cheap, after all. I should know that, being a writer. I will have to prove to him I mean what I say with actions, when he returns.

I go to bed.

Thirty-nine

For once my sleep is dreamless. There are no nightmares of being buried alive; nor do I awake with crying echoing in my ears, or shadow-girls in the corner of the room.

I wake around two a.m. My mouth is dry, the start of a hangover headache banging in my skull. As I feel around for my glass of water, I catch sight of something that makes me sit up, heart hammering in fear. I'm frozen for a second, unable to move. I gaze in horror from my bed. My sights are fixed on the dressing table opposite, its mirror illuminated by the moon that peeks through the dormer window. Something is written on the mirror in lipstick.

Never Have I Ever lost someone I love. Your turn Sam.

Mo? Caleb.

I toss the covers aside and run across the landing to Caleb's room. Before I even get there, I know I will find him gone. The little bundle under the covers is missing, but impotent hope means I snatch up his coverlet anyway. He is not in his cot.

Caleb is gone.

'Caleb! Caleb, sweetheart, come out for Mummy!'

Panic-struck, I check under the cot, then take in the room, trying to spot him. I open the wardrobe, push over his toybox, in case he's somehow got out by himself and is hiding. Then I spot something else. It's right in the middle of the new cream carpeting, placed so painstakingly it has to be on purpose.

A black, sooty shoeprint.

'Aimee, are you here? You bring my boy back!' I scream.

I find another on the landing that I'd run straight past in my panic. It points towards the stairs, as obvious as an arrow. There are more on the stairs, past the second storey towards the ground floor. Like I'd said throughout this farrago, Aimee has always had a flair for the dramatic. But does this mean she is actually here, or one of her minions?

Adrenaline surges around my body as I try and make sense of what message Aimee could be sending me this time. I'd obviously got it so badly wrong that Aimee didn't want to confront me after all.

She has my son!

I emerge from the stairs in the hall, where I find the trail again. Looking ahead, I realise it leads towards Mo's man-cave in the old coal cellar. It only has one door in and out. Is she leading me into a trap?

I grab a knife from the kitchen, just in case. I hesitate at the top of the stairs before gripping the banister and making my way down. The smell of old smoke becomes stronger, step by step.

'None of this needs to happen, Aimee!' I holler ahead. 'Just let Caleb come to the bottom of the steps. I will let you go. I swear.'

I burst into Mo's man-cave, hoping to grab the element of surprise. Instead, it is me who is shocked.

The draught is worse now. A chilly breeze rattles

around the room, rain soaking into the burned rug Lindy and I had rolled out for Mo along the floor. Too late, I grasp how Aimee has been coming and going in my house.

The coal chute.

I move forward, momentarily unable to process what I am seeing. Just as I had thought, I'd been as fastidious about security as I'd always been in London. But I'd forgotten one key detail, because I hadn't even noticed it. The coal chute cover is white-washed just like the room's walls.

Hiding in plain sight.

The chute stands open now, taunting me: in the past, the coal merchant would have opened it up and nuggets of coal would have cascaded into the cellar below. I can see the back of the shiny aluminium chute snaking up into the garden above. The white-washed plywood cover is discarded next to Mo's desk. I'd never thought about how the chute leads from the small cellar, up into the garden and vice versa. No wonder it had been so damn cold in the house; cold air has been moving around the ground floor.

I approach it, knife ready. Just in case Aimee is still in there, waiting to jump back down. She's not. Just two foot by four foot across, a child, or a very thin woman, could fit through easily. Choking on a sob, I hear my own snivelling cries at last. A hundred different scenarios race through my brain: Caleb, his face covered in blood. Or pitched from the headland, into the sea. Or in the dark and alone, crying for me.

My precious boy.

I look down at my feet. Another note lies on the white-washed bricks. Everything has led to this moment. I had brought him here, straight into the mouth of danger, then failed to keep him safe. What kind of mother am I?

I snatch up the note.

You know where to go.

Forty

I'm tucking my pyjama bottoms into my boots to leave the house before I even think it through. I falter in the hallway. The panic in my chest flutters back and forth like a bird in a cage: I take small, short gasps. I feel light-headed. I grab the banister and stumble upwards. I fall to my hands and knees. I hiss with pain as friction burns the palm of my bad hand. I suck it up and keep going.

Back to my bedroom. I grab my phone from the night-stand where it's plugged in. Mo's name flashes up on the screen. I hesitate, my finger hovering over it. There's a notification with his picture. I click on it, noting it had been sent about forty minutes ago. The text fills the screen:

We can get through this. I love you so much.
Going to the airport now. I'll be back as soon as I can. Xxx

I'm confused for a second; how could Mo know Caleb is missing before I do? Then I recall spilling my guts out to Mo on voicemail just three or four hours earlier. It seems so long ago. Then, anything had seemed possible. Now our little boy is missing, on my watch. He could be dead. No. Aimee might be a psychopath, but she couldn't hurt a child. Could she? I can't concentrate on the thoughts clamouring their way through my brain.

Caleb must be so scared, he's with a stranger. What the hell am I doing? I should call the police!

I know I can't. On the back of Aimee's note by the coal chute, she had scrawled, *COME ALONE* in capital letters. She doesn't say what she would do to Caleb if I call them, but she doesn't have to. I understand the threat as easily as I need oxygen to breathe. If it's Aimee who has Caleb, she might not be alone; one of her family members could be helping her, maybe even more than one. Dyers hate the police. The sight of blue lights could make them do anything. I can't risk Caleb's life. I have to do what she says.

I must go by myself.

I clatter down the stairs again, grabbing my car keys as I go. I make it out into the night, looking up at the skies. It's only the first few days of September, but the air is already autumnal. Leaves skitter across the lawn in the breeze. Against my will, the night of the summer party returns to me as I run towards my car.

The sound of teenagers whooping and singing to the Foo Fighters' 'I'll Stick Around'. Fairy lights strung up in the trees; plastic barrels of water to keep beers and bottles chilled. Unlike the very cold Spring Break Blowout, the turn-out was bigger; more alcohol was flowing. Aimee had already gone off with one of Felix's friends but returned. Her hair was mussed up and her make-up smeared; there was a dreamy expression in her eyes.

Maddy and Ruby did a weird combination of the River Dance and the Can-Can around the bonfire with Holly and some of the other younger girls. Holly flung her arms around her bolshy friend Jess. Now they were all spinning, round and round, cackling with glee. I watched, a wistful smile on my face.

Whatever had happened since the Never Have I Ever *game began, I would miss when I moved to London.*

The spell of the past breaks as I press the key fob in my hand. The vehicle's lights turn on automatically, the alarm system chirruping softly as the doors unlock. It had been that past vision of Holly at the bonfire that had returned to me, in Caleb's room. Holly had revealed herself as N1Fan in Costa the other day; could she have taken Caleb? I banish the thought. I need to focus. This has had Aimee's fingerprints on it since the beginning.

I slide into the driver's seat, my breaths harsh and rasping. I swipe through my phone, activating its Sat-Nav app, before putting it in the holder on the dashboard. I attempt to put the key in the ignition with shaking hands. It takes me three tries. As the engine finally kickstarts to life, I do a wonky three-point turn off the driveway, following the robotic voice of the Sat-Nav as it guides me towards my destination.

I try to take soothing breaths as I drive, calm the thundering of my heartbeat in my chest. I can hear the blood pounding in my ears. I have that sense of being outside my own body again, looking down at myself. I'd felt like this so often as a teenager, usually before being egged on to do something outrageous by Aimee. Now she is forcing me into something against my will all over again. I feel the familiar sting of tears. I grind the heel of my good hand into my eyes, gritting my teeth. I can't give up now. My little boy's depending on me. I can't bear the thought of Caleb scared, or worse, hurt by Aimee.

The streetlamps disappear as I turn into a small road, a canopy of trees blocking out the rain and moon above.

The headlights illuminate only a few feet ahead of the vehicle. The inside of the car is plunged into the gloom. My face is lit only by the instruments on the dashboard, the screen of my phone. My fear begins to recede as a dark, furious calm settles over me. I had spent years beholden to Aimee and her whims when we were teenagers. She'd bullied me mercilessly, having me second-guess everything about myself; my friends; my place in the world. She'd taken it all. Now she wants my child as well? *Never.*

It all ends, tonight.

Whatever had happened between me and Aimee in the past, Caleb is an innocent. So is Mo. I'm a lioness, going to rescue my cub. Enough is enough. A gate looms out of the darkness, lit up by the car headlights:

EASTERBROOK FARM

Where it all began.

Forty-one

My boots squelch in the mud as I leave the car at the gate. I can't take the vehicle any further. Huge chains are looped around the gate and its fence posts along with liberal twists of barbed wire. Next to *EASTERBROOK FARM* are various hand-painted signs reading *KEEP OUT* and *NO TRESPASSING*. They are decaying, broken down, letters missing in places. The gate itself is rusty; it hasn't been opened in years.

I can't see any lights on up ahead: where are the old barns, the main farmhouse? I can't tell. I can't even hear the soft whisper of the tide beyond the headland. The last time I had been here, the bonfire could have been seen for miles around. In my mind's eye, I see Will's older brother Felix slosh a can of petrol over the remaining unburned parts. The conflagration grows even higher. Felix was *technically* supervising the fire: he was standing next to it, but he was no responsible adult. He brought out a metal flask of whiskey and cigarette lighter from his pocket. He swilled alcohol around his mouth, then spat it out over his open lighter flame, creating that plume of fire like a 'dragon's breath'. It made the two younger girls next to him, Holly and her friend with the auburn hair, scream with delight. His legendary status as a party-giver was safe, much to Will's chagrin.

Now though, the drizzle soaks my face and hair. Wind whistles in my ears as my heart pounds in my chest. I have no coat; I am already cold, my pyjamas sticking to my bare skin. Leaving the car door open, I use the light to make my way around to the car boot. I pull it open and scrabble about inside.

I am grateful to Mo that he plans ahead so much. Inside is a large torch, a snow shovel and a selection of other tools. I grab the shovel, but it's too heavy to hold with the torch as well. I can't leave the torch behind, so I need to find a substitute weapon. Metal clinks as I search through the tools. I discover a telescopic wheel wrench, for undoing the bolts on tyres when changing them. It's still in its wrapper. Despite everything, I feel an absurd, simultaneous rush of both sympathy and affection for my husband as I pull off the plastic and cardboard. Typical Mo: he knows what he needs but has no clue how to use it. Another thing we have in common.

I turn the torch on as I shut the boot and the car door. The darkness rushes in at me, but I am single-minded, my sights set up ahead. I post the wheel wrench through a gap in the fence and put the torch in my mouth as I clamber over, as gingerly as I can. The bite of steel wire pierces one of my palms. I feel, rather than hear, the rip of fabric as my pyjama leg catches on some more barbed wire. But these are minor concerns. My attention is still fixed on where I think the farmhouse should be, or at least one of the barns.

The torchlight dances on the ground as my boots slosh through the mud. Though I sweep it left and right, I can't see any animal prints up ahead, nor any animals in the fields. Has this place been abandoned? As my boots find concrete, I stagger onto something metal. Red flashes up from under my feet in the light of the torch. It's another abandoned *KEEP OUT* sign, but official this time. It reads *POLICE – FOOT-AND-MOUTH AREA STARTS HERE.* Of course. The Jacksons had been affluent but had taken a battering like most beef and dairy farmers in the nineties, thanks to the spectre of so-called 'mad cow disease'. Reeling from that assault, foot-and-mouth must have been the final nail in the coffin.

The moon finally appears from behind cloud cover, illuminating the courtyard in its pale light. The farmhouse is revealed, its single-pane windows broken eyes. A faded *FOR SALE* sign boards up one of them. The front door hangs off its hinges. From a safe distance, I peer into the dark corridor. Like most old rural farmhouses, the building is low and dark and labyrinthine. There will be plenty of places for Aimee to hide in there. The old barn, where Will and Felix held the big summer party, looms out of the darkness to the left of the old farmhouse. I decide to check there first. My left fist tightens around the shiny new wheel wrench.

I creep towards the big doors of the barn, which are ajar. I pause, trying to listen out for Caleb's voice, or for his crying. I am both hopeful and alarmed to hear nothing from my boy. Does this mean he's unconcerned and waiting for me? Or that he's dead? I dare not follow this thread in my mind to its conclusion. I will fall apart and lose my nerve.

My weapon dangles by my side, ready to swing over my head like a baseball bat. I know I will bring it down on Aimee's skull if I must. I pray I don't have to. I don't pause to open the rotten, wooden doors; they'd scrape across the concrete and alert anyone inside. I click the torch off, just in case, and squint into the gloom, waiting for my eyes to adjust. A pang of nostalgia pierces through me as I spot one of those plastic barrels we used to store our beer in; there's even a string of old lanterns, broken on the floor.

I blink; ghosts of the past appear like bright spots in front of my eyes. The gloom becomes warm and welcoming, like I'd stepped back in time. Groups of teens sing and laugh, arms round one another. Ruby and Maddy are there, the kiss at the Tunnels party and Aimee's cruel dare consigned to the past. They dance in the middle of a circle of haybales. They're taking off Mia Wallace and Vincent Vega's routine at Jack Rabbit Slim's in *Pulp Fiction*. All our friends clap and hoot.

'It never needed to be like this. This is your fault, Sam.'

Aimee is right next to me, smirking as ever. I startle, flinching away from her. Pain bursts through my shoulder as I back, hard into one of the barn doors. As my mind reels, more memories flood through my panicking mind, crowding out my rational thoughts.

At the summer party, I flitted in and out of the throng, the outsider as usual. I jumped up and down to the music. Then I staggered off to find more to drink. Too late, I realised I'd left the other party-goers behind, meandering off the well-worn path between the bonfire and the barn. Damn it. *With only the blind optimism of the very tipsy, I trudged onwards for another five minutes or so into the almost pitch black. I lurched backwards from shadow that loomed out towards me: just an outcrop of rocks.* Phew.

A small copse of trees extended their branches, their twigs scraping my skin. Purple darkness swirled in front of my drunken eyes; I could barely see my hand in front of my face. I giggled, then a wave of sadness engulfed me again. This was my last party, ever; my old life was over. This time next year, I would be somewhere else, with God knows who. Getting lost in the dark felt like the creepiest metaphor ever when everything felt so uncertain.

Involuntary tears sprang up in my eyes. I reeled forwards into the darkness, but my foot found only air. I windmilled my arms, just as a tall shadow lurched out of the darkness, crashing into me. There was the sound of something metal, as my shoes kicked it. Corrugated iron? My inebriated brain could barely make sense of any of it. Panic burst through my mind as a last thought surfaced.

I'm falling.

'Watch out!'

But I hadn't fallen. Instead, hands had grabbed me as we'd stumbled. We both fell onto the grass and gorse with a whoomph. *I giggled as I heard a male voice utter a soft curse, then shrieked as I sensed, rather than heard, the soft fall of earth into a darker patch of shadow nearby. Whatever it was, we'd just missed it by a fraction of an inch.*

'Sam? That you?'

Even though I couldn't see his face, Mike's voice was instantly recognisable, like a hug from an old friend. Music still thumped from the barn and farmyard beyond, though whoever was DJing had to be going for a break in the moshing. Teens wailed 'Mr. Jones' by the Counting Crows, into the night.

'What the hell just happened?' *I felt his rough fingertips on my face in the darkness.*

'You nearly walked straight into a dried-up old well, you idiot.' *Mike's words were playful, despite his rebuke.* 'I saved you!'

273

'My hero,' I laughed.

All inhibitions gone thanks to alcohol, I rolled over, so I was lying across his chest. I pressed my lips against his, my tongue teasing his mouth open.

'Oh, hello.'

I was sure I could hear the smile in his voice as I broke off the kiss. I grinned too, even though I knew he couldn't see my face either. I'd felt reckless; it was my last night ever in Devon, with my old friends. I wanted it to include Mike, too.

'Let's go somewhere.'

Abruptly, Mike's hands snaked out of the darkness, pushed me off him. 'You forget what happened last time, at the Tunnels? You made out with Will right in front of me.'

My drunken brain took a moment to catch up with Mike's words. I couldn't work out why I was on my knees in the grass again. I chuckled, trying to save face.

'That was ages ago.'

'You think it's funny?' Michael sounded like he couldn't believe what he was hearing. 'You think you can just pick up where you left off? I should have known with you.'

What the hell was that supposed to mean? I pushed down my own hurt and sent out a pre-emptive strike.

'As if. Call it one for the road. I'm leaving tomorrow, you won't see me again.'

'Oh, fuck you, Sam.'

'Fuck you, too!'

There was no answer.

Even without being able to see him in the dark, I knew Mike had stomped off, without me. I swung around, moving forward inch by inch, still trying to get my bearings. I didn't get very far. I screamed and flinched as another shadow loomed out of *the darkness. My terrified brain turned its expression into a demonic face, its eye red like fiery flames.*

Aimee was standing right next to me, her torch under her chin, her visage twisted in a hideous mocking jeer.

I gasp as reality returns to me, stinging like a slap in the face. The decaying barn is deserted. The stench of old animal shit, damp and decomposing haybales makes me wrinkle my nostrils in distaste. As this realisation surfaces in my brain, teen Aimee's presence breaks like a soap bubble. She disappears.

I circle the old barn, then the 'new' barn that is now in as poor a state as the first. Inside, it's deserted too, all its farm equipment gone. The cattle stalls stand empty. There are no vehicles under the car port, or out the front of the farmhouse. The bailiffs would no doubt have stripped the place to raise as much capital on the Jacksons' debt as possible. I turn my attentions back towards the farmhouse. I don't want to go inside. I have no choice.

I have to, for my precious boy.

Forty-two

I tuck my soaking-wet hair behind my ears. I creep towards the front door of the broken-down farmhouse and slip inside. The hallway is wide, with four doors off it. I discover it's raining inside, too: there's a huge hole in the roof. I can see straight through, to the night skies and the stars beyond. Water drips down from a mezzanine landing, which is broken off. The wooden stairs have collapsed entirely: they lie in a pile of timber and rubble against the wall. There's no way Aimee could have got Caleb up there. That's something, at least.

My foot connects with a loose floorboard and it creaks under my weight, like something from a horror film. I am past caring. Aware the element of surprise is long gone, I crash into the hallway wielding my wheel wrench like a club, hollering as I go.

'Aimee, you bring Caleb out to me. Now.'

No answer.

I check each room, closing the doors as I go. That way Aimee can't circle through the house behind me, without opening one. In the living room there is just a faded old armchair, which erupts with mice that race for the skirting boards as my shadow falls on it. I give an involuntary cry of disgust, waving the wheel wrench after them in a futile gesture of aggression.

There's a second reception room, but again there is nothing inside bar a couple of old seventies-style sideboards with a few sad, presumably worthless figurines on top. Next to that, a downstairs toilet, with one of those old-fashioned hanging cisterns and a stained sink. A sliver of Body Shop apple soap is left in the soap dish, another echo of a simpler time.

Force of habit makes me reach for the light switch in the kitchen. It doesn't turn on. I sweep my torch across the big room and jump backwards as eyes are reflected back at me. They're not human, but animal: a small, mangy fox cub stops eating its pathetic rat meal and freezes where it is. When it realises I am not going to come blundering into the kitchen, it makes a break for the back door, squeezing out through the cat flap.

Tears of angry frustration burst from me now. I pull the note Aimee had left by the coal chute out of my pyjama pocket: *You know where to go.* I'd felt sure she would have brought Caleb here, back to Easterbrook Farm. It's the scene of Aimee's crime. But it looks like I am wrong. Panic engulfs me. Have I fallen into another of Aimee's traps? Perhaps she has sent me here on purpose, so she can do whatever it is she wants with Caleb, unhindered. *Please, no.*

'Your face!'

Up in the copse in the dark by the old well, Aimee had dissolved into giggles. I sighed with relief. She no longer looked like a demon to me, even though I knew her heart was as black as any creature of the night's. She hooted with laughter, clapping me on the back. I knew she wasn't laughing with me, but at me, but I played along anyway. As always.

'How about drunk Twister in the barn?' I grinned.

Aimee shook her head in disapproval. 'Oh, Sam. Have you forgotten already?'

Trepidation felt like a brick in my stomach. 'Forgotten what?'

Ruby appeared next, face flushed and happy. Maddy was not far behind. On the horizon behind them, Felix Jackson had set a whole petrol can alight. Will kicked it across the field as a small crowd gathered, egging both brothers on. Looking back now as an adult, I marvel at how neither of them ever lost a foot. Pure dumb luck.

Aimee stood aside and indicated two drunk girls in denim shorts in the distance. They spun around and around next to the bonfire, near-empty beer bottles in their hands. One was Holly 'Blobby', Ruby's sister. The other, her friend with the auburn hair.

'Jess Pedlar again,' Aimee drawled. 'I'm sick of that little cunt and her lies about my family.'

Aimee fixed Ruby and Maddy in her sights. 'Hey girls, how about that dare of dares we talked about, tonight?'

Maddy shrugged, non-committal. Ruby looked on, slack-faced. I feigned nonchalance too. I wanted to ask Aimee what she was going on about, but I kept my lips sealed. Last time I'd questioned her, she'd thrown a drink in my face, almost put another Never Have I Ever dare on me. Aimee had always been extra malicious when she'd been drinking. Jess could handle herself, that much was obvious. She was not afraid to stand up to Aimee; she was brave. That was why Aimee couldn't stand her. Simple. Thinking about that night twenty-three years on I wish I had queried her in more detail, but it had been my last party; my last ever night with Ruby and Maddy. I hadn't wanted anything to spoil it. That was understandable. It wasn't like I'd even known Jess or Blobby, not really.

'Then we're agreed.' Aimee grinned, her round face spotlit as

278

the moon reappeared from behind its cloud covers at last. 'It's time.'

I was none the wiser. 'What's the dare?'

All four of us looked to each other. My stomach twisted in protest, but I forced myself to concentrate. Because as always, I went along with Aimee. All four of us put our hands in a circle and recited Aimee's dare.

'Never Have I Ever taught Jess Pedlar a lesson she won't forget.'

Now, searching Easterbrook Farm to rescue my only child, I find myself muttering the same. Regrets ricochet around my mind. None of this should have happened. I should have been stronger. What if I had stood up to Aimee before it even began? Maybe I could have stopped what happened that night. Caleb would have been safe from this vendetta. Nausea paints the back of my throat. Maybe I am already too late. Dread in my heart, I turn the torchlight away from the farm, towards the headland beyond.

I know where she's taken my boy.

Forty-three

My realisation made about where Aimee has taken Caleb, I can't get there fast enough. I blunder about in the rain, shining my light around the farmyard, slip-sliding my way across the muck. Dark shapes loom out of the gloom as I trudge through the thick mud, past the barns, back out towards the headland.

There were the old lights, designed to lead back to the barns and the farmyard.

There was Felix Jackson holding court with his awesome dragon breath.

There was the bonfire.

There's a massive pile of kindling still there. At least, that's what I think it is, until I gain more ground and my weak torchlight picks out the details.

I scream.

Adrenaline floods through me, leaving me weak in its wake. The pile is made up of the bones of slaughtered farm animals. I remember the huge pyres of carcasses I'd seen on the news during the foot-and-mouth crisis, the black plumes of smoke spiralling up into the sky. Now weathered and worn by the passage of the last eighteen years, broken down and dark with age. The skulls of cattle and sheep, empty eye sockets and open mouths, left to moulder on the hillside. Creepy, yes, but they can't hurt me.

My boot sticks and suddenly my foot is free. I fall, face and hands first in the mud. The bandage on my hand is soaked instantly. Shrieking with frustration and fear, I stagger up again, making a grab for my torch. I use a clean patch of my pyjama top to clean the lens. I breathe a sigh of relief as it switches back on. I won't get far without it, though I am not getting far enough, quickly enough, even with it.

I mentally catalogue everything in front and behind me, working out exactly where I am in the darkness. I need to be able to get back to my car, when – not if – I get Caleb back. He will be cold, frightened. I can't delay. Still I flounder. I am finding it difficult to pick out the details in the darkness. I know panic is creating a fog inside my brain.

I have to make it back to the copse, where I last saw Mike that night.

I stand still, try to catch my breath as the drizzle adds to the mud soaking through my thin pyjamas. As panicked, rasping breath goes in and out, I find myself zoning out from the chilling wind of British summertime up on the headland; from the pain of the cold in my extremities; from the darkness surrounding me. I have to get my bearings. I can't waste any more time, going in the wrong direction.

Finally I work out where I am. It's enough to discern where I need to go.

There.

I run, as fast as I possibly can towards my son. I fight my way through the mud, up towards the headland and the small outcrop of rocks at the top. It feels as if the land itself is fighting me. The torchlight bounces on the ground. Pain works its ways up my calves, into the backs of my legs and pelvis. Water sloshes in my boots, my feet feel numb. But still I don't give up. I gulp in air and rain, my face burns with the cold. It's only the start of September, how can the temperature have dropped and the weather turn so rapidly? This ridiculous, incongruous thought is chased away just as quickly. Aimee has my baby. I have to get to him, save him.

What if I am too late? Please God, no!

I slow down as the copse of trees swims into view. It's bigger than I remember it, but that's because over two decades have passed since I was last here. The juvenile saplings have been left to their own devices and are now strong, robust ash trees with gnarled trunks and prominent roots lifting up out of the ground. Some of their leaves are turning for the autumn: on the ground, a mix of red and yellow leaves mark my way like over-sized confetti.

'Aimee!' I attempt to tighten my grip on the torch in my left hand. My hands are so cold, I fear it will slip right through my fingers. 'Aimee, you come out here. Now!'

Still no answer.

I knew there wouldn't be. She would want to do this, standing over the very place we'd last all seen one another. That flair for the dramatic she has will have demanded it. I can see a soft light flickering inside the copse. She is in there.

Let my boy be in there, too. Pleasepleaseplease.

I take a deep breath, steeling myself. This is it. The wheel wrench hangs loosely in my injured right hand. I wonder if my hand is too badly burned to grip a weapon properly, or even if I have it in me to fight back at all. Yes, DI Robyn Dallas would do whatever it takes, even if she was injured. So will I.

Under the ominous, creaking branches of the trees, I stride into the copse. I keep my arms up, ready to bring the wheel wrench down on skulls or bodies, sure she or some other Dyer family member will come running at me.

No one does.

I falter. Inside the copse, there seems to be only shadows. But then my eyes start to pick out the details. In the centre of the trees, an old storm lantern: a large, thick wax candle flickers behind the glass. In the flickering light, a person's silhouette. It rocks back and forth, humming an old nineties Ibiza tune, its face in darkness.

'Aimee?' My voice cracks.

The shadow steps forward. My eyes are drawn to Caleb in its arms, checking to see if my precious boy is all right. Dread settles over me again as I note his eyes are closed. Is he asleep, or dead? No. I can't think like that. His cheeks are red with cold, his lips pink. I am gratified to see he is in his weather-proof all-in-one; his abductor had obviously planned ahead for the atrocious weather. I long to reach for him, grab him back, but I daren't. The sight of him, so near yet so far, fills me with both fear and fury.

'*There* you are, Samantha,' the shadow says.

As the light illuminates the shadow's face, realisation cascades down on me with icy clarity.

Forty-four

The vagrant woman I'd seen around town is right in the centre of the copse, Caleb in her arms. Aimee *had* been hiding under all our noses, just as I'd thought. Her belongings are abandoned beside the storm lantern in their many laundry bags. I take no pleasure in being right in my deductions, though I am relieved this probably means no other Dyer family member will be with her. Dread prickles through me at the thought of my child in this madwoman's grip. I have to keep my cool. There's no telling what she might do to him.

I force authority into my voice. 'Give me back my son.'

Aimee just flashes me that maddening smile.

'Typical Samantha Russell. Golden girl. Never has to take responsibility for her actions.'

Aimee's voice is not like I remember it. The gloating, comic-book villainy of my memories is gone. Now she just sounds weary. She is still frighteningly thin, her hair scraped back in that greasy ponytail. But I know Aimee of old; this could go either way.

'Please. Give me my baby.'

I dare not attempt to just grab my baby back. I stagger forward, extending my arms for him, making Aimee jump back in alarm. I drop the wheel wrench and the torch on the ground, holding up both my hands to show I am unarmed, like a cop in a movie.

Aimee takes a step back. I'm shocked to see her hold my boy's face to her bony shoulder, as if I am a threat to him. My arms ache to hold him, protect him from her. Frustrated tears form in my eyes and spill down my cheeks.

Even so, I am glad to see him stir. He waves his little arms around, then slumps again, asleep. It distracts her. She closes her eyes. Her mood changes are worryingly abrupt.

'Takes me back.' She smiles, beatific as she inhales Caleb's baby scent from the top of his little skull.

Aimee kicks something aside by her feet. I hear the muffled, metal *thumph* of corrugated iron. I'd missed it in the darkness. Twenty-three years of mud, leaves and mulch had obscured it from view. Sour dread pools in the back of my throat, pouring like lava into my roiling stomach.

The old well.

Panic flares between my shoulder blades. 'I'm not getting in there.'

'Who said it was for you?'

Her arms tighten around Caleb, still asleep in her arms. It forces an alarmed realisation in me: *does she want to put my baby down there, in the dark?* I see Aimee heft my son's prone body up in the air like a sack of grain. He falls through the air as I make a fruitless snatch for him. He disappears into the chasm below us, shattering his tiny bones on the way down. An endless loop of horror.

I raise both hands in a pleading gesture. 'Wait! Wait! Please don't hurt my baby!'

Aimee's face slackens in shock as she takes in my fear. 'You think I would hurt a *child*?'

Too late, I realise my mistake. An incredulous bark of a laugh escapes her.

'This is typical. Always, my fault!' Aimee spits, 'I never asked for this, I got pulled into it anyway. First by Dad and Uncle Bill, then by the rest of you.'

My confusion peaks as her pace quickens. How can Aimee think this was anyone's fault but her own? She was the one who had started it all, who insisted we continued. I was the one who never wanted any of this! Anxiety makes it difficult to breathe. I swallow ineffectively against the hard lump in my throat.

Aimee tilts her head at me, like I am an intriguing specimen she's watching for some kind of science experiment. 'You thought you could leave all this behind you. Reinvent yourself, follow your dreams, become this big writer. You think you're a good person, Samantha. Well, I'm a reminder . . . You're not.'

She moves towards me and for one beautiful moment I think she is going to put Caleb in my arms. But she turns away, snatching him from my grasp again. My arms ache for my baby; it physically hurts me to be so close, to have her keep me away like this. A choked sob bubbles up from inside me, but something else flickers in recognition at Aimee's words, just like it had when Maddy had put the phone down on me.

'You lied to everyone about what really happened that night. Hell, you told yourself that lie for twenty-three years. Believed it too, by the sound of things.'

'No,' I whisper. 'That's not true.'

Aimee turns her back on me and marches back to the well. She kicks at the corrugated iron at her feet, her progress hampered by my baby in her arms.

'Give him to me,' I say. 'Please, Aimee!'

'Stop calling me that.'

At her feet, twenty-three years of mud, moss and mulch have created a seal on the corrugated iron covering the well. She kicks at it again, and again. Finally, she is able to slide a toe underneath the metal. She hefts it off, booting it away.

She points at the well with her free hand. 'Look.'

'I don't want to.' My voice sounds petulant, like a child's. 'Do it.'

I stay where I am. The last vestiges of defiance surge within me. 'So you can push me in, you crazy bitch? No chance.'

'Look, damn you!'

Her raised voice echoes around the copse, making me flinch. Caleb awakes in her arms, his little face crumpling with fear. His whimper of fear becomes full-blown cries immediately as he picks up on the tension and confusion in the air. I hate her even more for scaring my baby.

My heart hammers. Nausea threatens as dark shadows play on the periphery of my vision. I know I should wrestle Caleb off her, then turn and run out of the copse; take him back to the car, lock us in. But even if I am able to grab my boy back, I am soaked through. Caleb is too heavy for me to run with. My injured hand will hamper my ability to hold on to him. Aimee would catch up with me easily. She could have a knife, for all I know.

I better do as she says.

Keen to get this nightmare over with, I approach the well with caution. I ensure Aimee is in my sights the whole time, on the opposite side. I can't risk her getting behind me, pushing me in. But she makes no attempt to move, or rush at me. She stares back, her own hair and clothes rain-soaked, her chest heaving. Caleb grizzles in her arms, perturbed.

I make it to the edge of the well without incident. I tear my sights away from Aimee and look into the darkness, as she'd instructed me to. Aimee retrieves the storm lantern, holding it up with one hand, illuminating the dark chasm below us both.

I blink, unable to process what is in front of me for a moment, before picking out the details. Inside the well, bones. They are weathered and old, just like the farm animals' back near the farmhouse. But there's a couple of key differences. Blackened rags cling to them; as do ragged strands of hair that once were purple, twenty-three years ago.

I scream.

Forty-five

'How?'

I regard the grown, vagrant Aimee at the top of the well, unable to process what I am seeing. She can't be a ghost though; she is flesh and bone. She is still holding my boy.

'This isn't possible!'

'You left her here to die. All alone, in the dark. You killed her.'

I can't take in the woman's words. Who the hell is at the bottom of the well? My horrified brain picks over the evidence in front of me. The remnants of old fabric, the darkened bones.

'I don't understand.' My mind refuses to process the awful scene.

'*Think.*'

The night of the summer party was clear and humid. As if in slow motion, I saw myself grab a large, fist-sized rock, covered in moss. Like I was watching myself from above, I pitched it at Aimee.

The girl who made my life a living hell since Year Nine. The girl who did nothing but get between me and my friends, spreading her poison wherever she goes. I wasn't thinking ahead to what happened next; I wasn't thinking at all. I just wanted her out of my life.

Direct hit.

All those rounders lessons had paid off. The rock sent Aimee spinning. A strange mixture of triumph and relief surged through me, but it was short-lived. Aimee's eyes rolled back in her head and this time she fell further forward, snatching at the air as she went down.

Straight into the old well.

My eyes lock with the homeless woman's as another realisation forces itself to the surface of my brain. When I'd called the woman in front of me by Aimee's name, what had her reply been?

Stop calling me that.

'Wait. You're not Aimee!'

The vagrant woman gives me an eerie, gummy smile. '*Finally.* Who am I?'

I take in her drawn face; she rolls her beady blue eyes at me, almost good-natured. It's a small action, but I see the Dyer in her. The missing piece of the puzzle slots into place at last. It had been hiding in plain sight all along, just like her.

'Jess Pedlar.'

The two words jump out of me like a magic spell. As soon as I utter them, a million connections fire in my brain. It seems so clear now: 'Jaye' for Jess. She had seen me around town, realised I was back. Watched me from afar. She would have been small enough to come and go, via the coal chute. She was the one who had crept around my house, intimidated me. Deleted my book, set Mo's desk on fire. She'd made me think Aimee was after me.

'Why?' I whisper.

Jess purses her lips. 'Dig deep. You know why.'

My desperate mind zips through everything I learned in my investigation. My memories had been like shattered glass, or the fragments of a kaleidoscope. Now the pane was whole; the colours aligned for the first time. I have been on the run from the truth, what I'd done to Aimee, for twenty-three years.

'But Aimee got out.' My voice is flat, like I am reciting by rote.

Jess tilts her head. 'Did she?'

Never Have I Ever taught Aimee Dyer a lesson she won't forget . . .

Forty-six

We'd all been in agreement, for that last *Never Have I Ever* dare. At least, that was what Aimee insisted, as the mournful guitar of 'Under the Bridge' by The Red Hot Chili Peppers sounded around us. None of us had wanted to do it. Aimee had hated Jess, so what? Whatever beef she had with her, it wasn't our fight. Yet all three of us had folded to what Aimee wanted. Just like always.

It hadn't been difficult to tempt Jess away from the bonfire and Blobby. Holly had drunk too much and passed out. Mike had said in a reproachful voice that he'd watch over her. I'd shrugged, avoiding his gaze. Then I'd gone and told Jess Aimee wanted to speak with her up at the copse. Her face lit up. It was like she'd been waiting for Aimee to call on her for some reason. I didn't have time to consider what this could mean; I didn't care. I just wanted it over with.

We walked up from the party, leaving the thumping music behind us. I could see a light flashing from among the trees. I went first into the copse, holding a lighter aloft like the Olympic torch. Jess and Ruby trailed after me, keeping close and shivering as the temperature dropped. The other light vanished from sight; it was pitch black inside. Of course, it was just Aimee messing with us as well as Jess, but even so I felt spiderwebs of trepidation dance across my neck and shoulders. School playground legends of escaped mental patients and mad axe-murderers in country locations whizzed through my brain; so did visions of blood and amputated limbs.

Then all three of us were bathed in bright, white light. Shadows moved forward from the tree line towards us, their arms and legs elongated and spindly. I struggled to decipher what we were seeing. My initial worries about serial killers were abruptly replaced with more urgent concerns about extra-terrestrials: The X-Files always seemed to have UFOs landing in the middle of nowhere. But then my eyes became accustomed to the assault of light. The elongated bodies of shadows receded, switching to form something altogether more human, holding a lifeboat searchlight.

Aimee and Maddy.

'Hello, Jess.' Aimee ambled towards us. 'Rubes. Hold her.'

Ruby looked undecided for a microsecond, as Jess shrank away from her. Ruby shot me a pointed look, so I grabbed Jess's right arm as Ruby took hold of her left.

Jess looked to each of us, her face slack with betrayal and shock. 'What the hell are you doing?'

Then fury twisted her mouth and she began to shout and swear as she kicked out with her legs. Both of us were taller and stronger than her; it was no use. Jess was gutsy enough though for us to have to hold on with both hands. It was like trying to hold on to an eel. Not for the first time, I was filled with admiration for this girl.

'Jess Pedlar, you stand accused today of being a total pain in the arse. How do you plead?' Aimee dipped her face towards Jess's.

The younger girl growled and gnashed at all of us, her anger making her words unintelligible.

'Awww, Jess! Did you think you'd get away with dissing me?' Aimee giggled. 'Always, thinking you can stand up to me. As if!'

I willed Jess to give up, acquiesce. Aimee was the type who needed to win. If Jess just backed down, then Aimee would soon get bored and let her go. Maybe we could salvage the rest of the night. We could all get back to the party, the warmth of the bonfire.

'Screw you!'

Jess hocked up a gobful of phlegm and spat in Aimee's face.

I'd almost laughed; God knows Aimee had deserved whatever Jess was able to dish out. Then I discerned the flash of humiliation in Aimee's eyes vanish, swiftly replaced by dark fury. My stomach went into free fall. Whatever Aimee had planned for Jess, it just stepped up a gear. Jess had made it fifty times worse for herself.

Aimee wiped her face with her sleeve. She leant in closer, hissed in Jess's ear. 'Now you've done it.'

We propelled Jess away from us. She froze where she was, panic written all over her face. Tears threatened, too: I could see the humiliation would break her. But still I did nothing to stop it, to help her. I might not have been the ringleader, but I was a bully as much as Aimee.

'Okay. Strip. Now.' Shadows dappled Aimee's face, from the searchlight and the movement of the trees.

'What?' Ruby grabbed at Aimee's sleeve. 'Aimee, no. C'mon.'

Aimee shook Ruby off, shooting her a contemptuous glance. 'Never Have I Ever taught Jess Pedlar a lesson she won't forget, remember?'

'Yeah, Ruby. We're just freaking her out, remember,' Maddy echoed.

Aimee turned her attentions back to Jess. 'I told you, bitch. Do it.'

There was a glint in the moonlight as Aimee pulled something metal from her pocket.

A knife.

Ruby and I took a step back, appalled. Even Aimee's one-woman fan club Maddy had the grace to look alarmed. Snivelling and afraid, Jess started to peel off her clothes. Seeing the moonlight on her pale skin sent waves of nausea through me. I looked away like a coward, studying my shoes as Aimee offered Jess jeers of encouragement.

'Check out those chicken wings!' Aimee plucked at Jess's skinny arm, poking at her hip bone that jutted out as she pulled down her jeans.

Ruby elbowed me in the ribs, sending me a silent appeal. But I had justified my lack of action to myself. What could we do? Aimee had a knife. If we stepped in and denied Aimee her revenge, anything could happen. It would be okay for me; I was leaving for London in the morning with my parents. But Maddy and Ruby had to stay behind in Devon with the mad bitch. I told myself I was thinking of them.

I took Ruby aside, muttered in her ear. 'C'mon. Just let Aimee have this. It will be over quickly. It could be worse!'

Ruby pushed me away from her. She looked me up and down, disgusted. 'What the hell has happened to you, Sam?'

Tears tracked down Jess's cheeks, all trace of her earlier fury gone. Aimee circled her, still poking and mocking. She invited Maddy to join her, though she gave some excuse about needing to hold the searchlight. Ruby pulled off her own hoody, offered it to Jess.

'Erm, what are you doing?' Aimee demanded.

Ruby's voice was clear and unapologetic as she rounded on Aimee and the rest of us. 'Okay, that's enough. You've had your fun, Aimee. Let her go, now.'

Aimee smiled in challenge. 'Oh Rubes. That was just the warm-up act.'

'What is wrong with you bitches!' Ruby yelled.

She marched off towards the trees, leaving us all behind in her wake. Aimee cackled as she saw her go.

Aimee kicked aside dead leaves nearby. 'See you real soon, Rubes!'

I did not like the sound of that. I wished I'd never told Aimee about this isolated spot on the headland or agreed to lure Jess here. Ruby was right, there was something wrong with me. I was a coward.

Maddy shone the spotlight on the ground by Aimee's feet, revealing a large piece of corrugated iron. I could also see a selection of large rocks, weighing it down. Aimee grabbed for them, casting them aside so she could yank the iron off the ground. With a warrior's battle-cry, she hefted it off the earth. My curiosity piqued, I peered into the mouth of the hole. Too late, I realised with a sickening thud what Aimee's endgame was.

'Here we go, girls!' Aimee announced. 'Time to make good on our dare!'

'No.' Jess's eyes widened as she finally made the connection. 'I'm not going in there! No!'

She did not make any attempt to collect her clothes. She dashed off towards the trees, her white body like a streak of lightning. I was glad to see her go and made no attempt to follow; neither did Maddy. But Aimee speeded after Jess, catching her quarry easily. Jess squealed like a fox caught by hounds. Merciless, Aimee twisted Jess's arm behind her back, then frog-marched her back towards the well, shrieking and pleading, the knife at Jess's throat.

'No! Please, Aimee! I'm claustrophobic!' Jess bucked and writhed, trying to escape Aimee's grip.

'C'mon! Maddy! Sam!' Aimee panted like a marathon runner, caught up in the adrenaline of it all. She forced Jess down onto her knees. 'I'm sick of this cow's lies about my blood.'

'It's not lies!' Jess screamed, though Aimee pressed her face into the soft earth before she could say any more.

'C'mon, guys! Never Have I Ever *thrown Jess Pedlar in the well.*' Aimee had a wide smile on her face, like she'd just proposed doing something normally illicit, like underage drinking or tomb-stoning off the pier. 'Finally, a solution to this cuckoo in the nest.'

'You're crazy,' Maddy whispered.

It was the first critical thing I'd ever heard her utter in Aimee's presence. But it wasn't enough to spur Maddy into action. She just stood there, frozen to the spot like a rabbit under the sly gaze of a fox. My whole body felt like it was filled with concrete; I didn't think I could lift a finger.

'Fine. I'll do it!' Aimee huffed.

Aimee hauled Jess to her feet. This seemed to launch Maddy: screaming, she raced towards Aimee, arms out in a futile attempt to catch Jess. But I could see she was on the wrong side of the hole. Even if she reached the mouth of the well in time, Jess would pitch straight in.

Jess kicked out with her long legs, knocking her head against Aimee's chin, stunning her momentarily. This distracted Aimee just long enough for me to grab one of the rocks that had weighed the makeshift well cover down. It was large but fit in my fist with the familiar weight of a rounders ball. Calling up my years of experience on the school rounders team, I moved into a pitch position. Aimee hollered and shoved Jess towards the well, just as I took a deep breath and threw the rock directly at Aimee's head.

The rock sent Aimee spinning. Jess let out an involuntary shriek, jumping backwards and out of harm's way. Then I saw the confusion in Aimee's eyes as she lurched sideways, then fell to her knees. A strange mixture of triumph and relief surged through me.

It was short-lived.

Aimee's eyes rolled back in her head. This time she fell further forward, snatching at the air as she went down.

Into the well.

As Aimee had fallen, time was suspended for a second. Then shock hit, snatching our breath and making our hearts jump up in our throats. We'd stared at one another, unable to believe what just happened.

Maddy's voice cut through the night. 'Sam, you killed her!'

Time began again. Both of us abandoned the shivering, shocked and still half-dressed Jess. We ran forwards to the mouth of the well and peered into the darkness, afraid of what we might see below, yet unable to do anything else.

'Aimee!'

Forty-seven

Back in the copse in the wind and rain, I can't take my eyes off the rotten bones below. Horror stops me collecting my thoughts together. All I can think of is what Jess is telling me: I had left Aimee to die. How could I have done that?

I'd been on the run from that night my whole life. I couldn't face what I had done. It's why I'd cut off contact with Maddy and Ruby when I went to London; why I'd never returned Maddy's calls or written back to her.

It's why I'd never told Mo about my teenage years; why I'd been so keen to keep him away from finding out more about *Never Have I Ever*. It had been nothing to do with the strain our marriage was under at all.

But, wait. Like in the farmyard when I was panicking which direction to take, I slow my breathing down. I have to think straight. It's the only way to the real truth. I close my eyes. The years fall away, so does rain and wind biting at my face, chilling my bones. Even Jess and Caleb disappear. They are replaced by ghosts of the past. I see myself, Jess and Maddy racing to the mouth of the well. Maddy holds the searchlight above her head, sending a pillar of light into the shaft. We peer into its depths. We're terrified of what we might see within, but we are left with no choice.

★

'You stupid bitch, Sam!'

At the bottom, Aimee held one arm up to shield her eyes from the searchlight. If she had passed out because of my blow to her head at the top of the well, it had just been momentary. There was a bead of blood running down the side of her face, but she was very much awake. She was on her knees, scrabbling around in a gross combination of slime, moss and old leaves.

Seeing her alive, gratitude almost floored me. I would never have imagined I could be glad to be insulted, or weak at the knees at the sound of Aimee's voice. Just as quickly, my mood turned. Safe at the top of the well with the others, I recovered my nerve.

'You're the stupid bitch. You just had to take it too far, didn't you!' I felt my chest puff up with bravado.

'Stop it!' Maddy wailed.

I can't have done this. 'Aimee was alive. You're lying.'

Jess's face is deadpan. 'I never said just the stone killed her.'

Doubt pierces my psyche again. No, Jess is lying. She has to be. She is trying to set me up. It's true I behaved badly; we all had. I should have stood up to Aimee sooner. I was no ringleader; nor had I caused Aimee's death. This is not my fault. But why is Jess trying to blame this on me? I'd saved her that night!

'You should be thanking me, you stupid bitch!'

The relief I feel as those angry, toxic words tumble from my lips is indescribable.

I take cleansing breaths, smelling the peat and petrichor in the air. I recognise the pent-up aggression I've been carrying with me for weeks, since this whole farrago started. Injustice surges through me: *I had saved Jess!* She wouldn't be standing in front of me right now if I hadn't. Her life might have been shit since I'd seen her last, but that wasn't all up to me. Aimee had wanted to *kill* her, for God's sake! Finally, the anger I had been striving to keep in check for Caleb's sake floods through me.

Yet Jess just smiles and closes her eyes. '*There* you are.'

As I watch her blissful face, confusion spears me in the chest once again. It's like I have given her a gift. She opens her eyes, fixing me with those beady blue eyes.

'What do you mean? "*There* I am"?'

Jess fixes me with that impassive stare of hers. 'The *real* you. You're a fantasist, Sam. Pretending that they bullied you, that you were a victim. That you weren't one of the ringleaders of that group. It was you and Aimee, egging the other two on. You have rewritten history, to suit yourself. I bet you do it all the time. Tell yourself that the things that went well were your idea, that mistakes were someone else's. Your poor husband, how does he live with you?'

These words feel like an echo. Everything shifts into focus, like shafts of sunlight through a window after rain. Me, doing whatever I want, making accusations when it doesn't go my way; Mo, always blaming and doubting himself for disappointing me. I'd trained him to do this . . . No, I'd *bullied* him into everything. Maybe I wasn't as bad as Aimee, or even Wendy, Ruby and Holly's mum. But I'd railroaded him our entire married lives. I can see it all clearly:

Me, viewing houses on Rightmove, printing off details
Presenting them to Mo, my favourites highlighted for him
Texting him links to local schools and smiley, cajoling faces
Getting Lindy to 'have a word' aka go on and on at him for hours

301

Showing him pictures of the quay and Verity
Sending him yet more links to psychological studies about children
who grew up in the city versus those who grew up by the sea

It must have been a bridge too far, because Mo had finally fought back. He'd been right. It *was* all me, wanting to come back to Ilfracombe. But why would I want to come back, other than for Caleb? Had some dark part of me wanted to tackle the past, figure out what had really happened with Aimee?

Aimee pulled herself up to a standing position via the well wall, screaming and flinching when a chunk of it came apart under her fingers.

'Just get me out, will you?' she whimpered in a small voice.

No more of the ancient old well came crumbling on top of her. Aimee was holding her right arm to her side; perhaps she'd hit it on the way down or hurt her ribs. Maybe both. In her makeshift prison cell, Aimee seemed smaller. I couldn't believe we'd all been beholden to her for so long.

Maddy set the searchlight down. 'Hold my feet.'

I could follow her logic; we'd form a human chain, suspending Maddy to grab Aimee and haul her up. As Maddy lay on the ground in preparation, I dithered.

'No.' I grabbed her sleeve. 'She can't get away with this. Look what she's done! Aimee was the one who deserved to be taught a lesson.'

I indicated Jess, who was sitting nearby, now dressed in Ruby's hoody. She'd drawn up her knees under her chin, pulling the hoody over them and down to her feet. She looked like a little kid. Jess stared into the darkness, still shivering, her focus elsewhere.

'Screw you, Sam!' Aimee hollered from inside the well. 'Screw all of you bitches! I'm not going to forget this. When I get out of here, I'll kill all of you!'

I whistled. 'Wow, you've learned sweet F.A. from all of this, haven't you?'

I kicked at the edge of the well, sending a small shower of earth down on Aimee below. A cacophony of colourful insults flew back up at me.

Maddy looked like she might throw up. 'We can't just leave her down there.'

I smiled, trying to reassure her. 'Of course not, just 'til morning. It's only a few hours away now anyway. It's the least she deserves. I'll come back, let her out.'

'Promise?' Maddy wrung her hands.

'I give you my word,' I said.

Jess fixes me with those Dyer blues. 'You said you would come back for her?'

'I did.' I can hear the earnestness in my voice, even though Aimee's remains in the well contradict me. 'I swear. I came back in the morning.'

'Lies!'

This is why Maddy had put the phone down on me; why she'd blocked me. This is why she had asked me if I'd kept my word on the phone. She hadn't believed me. She'd only thought Aimee was stalking me out of revenge, for being left in the well too long. Not forever. I cannot accept that Aimee couldn't get out.

'I came back, I swear.'

'That evidence says . . . you're a liar.'

This variation of DI Robyn Dallas's catchphrase sounds

jarring, coming from Jess's lips. She really has done her homework on me. She has taken a fine-tooth comb to my life, my routines, even my writing. This can't just be about revenge. Jess has to be after something specific from me, to have gone to all this trouble.

'Tell me what you want, Jess?'

Jess just smiles as if she hasn't heard me speak. I've lost all track of time. How long have we been standing in the copse for? I'm only in my thin pyjamas. I'm drenched, covered in mud, freezing. I can feel my injured hand throbbing, strangely hot against my cold flesh.

She reaches out a hand to Caleb, smooths his blond curls. I feel a stab of absurd betrayal when he smiles at her. 'Reminds me of my boy. He was such a beautiful baby. My Ethan.'

I seize on this information. 'I met him, on the pier. Big lad, blond hair. Lovely smile.'

Jess stifles a sob. Sympathy leaps out of me next, against my will. It feels like a strange contrast against the pure hatred I feel for her as well, for taking my baby. This woman is so pathetic, so broken. She's been cast aside by society, by her family, *by us*. I had barely given a thought to Jess Pedlar in the last two and bit decades. Even so, my mind reels at the strangeness of the situation. The last time I had seen Jess twenty-three years ago in this copse, I had saved her from Aimee. Why is this happening?

Jess raises her eyes skywards. 'It's why I started drinking. I lost everything! My home, my boyfriend. Even my own son. Do you know what that feels like? Of course you don't. People like you get what they want. People like me, well. You never get yours. You can see how I've ended up.'

'You mean people like Aimee. She hated you for being her sister.'

'*Half*-sisters,' Jess spits, but she does not counter my deductions. She laughs. 'I did think you would join the dots a bit quicker. You are a mystery writer after all.'

'When did you all find out?'

'Frankie told us when I was in Year Seven at Ilfracombe, around the time Aimee got expelled from West Buckland.' Jess sighs. 'Did a big confession before he went to bloody jail. Mum was useless. They both left me to deal with this crap from Aimee. I thought we could be friends. I wanted to be friends. But you know what Aimee was like.'

The black-and-white headline from Frankie's court case sears through my brain. Jess had lost her dad but gained a sister. Frankie had vanished from her life while her mother watched, impassive, from the sidelines as the Dyer family imploded. Aimee must have hated the fact Holly was friends with Jess; her unwanted half-sister always being on the periphery of our friendship group.

I try again. 'I helped you, that night. Don't you remember? I saved you!'

Jess laughs, incredulous. 'Have you not been listening? That night destroyed me. I wish you *had* all killed me!'

That can be arranged.

The thought surfaces in my brain with shocking clarity. Soaked and standing ankle-deep in stagnant water, I realise the true, visceral potency of motherhood for the first time. The *Verity* statue flashes into my head again. Women have lifted cars off their offspring; run into the middle of busy roads after them; given them whole parts of their own bodies and sanity. I realise I would claw this woman's face

305

off, stab her, bludgeon her, burn her if it meant I could have Caleb safe in my arms. I am not a lioness or avenging angel, just a mum.

'Is this some Dyer family honour thing?' I grab hold of a thread, glad of a possible explanation for Jess's behaviour at last. 'Aimee tried to kill you. They all left you out in the cold. They abandoned you. They don't care about you.'

Jess stares at me with shining eyes; I know I have pressed a nerve.

This is the Jess Pedlar I remember: Holly's petite friend with the throaty laugh, the auburn hair. More involuntary sympathy courses through me. She'd been left to deal with too much as a vulnerable fourteen-year-old. Guilt comes next as I recall Michael's explanations of how 'Jaye' is the local bag lady, sleeping rough for years. She has nothing, not even her real name. The bullying has obviously taken its toll on Jess's frail body, on her mind too. What happened twenty-three years ago changed the direction of her life.

'Aimee was a monster,' I whisper.

'Yes.' Jess's eyes glitter with tears. 'She was. But she was still my half-sister.'

Her voice is as cold and hard as the biting wind. 'You left her. You killed her. How else do you explain her body still being in the well?'

'No,' I insist, 'I wouldn't do that.'

'Yet you did,' Jess says. 'See, I had to go back, too. With everything that happened that night, I left my jacket at the well. I went back. And guess what I found.'

I *can* imagine. My treacherous brain paints what was waiting for Jess in hideous technicolour, like my own private horror movie. I can see Aimee's dead body slumped at the bottom of the well: her pale, grey flesh; blue-tinged lips;

her staring, glassy blue eyes. But Aimee had been alive, breathing when I had last seen her. Jess cannot play her mind games with me.

I stand certain. 'I didn't do this. I didn't kill Aimee.'

Forty-eight

As the party wound down at Easterbrook Farm and teens crawled into sleeping bags around the remains of the bonfire, I did as I'd promised Maddy. I returned to the well.

Entering the copse up on the headland, I could hear Aimee's rasped shouts for help. I left her for a few more moments as I tied the end of the rope I'd brought to a nearby tree. This would help haul her out; I looped the rest around my shoulder.

When I heard crying, my conscience finally got the better of me. I peered into the well and found Aimee shivering and snivelling at the bottom. Her left arm was wrapped around her side. I even felt sorry for her, especially when she regarded me with tears in her big blue eyes. I couldn't recall ever seeing Aimee cry before.

'Sam! Thank God. Please, throw the rope down?'

Birds recited the dawn chorus with gusto, even though the well was still overcast by the trees. I could see fury flicker in Aimee's face, though she tried to hide it. Crouching down on my haunches, I assessed the situation. Her look of anger morphed into uncertainty.

Never Have I Ever *taught Aimee Dyer a lesson she won't forget.*

In the copse, morning is arriving. I can hear the harsh call of a crow, warning us to keep away from its nest. I know how it feels. My baby is still out of my reach. I am wet through and cold, shivering and sniffling. I just want to go home and take my boy with me. Inexplicably, Michael's smiling face swims up in my subconscious; I'd tasked him to find out if Aimee's disappearance after the party had been resolved. Michael told me Aimee's parents had come into the station, said she had turned up. That she'd gone to Australia. That had obviously been a lie, but it's clear the Dyers must have believed it. Ruby, too.

'Aimee sent a note home?'

Jess snorts in derision. 'That was me, obviously.'

'Sounds like guilt to me.'

'Too right it was guilt. I didn't want my aunt and uncle and cousins to suffer. I was trying to spare their feelings.'

'You should have just told them what really happened.'

Jess rolls her eyes. 'And have you try and blame it on me, say I was an accessory? We all believed you when you said you would go back for her.'

I have to take her point. Jess had abandoned Aimee originally down the well, just like Maddy, Ruby and me. Unlike the rest of us, she had a double motive: the *Never Have I Ever* bullying, as well as jealousy Aimee was Frankie's love child. I'd done enough research into barrister antics in the courtroom for DI Robyn Dallas to know they would have spun it as Jess being the ringleader somehow, especially given the Dyers' shady reputation in town.

Then something else clicks. There's another reason I'd thought Aimee had managed to get out of the well back then. Jess had handed it to me on a plate, just as she had Bill and the rest of the Dyers.

It was Moving Day, barely twelve hours after the party. I was lying on the bare mattress on the floor of my bedroom, my mood

309

as black as the mournful clothes I was wearing. I pushed away the stinging nettles of guilt about leaving Aimee that had plagued me since the early hours. I reminded myself that Aimee had ruined my last night in Devon, the last party I would ever have with my friends. She deserved everything she got. It wasn't like she couldn't haul herself out. Maybe this would teach her the valuable lesson she needed.

All around me, the walls were bare: my pictures had been taken down; my sports trophies and certificates safely stashed away. My posters of Brandon Lee in The Crow *and 'ironic' tribute collage to the Spice Girls had been rolled up in cardboard tubes. My collection of snow globes were in boxes; so was my* Sweet Valley High *collection; even a Teddy Ruxpin I'd had as a little kid but hadn't been able to part with. I would shove it under the bed every time Ruby, Maddy and Aimee came round. Now he was wrapped in newspaper like a precious ornament.*

The hustle and bustle of removal men sounded throughout the house. I could hear swearing, whistling and general chitchat as three huge men trudged up and down the stairs. I hated seeing the furniture taken from the house to the big van on the driveway, so I'd retreated, thinking it would take them hours before they got to my room. But it turned out it did not take long to dismantle someone's whole life. There was a knock on the door. My room was next.

'C'mon then, you.' Lindy's voice was soft as she ushered me out.

I put up no resistance, clumping down the stairs, morose and tearful. I had thought I would be happy to move from Devon, leave Aimee and the others behind at last. Instead, I felt I was already missing a part of myself, cut adrift. There was already an echo; the house was almost empty. Ghost home.

The snap of the letterbox sounded like a gunshot. I stiffened as a single envelope, hand-delivered, dropped on the mat. I snatched it up, certain I knew who it was from already. I'd been waiting for this. Removal men tramped past me, carrying my boxes. They laughed and joked amongst themselves. They didn't notice me sitting cross-legged on the hallway carpet, staring at the envelope in my hands. I tore it open; a piece of paper fluttered out, its hateful words displayed.

Never Have I Ever been punished for what I have done.

In the copse, I square up to Jess. There's an alternative version to Jess's story; something else that has been staring me in the face. It seems so clear now.

'You're lying.'

Perhaps Jess feels her advantage slip away, because her lip wobbles like a child's. 'I'm not.'

Seeing her begin to crumple gives me the answer I need. She *is* lying. Relief fills every pore, my fingertips tingle with it. Jess is just like Aimee in more ways than one. I can see it so clearly now. I'd taken Jess's word for it that Aimee was already dead when she found her in the well.

'It was you who killed Aimee,' I say.

Forty-nine

Jess does not sigh and give up her confession like Dallas's nemesis Elodie Fitzgerald, or any of her many evil right-hand men. 'You will literally try and twist it any way you can, won't you? You really are that deluded.'

She looks at me like I am the mad one. Now it's my turn to rise to the bait.

'*I'm* deluded?' I can't contain my incredulity. 'I'll tell you who the fantasist is, Jess Pedlar. You. *You're* the one who's been creating conspiracies, sending me out of my mind with worry over something that happened years ago. I was just a teenage girl who Aimee pushed too far. It wasn't right to leave her in the well, I get that, but it wasn't me who killed her.'

Jess raises her face to the skies, as if tired of me. 'I never wanted any of this. You all pulled *me* into that stupid game of yours, not the other way around. I've had to live with covering up a death, one *you* caused.'

'So *you* say.' I watch her shift Caleb from one hip to the other. 'If you could prove it, you'd have never been torturing me like this. You'd have gone to the police a long time ago.'

Stalemate.

Jess's nostrils flare in irritation, but she does not dispute my words. I feel a burgeoning confidence this will soon be over. Jess is up to her neck in this, just like I am.

I have won.

I just need my son back; to get my baby home, warmed up and into some dry clothes. Me too. I also need to secure my home, block up the coal chute. I can see the grey light of dawn receding, the sun climbing higher in the sky, peeking between the skeletal branches of the trees in the copse. I need to get home, before Mo does.

Make sure Jess Pedlar never wheedles her way into my life ever again.

I force authority into my voice. 'This is over. Give me Caleb.'

'I want money.'

Jess's voice is so quiet, I almost don't catch it.

'What?'

'You heard.' I can see that steely determination in her blue eyes again. 'Having to live with covering up Aimee's death, it's why I started drinking. To blot it all out. I tried so hard to move on, to forget. But eventually, I lost everything. My boyfriend, my home, my son. Think of it as compensation.'

'Drinking was your choice. I didn't make you.' My words feel hollow; my mouth is dry. 'Anyway, I don't have any money.'

'Oh, please,' Jess scoffs. 'You're the bigshot author. I've seen your books in stores, your face in the newspaper I sleep on at night! Pull the other one.'

'Honestly, Jess, writers don't make much. We're not all like J.K. Rowling or E.L. James. Most of us make a few thousand, here or there.'

'Well, it's still more than I have.'

Again, I have to take her point. Still, all my money from writing goes to pay the remainder of the debts we consolidated with the house move back to Ilfracombe. Even if I

313

had any spare money, Mo would notice me siphoning it off our joint account. That in turn would lead to questions from him that I don't want to answer. What if he believed Jess's screwball versions of events about Aimee's death over mine? Then he really would leave and probably take Caleb with him. He might report me to the police, too. Mo is a law-abiding citizen, deep down; prone to seeing things in black and white. It's the one thing he has in common with Michael.

'Look, I don't want much. Just enough to get a flat. Somewhere where I can get back on my feet, get my life back. Then my Ethan will come and see me again.'

A small part of me genuinely feels for Jess. I'd made so many sacrifices for my own son. I'd compromised my health, my time, my career, my marriage, even a good portion of my sanity. I had wanted Caleb so much, I'd known even in my darkest days it would be worth it. Would it always be so? I'd read about children growing into teenagers and then young people who hate their parents. I can't imagine what it would be like if Caleb grew up and didn't want to see me any more.

Then that dark part of me clamps down on my compassionate thoughts. That harsh voice tells me Ethan would no doubt have good reasons for not wanting to see Jess. I don't know what she might have done to him in the grip of alcoholism. Maybe she'd terrorised him, beaten him? At best she probably neglected him. Addiction always has collateral damage and children are on the front line. Even if I had any money and gave it to Jess, there's still no guarantee Ethan would want anything to do with her. That would be because of her own actions, not mine.

'I don't have that kind of money to give you, Jess. I'm sorry.' I make a last appeal. 'Come on. This is over. Give me Caleb.'

I flinch as one of her claw-like hands grabs me by the wrist. She forces me to look at her this time, a weird reversal of when I'd confronted her outside Kat's café.

'Then I will tell them all. Starting with your husband.'

Anger mobilises that primeval part of me. My shame and fear dissipates. That evening twenty-three years ago might have changed Jess, but it had changed me too.

'Give me my son back, Jess. Now!'

With an animalistic yell, I grab for her, determined to snatch Caleb back by whatever means necessary. Even as I attempt to launch myself, I know it's a folly. I feel my body move forwards, yet my frozen feet stick fast in the mud. I overbalance, pitching face first into a large muddy puddle. I gasp, tasting grit in my mouth and wiping stagnant water from my face and eyes. My injured right hand is agony now, the nerve endings shriek.

'Oh, Samantha.' Above me, Jess sounds genuinely drained.

I roll over, catching sight of something metal glinting in the mud. It's the wheel wrench, where I'd dropped it earlier.

My good hand snakes out and grabs it.

Fifty

With a guttural shriek, I wield the wheel wrench around, through the air.

From my position lying on the ground, it connects with the back of Jess's leg. She screams in pain and surprise, dropping to her other knee. Caleb slides down her hip, landing heavily on the ground. He emits a shocked squeal as the cold mud hits him, then screams in a combination of disbelief and anger.

'You should have just given him to me, Jess!'

I clamber to my feet. In the periphery of my vision I see Caleb roll over, his face red and his mouth curled in a snarl. *Who's Mummy's Boy?* I send him a silent apology; I will make it up to him. I check to see how close to the well he is. He is safe, for now.

There's something I have to do first, to protect him.

I turn my attention back to Jess. She scrabbles about in the mud, a red sea of pain evident on her face. She gasps like a stranded fish. I am both elated and horrified by the violence that had leapt out of me, like a dark shadow. I'd felt a snap of bone in her femur as it gave way. It must be agony. Good.

'You took everything from me,' Jess hisses through clenched teeth, making a clumsy grab for my ankle.

This again. Jess is so keen to stand in judgement of me, make out I am the one behind all her misfortunes. I had *saved her* from Aimee; Jess is the one who has thrown that gift away. I didn't do this to her, or to Aimee. Not me. Never me.

'You did it to yourself!'

I grab her forearm with my unburned left hand, attempt to peel her off my leg. Disbelief courses through me as well as adrenaline. How could I ever have allowed Jess to get under my skin, doubt myself? I had left Aimee alive. I might have walked away from the well a second time, but I'd left her the rope, the means to get out. Jess had been the one who had murdered her sister. Maybe she was watching and had pulled up the rope when I left. She must have been the one to re-cover the well. That was why she'd started drinking, unable to cope with what she had done. She cannot blame her actions on me.

Jess screams. She is sickeningly light. It's as if her bones are hollow, like a bird's. Perhaps it's sheer willpower that gives her strength, because prising her off is difficult. I am forced to kick out with my leg, sending her sprawling back in the mud. Still stuck myself, the movement makes me topple away, straight onto my back. Winded, I'm forced to stare at the white skies for a second as I listen to Jess's whimpers of pain and Caleb's cries.

Before I can roll over, Jess is looming over me again. 'You walked away. You hit her in the head and then left her to die!'

She grabs at my collar, her long, dirty talons digging into my neck. She pulls my face close to hers. The pain of the scratches from her long nails does not register. Between the cold I've endured and the blood pounding in my head, I am gripped by the moment, but also curiously detached. It is like I am watching a film.

'I don't believe you. You pulled up the rope I left for her. Entombed her down there forever.' I'm panting, like a marathon runner. 'You're a liar.'

'I am sick of everyone telling me what I am!' Jess lets go of me, falls away. 'Mum; the kids at school; Aimee; the rest of the Dyers; you! I only ever wanted to be part of a family. Why is that so difficult to understand?'

I drag myself to my feet. I gasp for air. Jess gazes up at me from the mud. Even in terrible pain, her blue eyes are still furious. I can see the Dyer determination in them; she will never let this go.

I blink. I feel like I am outside my own body again, looking down at myself. Forcing my body to go through the motions, against even the will of my mind, has always been something I have been able to do. Another flash of that broken little hamster, the blood in my palms; my injured hand throbs, along with the memory. Behind us, my little boy pulls himself from the mud and howls, sure his mother must hate him. What he doesn't realise yet is, I am doing this *for* him.

I have no choice.

I will do anything to protect Caleb, to ensure the Dyers will never breach our lives or home again. This nightmare has to end.

Whatever it takes.

'What are you doing, Sam?'

The element of surprise is mine. Jess can't believe my aggression. An absurd, disbelieving smile paints itself across her face. Her efforts to extricate herself from my grip are too feeble to shake me off. Any worries I'd had about Jess earlier were only because she'd been holding Caleb. She is weak, malnourished.

Jess's eyes are wide, fearful now. She stops slashing at me with her long nails; she grabs at my fingers, tries to prise them off, ineffectual. I am strong. She is sick, skeletal. She raises both hands in front of me, begging. It is another reversal, but this time I am in charge.

'Please, don't. Sam!'

Now Caleb is safe from her, I do not have to hold back. This is not an even match, but there's no time to consider the ethics of my actions now. In this fight, there can only be one clear winner. Me. I am prepared to fight. For the sake of my own family: the little boy still crying in the mud, the man on his way home to me right now.

This woman broke into my home, stole my baby.

She deserves this.

I let go of Jess. Not expecting it, she lurches forward. I grab her ratty ponytail, twisting it around my left fist so she bellows in pain. Back in my control, I drag her, slipping and sliding as I do so. She bends backwards, trying to loosen some of the pressure on the roots of her hair, the nape of her neck. As she realises where we are going, she attempts to dig her good foot into the mud.

'No. No!' Jess whimpers. 'Sam, please?'

My gaze set on my destination, I don't stop.

I can hear her saying words, but I process none of them. I cannot afford to. I draw on a primeval reserve of strength I hadn't known I still have. The only other time I've felt it was in labour, when I pushed Caleb into the world. Now it bursts through me again as my hand connects with Jess's bony shoulders and I push her away from me, as hard as I can.

Jess staggers forward dragging her bad leg behind her. She snatches at the air in vain, as if she can stop herself. As she topples, she twists so she's looking straight at me.

Our eyes lock.

Then she falls, her mouth twisted in a silent scream. She disappears backwards, falling out of my view.

Into the well below.

I rush towards the open chasm as present and past slide together again.

Aimee on her knees again, staring up at me from inside the well, eyes wide with fear.

'Or what?' I said.

'I'll do anything you say,' Aimee begged, 'I swear.'

I smiled, enjoying being in control for once. 'You promise you will stay away. You will never contact Maddy and Ruby again, when I'm gone?'

'I promise. I'm sorry, Sam.'

But I knew Aimee of old; her performances were Oscar-worthy. Even at the bottom of a well, bested and humiliated, she was bound to come back fighting. I might have been escaping her wrath by moving upcountry, but I knew deep down she would make Maddy and Ruby pay for this. Even if they didn't hang out with her any more, there was still lots Aimee could do to make them social outcasts at college, targets for yet more bullies. There would be nothing I could do either, not from London. That hard part of me shut these thoughts down: that's their problem. I'm leaving.

This prompted another realisation. I didn't want to help Aimee out of the well myself. I wanted to be as far away as possible. It was just pure common sense; self-preservation. No one can blame me for that.

I did a quick check: the rope was still tied to the tree; I'm not a monster. Aimee might have hurt her arm, but if she really wanted out, she could still make it. Let her figure it out.

'Have a nice life, Aimee.'

I stood up and walked away, Aimee's hoarse screams of pleading ringing in my ears. But as Aimee herself was fond of saying: are you really being bad if there's no one around to see it?

I expect to see Jess staring up at me from the bottom of the well, like Aimee had done all those years earlier. But she lies on her back, completely still. Her head is tilted at a strange angle, her face close to Aimee's remains; a parody of a loving kiss. I spare no time staring at her crumpled body. I pull the corrugated iron across, kicking mud and leaves across it.

I blink again and I can hear normally all of a sudden. Caleb's howls have downgraded to a miserable snivel. I run to him, scooping him up. He stiffens in my arms, arching his back, anger and fear still peaking in his small body. As I trudge back towards the car, I coo to him, smooth mud away from his face. Finally, he settles back against my chest, no longer trying to escape me. I am Mummy again. I always will be, after this.

As I traipse past the boneyard and the derelict farmhouse, I spot the car up ahead, where I left it by Easterbrook Farm's gates. As my actions sink in, an onslaught of guilt settles on me. I can see Michael's disappointed face. But he believes in a binary place, where there is right and wrong, good and evil. I can appreciate the nuance of a more morally ambiguous world. Jess started this. I saved that girl, but this is the thanks I get. She terrorised and intimidated me; abducted my child; made me afraid in my own home and my loved ones doubt me. I could have stood by and let Aimee throw her in the well back then. Instead she wanted to blame me for her life turning out badly since. Like Lindy always says, some people just can't take responsibility for their own bad choices.

I unlock the car, sliding Caleb into his baby seat. The poor mite is exhausted after his strange sojourn in the wilderness. I belt him in, sorting through the things I have to get done today. I check the clock on the dashboard; there's still time before Mo returns home. I should get there before he does. I need to bathe Caleb, get him some dry clothes. I also need a shower, new clothes; to redress my bandages.

I exhale as I sit down in the driver's seat, cradling my injured hand in my lap. Relief replaces guilt like a warm blanket. The threat is all over now. I take no pleasure in what I had to do. Like *Verity* down in the harbour, wielding the sword above her head, I had to be a warrior today. But real life is seldom as romantic as art, or statues. Real life is dirty, savage. I had done what was necessary. Now we can be the perfect family, just like we've always wanted. I would die for my child, my husband. Today I proved I would kill for them, too.

I close my eyes. I think back to Moving Day, to Lindy appearing at the front door of our old house, car keys in hand. Before she could see it, I had crumpled that first *Never Have I Ever* note I now know Jess sent me in my fist and joined Lindy on the doorstep. We had watched the removal men put the last of the boxes into the van, then close up the big back doors.

★

'Big adventure next! You said your goodbyes?'

I painted my own smile on for her benefit. 'Yes.'

Lindy reminded me of Pennywise the Clown: manic eyes, overly wide smile. My poor mum, who'd struggled so hard. I'd thought I was looking after her when I was a teenager. The reality was, she'd been looking after me; she'd always made sure I'd never truly realised what peril she'd been in. Such a warrior.

Lindy looked around the well-kept, neat front gardens. 'I'm really going to miss this place. But time for a change. Right, Samantha?'

'Right,' I echoed.

Lindy strode over to the car and got in behind the steering wheel. I'd hung back, pulling the front door shut, posting the front-door keys through the letterbox as Lindy had instructed me to. I took one last quick look at the house, then up and down the street. The hanging baskets, the bright white render, the small stone garden ornaments. I'd decided it was all so . . . provincial. I was not meant for smalltown suburbia like Ilfracombe, but for the bright lights of the city, far away from there. I could forget all about Aimee, even Ruby and Maddy. Reinvent myself, become somebody. Anything was possible now, I decided, as long as I was far away from Loserville.

I got in the passenger seat beside my mother. Behind us, the removal van left the driveway. Lindy looked in her mirror and backed out after it, leaving our old house in the rear-view mirror. I did not look back at my childhood home but muttered under my breath as Lindy flicked the indicator.

'Never Have I Ever been so glad to get out of here.' I threw the crumpled note from the open car window before Lindy could catch me.

*

323

My eyes open as my phone vibrates with a text on the dashboard. Mo's picture pops up, a short message and selection of kisses and emojis with it: *'Landed, on my way back. Should be with you in a couple of hours. Fresh start?'*

I smile, tapping my reply straight away.

Fresh start.

Acknowledgements

Writers often lead solitary lives, but unlike the rather self-important Sam, I would like to acknowledge it takes MANY people to make a book!

First thanks to my amazing editor, Eve Hall at Hodder, whose suggestions and edits were always on the button. Mad respect to my agent Hattie Grunewald and all the wonderful book agents at Blake Friedmann, especially Isobel Dixon. I will miss you all.

Thank you to Devon and Cornwall constabulary, who talked me through a variety of police procedures, including 'inactive mispers'. Thanks to those who have catalogued everything related to Mad Cow Disease and Hand, Foot & Mouth online. Cheers also to the 90s weirdos who have made a billion websites and videos dedicated to all things 90s. What a trip down memory lane! Any mistakes are mine.

To my unholy trinity of writing BFFs, many thanks to JK Amalou, Jenny Kane and Elinor Perry-Smith. Your unwavering support means so much. Elinor even trekked with me to the very top of Ilfracombe's Capstone Hill when we both had a hangover. That's dedication.

Thanks to my daughters Emmeline and Lilirose who escorted me on many more 'research' trips to Ilfracombe. The Coke floats in Johnny C's diner are AWESOME. I never get bored of watching you both doing back-flips on the green by the crazy golf.

Thanks also to my wonderful Bang2writers, especially the (self-named) 'Angel Bitches' headed up by Emma Pullar, Olivia Brennan and Liam Kavanagh. Your support on the chat thread is always such a tonic!

Respect to 'him indoors' aka Mr C. Babe, you really got on my tits for *reasons* whilst I was writing this book . . . But this was handy because Sam and Mo were having problems too. Ours weren't so bad, but thanks for the inspiration. Seriously, love you always.

Lastly, thank you to Damien Hirst for *Verity*. She might be controversial, but that's good art. Personally, I never tire of looking at her. I wish she could have made Ilfracombe pier her home when I was a teenager. I might have felt more inspired and less like I wanted to go off the rails! (Kidding.)

L.V. Hay

In the best books, the ending often comes as a shock.
Not just because of that one last twist in the tale,
but because you have been so absorbed in their world,
that coming back to the harsh light of reality is a jolt.

If that describes you now, then perhaps you should track down
some new leads, and find new suspense in other worlds.

Join us at www.hodder.co.uk, or follow us on
Twitter @hodderbooks, and you can tap in to a
community of fellow thrill-seekers.

Whether you want to find out more about this book,
or a particular author, watch trailers and interviews, have
the chance to win early limited editions, or simply browse
our expert readers' selection of the very best books,
we think you'll find what you're looking for.

And if you don't, that's the place to tell us what's missing.

We love what we do, and we'd love you to be part of it.

www.hodder.co.uk

@hodderbooks

HodderBooks

HodderBooks